TRANSFORMERS
BUMBLEBEE

Facebook: **facebook.com/idwpublishing**
Twitter: **@idwpublishing**
YouTube: **youtube.com/idwpublishing**
Tumblr: **tumblr.idwpublishing.com**
Instagram: **instagram.com/idwpublishing**

COLLECTION EDITS BY
JUSTIN EISINGER
AND ALONZO SIMON

PRODUCTION ASSISTANCE BY
SHAWN LEE

PUBLISHER
GREG GOLDSTEIN

Licensed By:

ISBN: 978-1-68405-229-5   21 20 19 18   1 2 3 4

TRANSFORMERS BUMBLEBEE MOVIE PREQUEL: FROM CYBERTRON WITH LOVE. OCTOBER 2018. FIRST PRINTING. HASBRO and its logo, TRANSFORMERS and all related characters are trademarks of Hasbro and are used with permission. © 2018 Hasbro. All Rights Reserved. © 2018 Paramount Pictures Corporation. All Rights Reserved. The IDW logo is registered in the U.S. Patent and Trademark Office. IDW Publishing, a division of Idea and Design Works, LLC. Editorial offices: 2765 Truxtun Road, San Diego, CA 92106. Any similarities to persons living or dead are purely coincidental. With the exception of artwork used for review purposes, none of the contents of this publication may be reprinted without the permission of Idea and Design Works, LLC. Printed in Canada. IDW Publishing does not read or accept unsolicited submissions of ideas, stories, or artwork.

Originally published as TRANSFORMERS: BUMBLEBEE MOVIE PREQUEL issues #1–4.

Special thanks to Sonal Majmudar, Tom Warner, Ed Lane, Beth Artale, and Michael Kelly.

Greg Goldstein, President & Publisher
John Barber, Editor-In-Chief
Robbie Robbins, EVP/Sr. Art Director
Cara Morrison, Chief Financial Officer
Matthew Ruzicka, Chief Accounting Officer
Anita Frazier, SVP of Sales and Marketing
David Hedgecock, Associate Publisher
Jerry Bennington, VP of New Product Development
Lorelei Bunjes, VP of Digital Services
Justin Eisinger, Editorial Director, Graphic Novels & Collections
Eric Moss, Sr. Director, Licensing & Business Development

Ted Adams, IDW Founder

WRITTEN BY
JOHN BARBER
ART BY
ANDREW GRIFFITH
COLORS BY
PRISCILLA TRAMONTANO
LETTERS BY
TOM B. LONG
SERIES EDITS BY
DAVID MARIOTTE

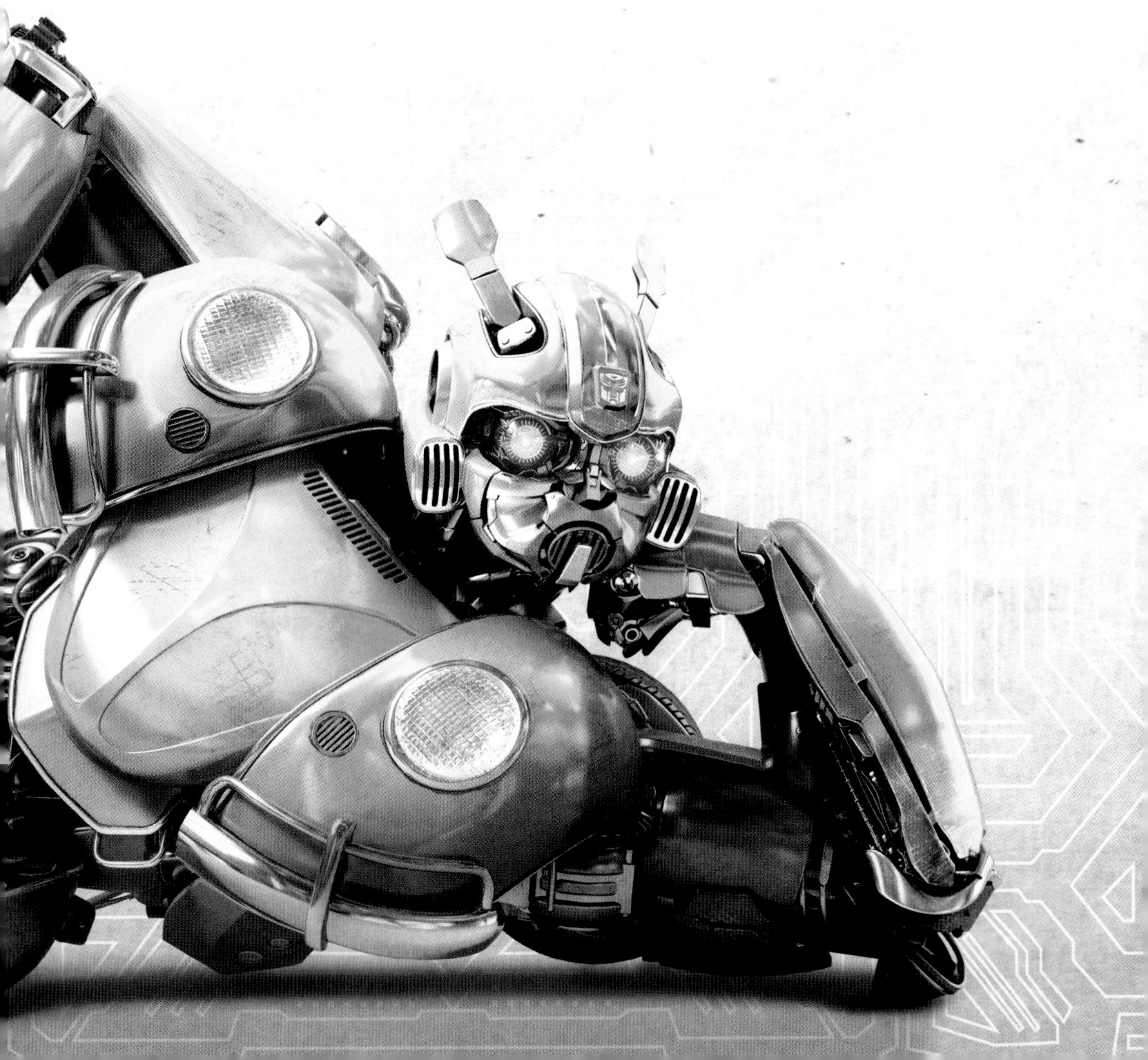

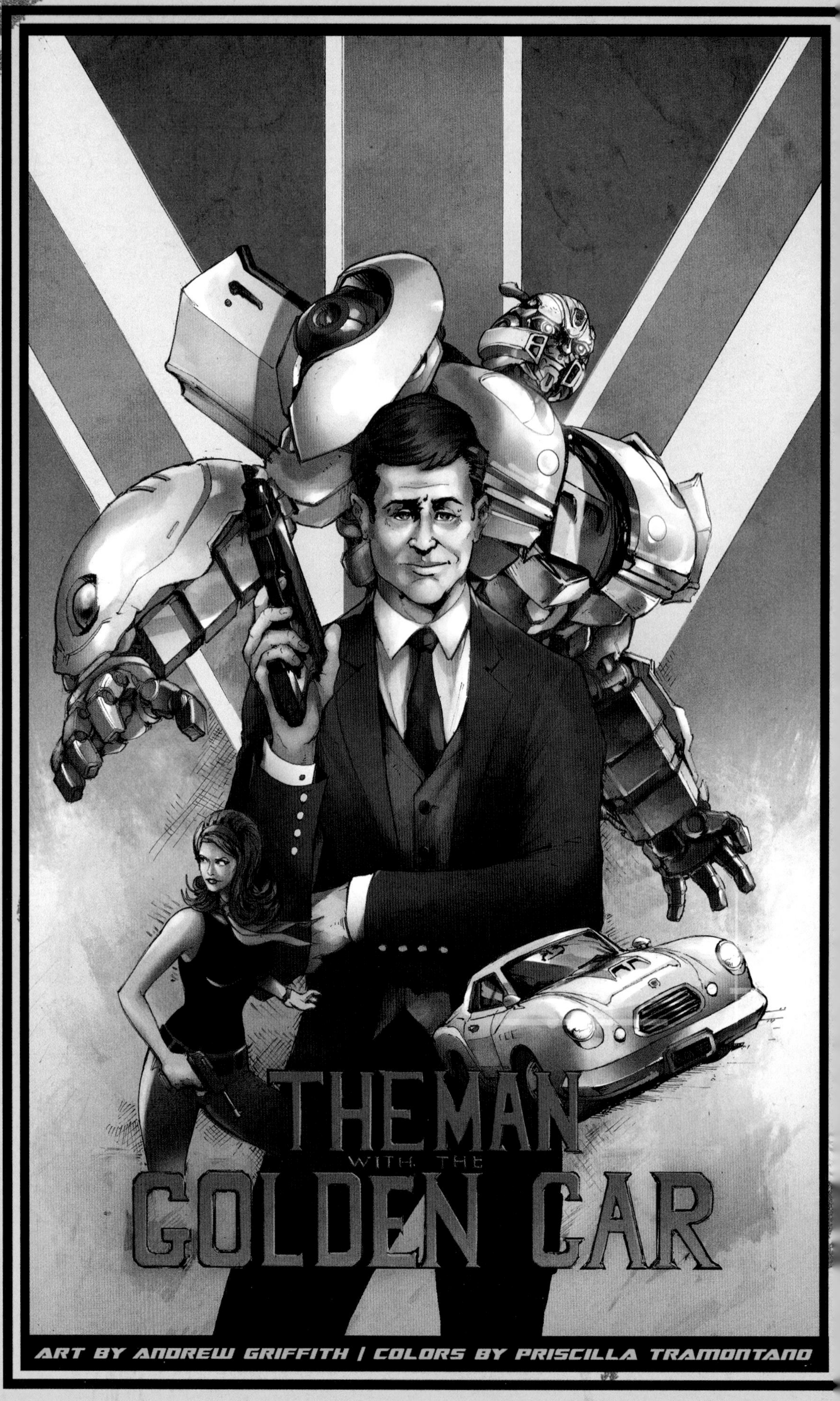
THE MAN
WITH THE
GOLDEN CAR
ART BY ANDREW GRIFFITH | COLORS BY PRISCILLA TRAMONTANO

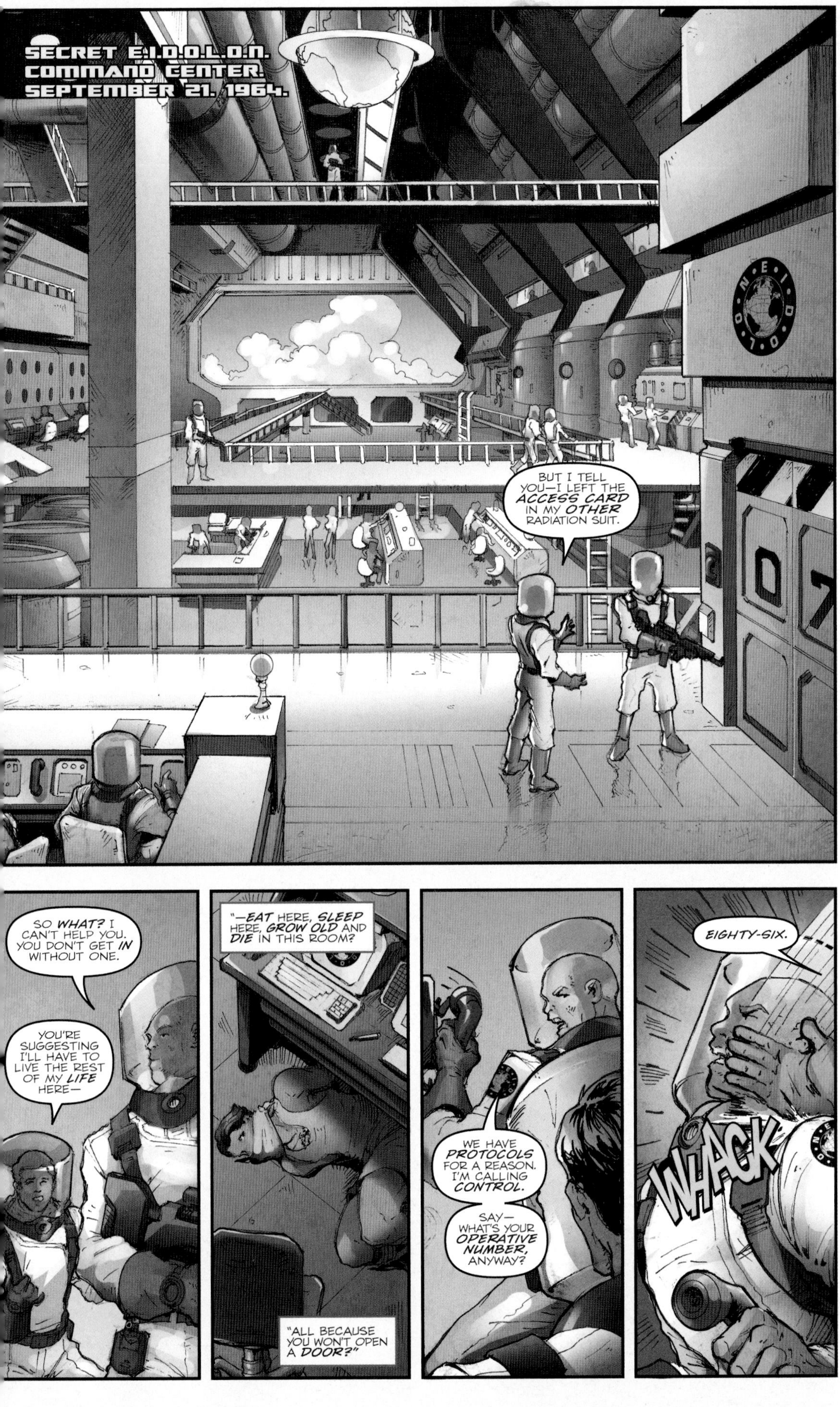
SECRET E.I.D.O.L.O.N. COMMAND CENTER. SEPTEMBER 21, 1964.
BUT I TELL YOU—I LEFT THE ACCESS CARD IN MY OTHER RADIATION SUIT.
SO WHAT? I CAN'T HELP YOU. YOU DON'T GET IN WITHOUT ONE.
YOU'RE SUGGESTING I'LL HAVE TO LIVE THE REST OF MY LIFE HERE—
"—EAT HERE, SLEEP HERE, GROW OLD AND DIE IN THIS ROOM?
"ALL BECAUSE YOU WON'T OPEN A DOOR?"
WE HAVE PROTOCOLS FOR A REASON. I'M CALLING CONTROL.
SAY— WHAT'S YOUR OPERATIVE NUMBER, ANYWAY?
EIGHTY-SIX.
WHACK

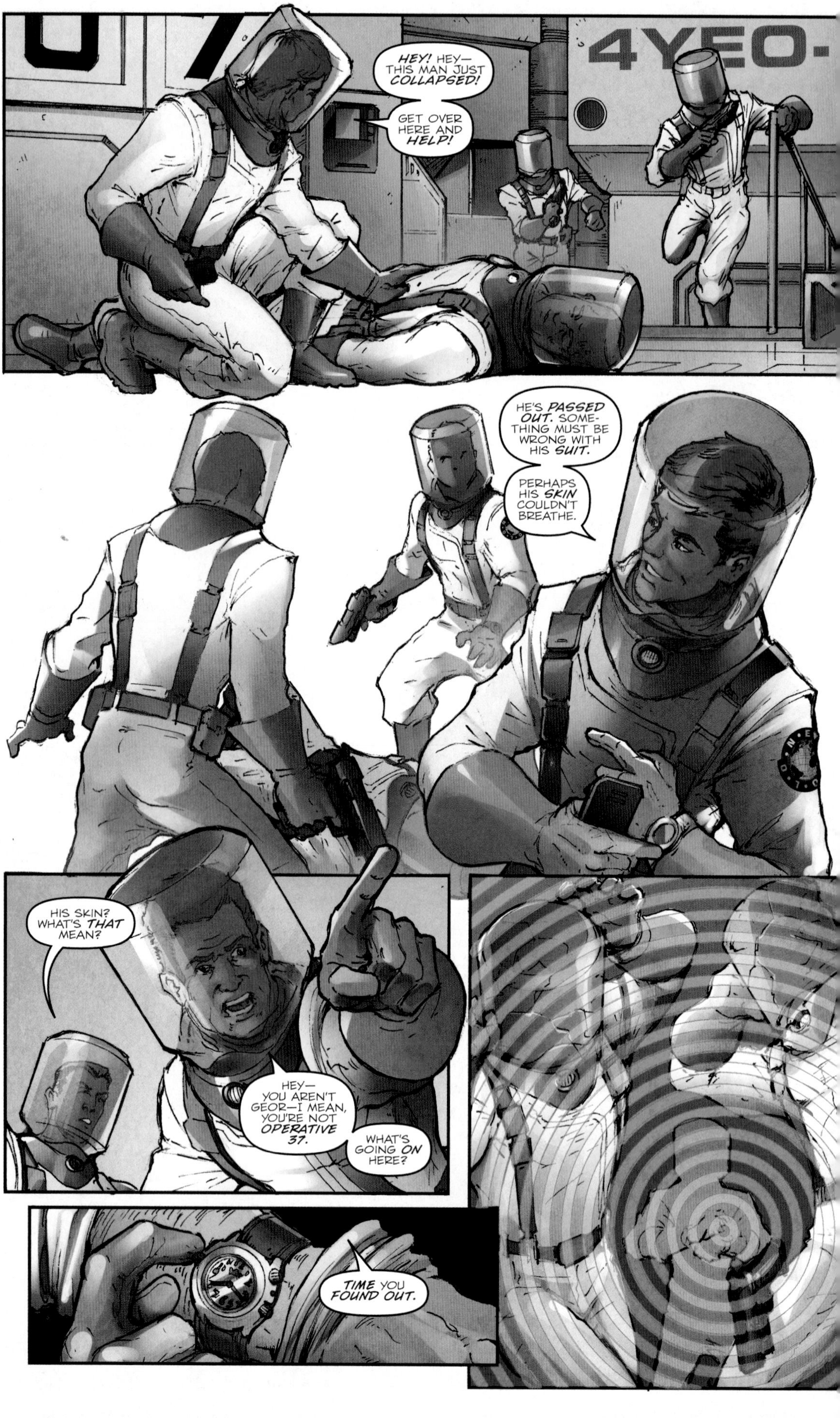
4YEO-
HEY! HEY— THIS MAN JUST COLLAPSED!
GET OVER HERE AND HELP!
HE'S PASSED OUT. SOMETHING MUST BE WRONG WITH HIS SUIT.
PERHAPS HIS SKIN COULDN'T BREATHE.
HIS SKIN? WHAT'S THAT MEAN?
HEY— YOU AREN'T GEOR—I MEAN, YOU'RE NOT OPERATIVE 37.
WHAT'S GOING ON HERE?
TIME YOU FOUND OUT.

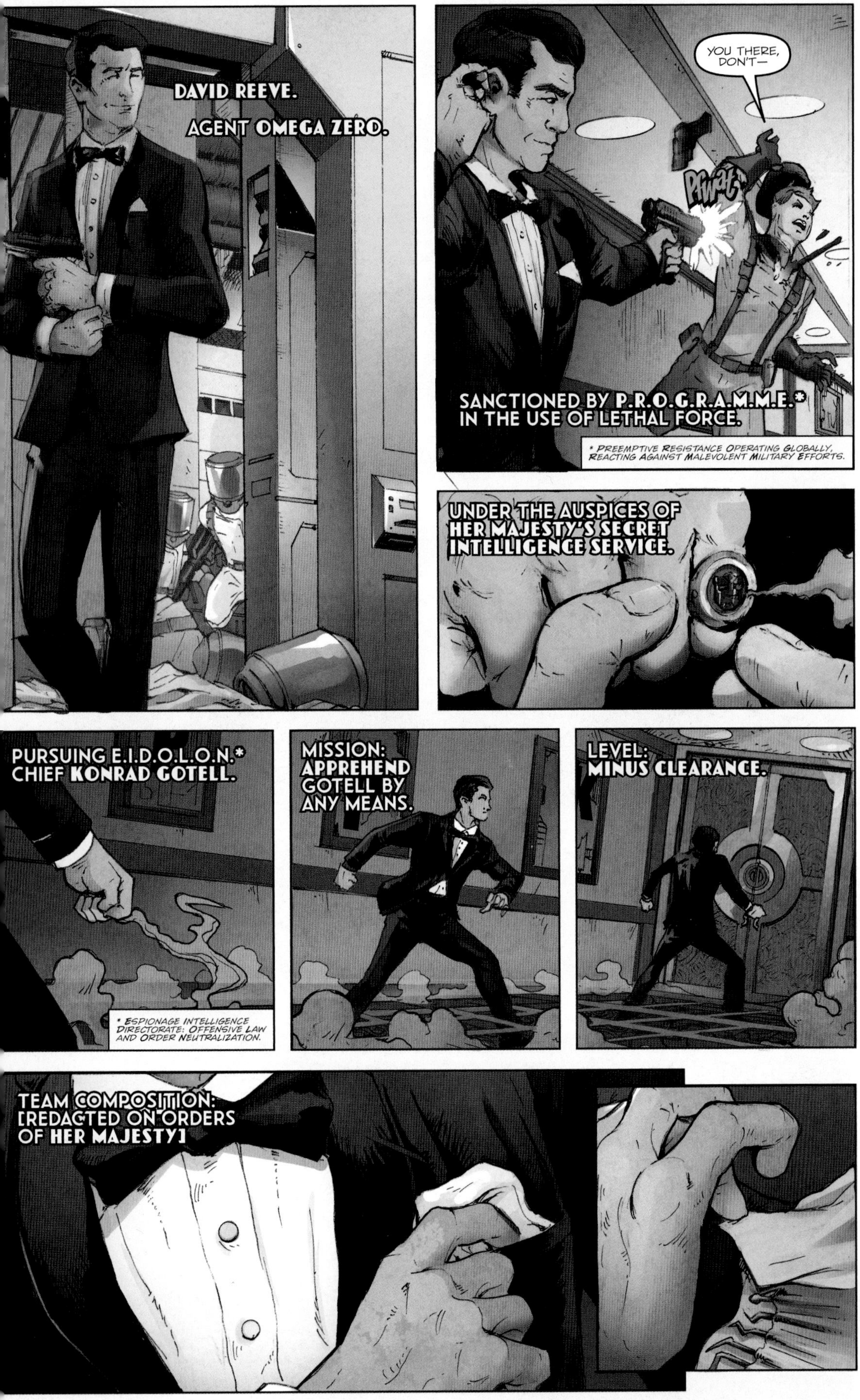
DAVID REEVE.
AGENT OMEGA ZERO.
YOU THERE, DON'T—
PFWAT
SANCTIONED BY P.R.O.G.R.A.M.M.E.* IN THE USE OF LETHAL FORCE.
* PREEMPTIVE RESISTANCE OPERATING GLOBALLY, REACTING AGAINST MALEVOLENT MILITARY EFFORTS.
UNDER THE AUSPICES OF HER MAJESTY'S SECRET INTELLIGENCE SERVICE.
PURSUING E.I.D.O.L.O.N.* CHIEF KONRAD GOTELL.
* ESPIONAGE INTELLIGENCE DIRECTORATE: OFFENSIVE LAW AND ORDER NEUTRALIZATION.
MISSION: APPREHEND GOTELL BY ANY MEANS.
LEVEL: MINUS CLEARANCE.
TEAM COMPOSITION: [REDACTED ON ORDERS OF HER MAJESTY]

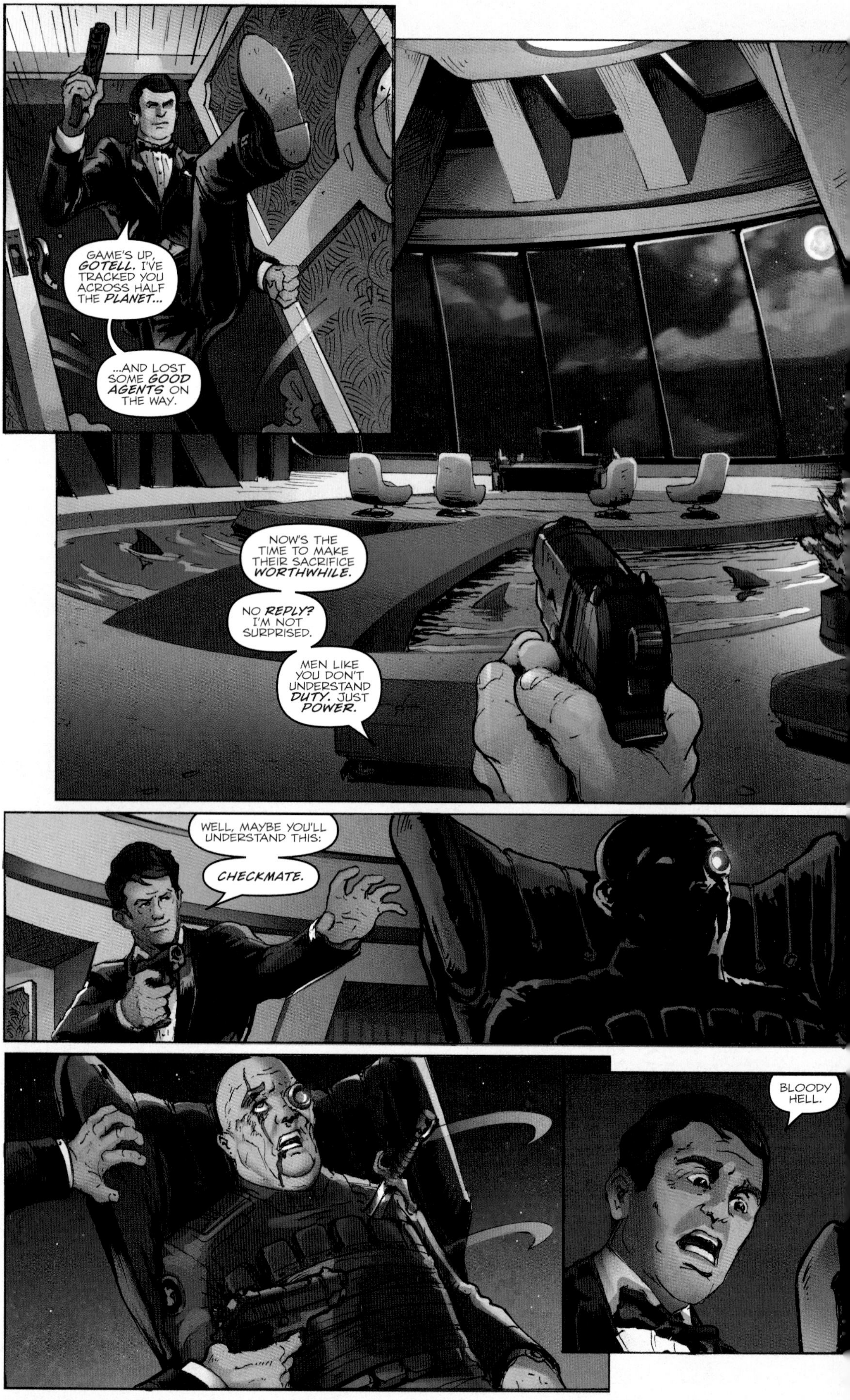
GAME'S UP, GOTELL. I'VE TRACKED YOU ACROSS HALF THE PLANET...
...AND LOST SOME GOOD AGENTS ON THE WAY.
NOW'S THE TIME TO MAKE THEIR SACRIFICE WORTHWHILE.
NO REPLY? I'M NOT SURPRISED.
MEN LIKE YOU DON'T UNDERSTAND DUTY. JUST POWER.
WELL, MAYBE YOU'LL UNDERSTAND THIS:
CHECKMATE.
BLOODY HELL.

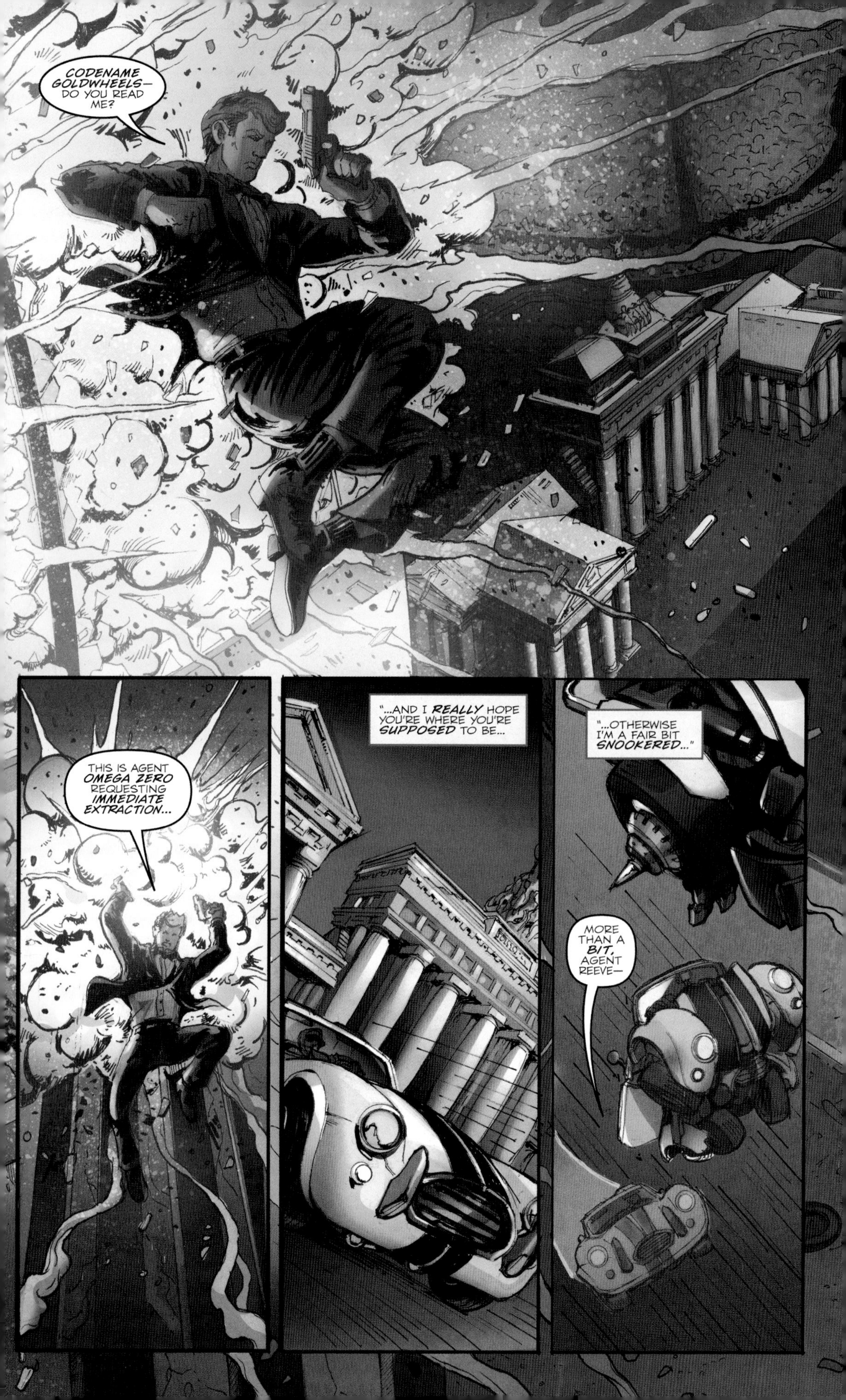

CODENAME GOLDWHEELS— DO YOU READ ME?
THIS IS AGENT OMEGA ZERO REQUESTING IMMEDIATE EXTRACTION...
"...AND I REALLY HOPE YOU'RE WHERE YOU'RE SUPPOSED TO BE...
"...OTHERWISE I'M A FAIR BIT SNOOKERED..."
MORE THAN A BIT, AGENT REEVE—

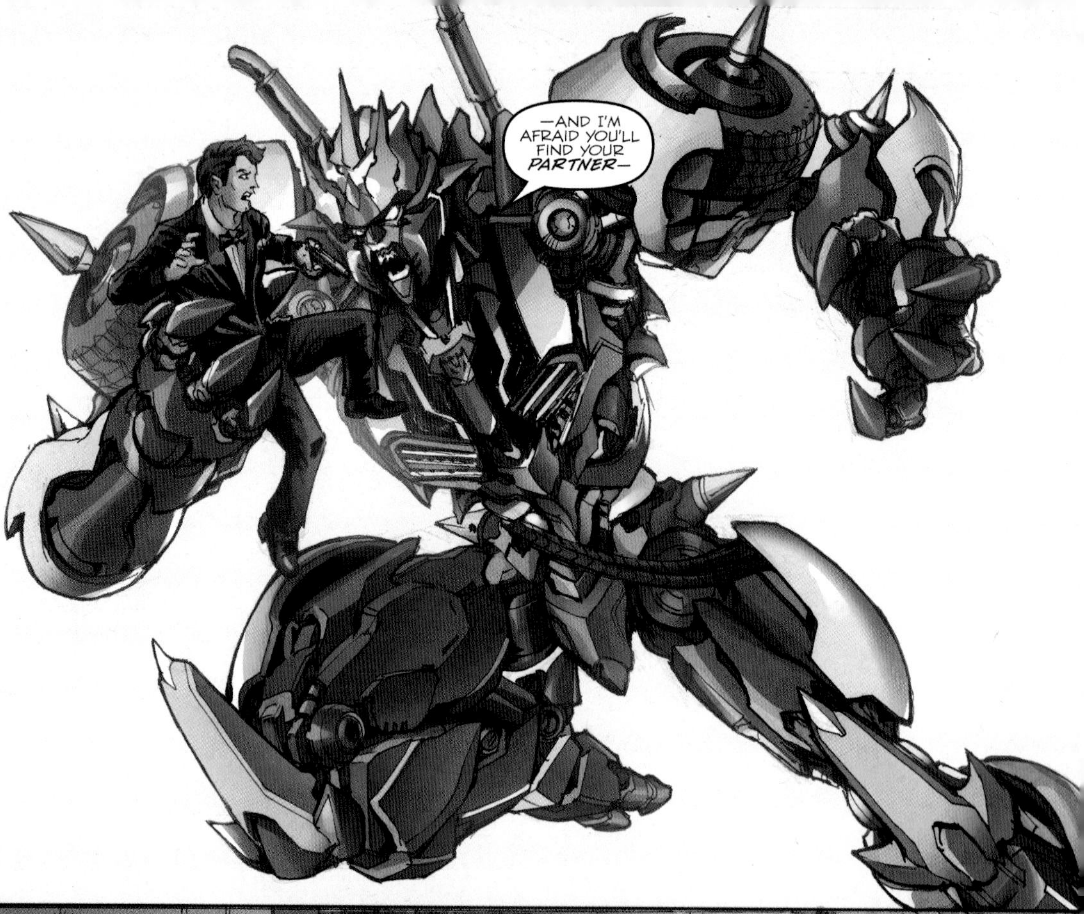
—AND I'M AFRAID YOU'LL FIND YOUR *PARTNER*—

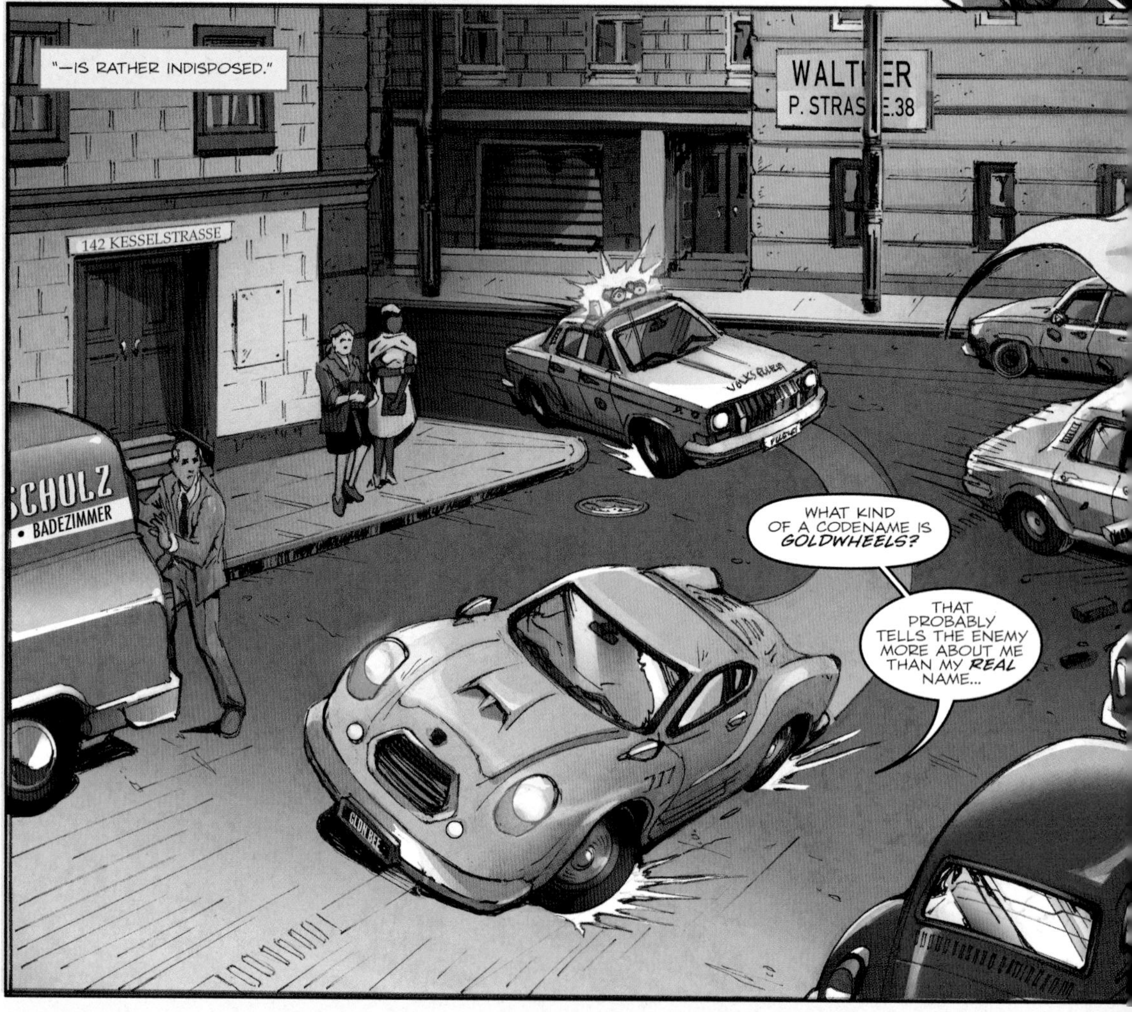
"—IS RATHER INDISPOSED."
142 KESSELSTRASSE
SCHOLZ
BADEZIMMER
WHAT KIND OF A CODENAME IS *GOLDWHEELS?*
THAT PROBABLY TELLS THE ENEMY MORE ABOUT ME THAN MY *REAL* NAME...

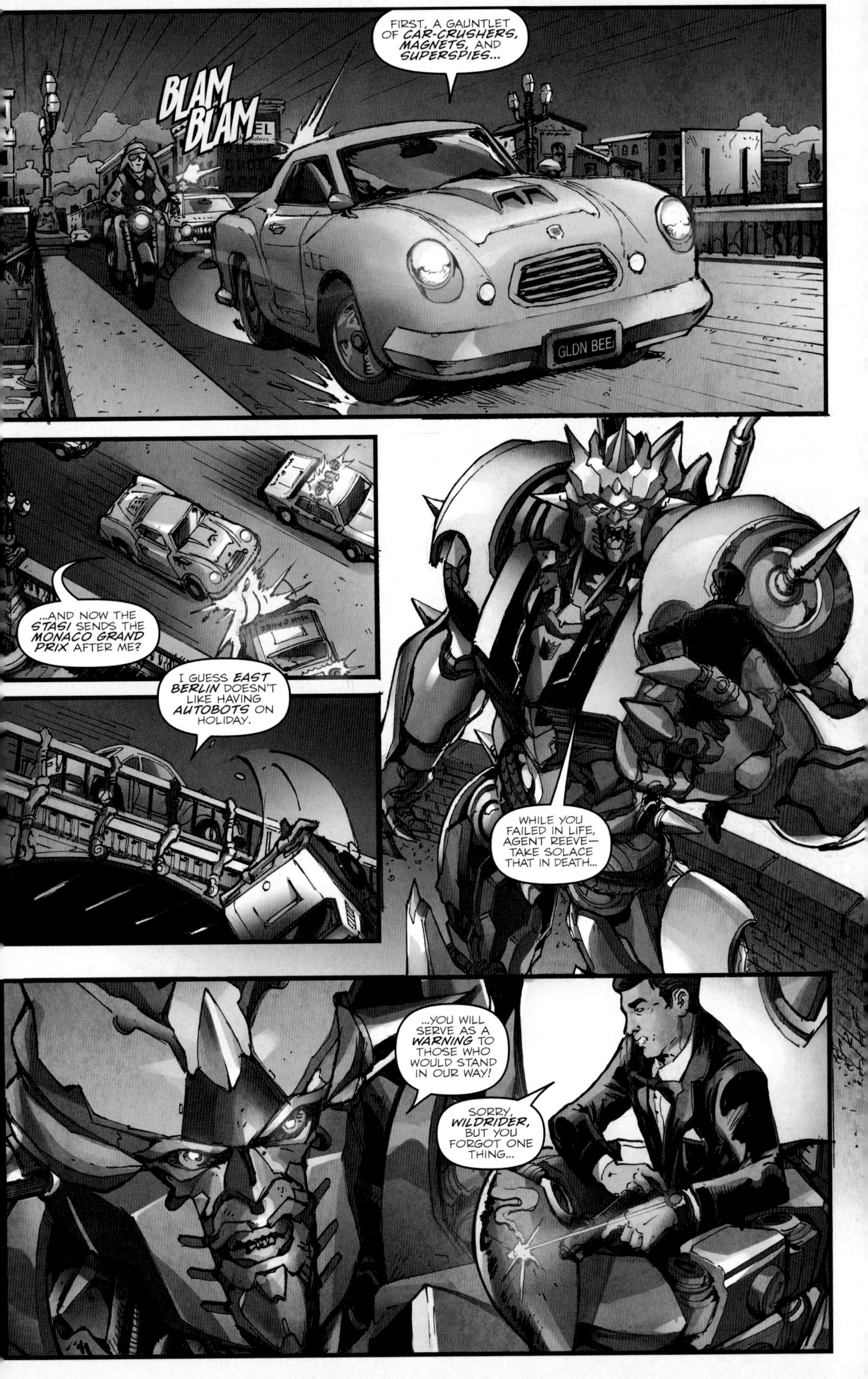
FIRST, A GAUNTLET OF CAR-CRUSHERS, MAGNETS, AND SUPERSPIES...
BLAM BLAM
GLDN BEE
...AND NOW THE STASI SENDS THE MONACO GRAND PRIX AFTER ME?
I GUESS EAST BERLIN DOESN'T LIKE HAVING AUTOBOTS ON HOLIDAY.
WHILE YOU FAILED IN LIFE, AGENT REEVE— TAKE SOLACE THAT IN DEATH...
...YOU WILL SERVE AS A WARNING TO THOSE WHO WOULD STAND IN OUR WAY!
SORRY, WILDRIDER, BUT YOU FORGOT ONE THING...

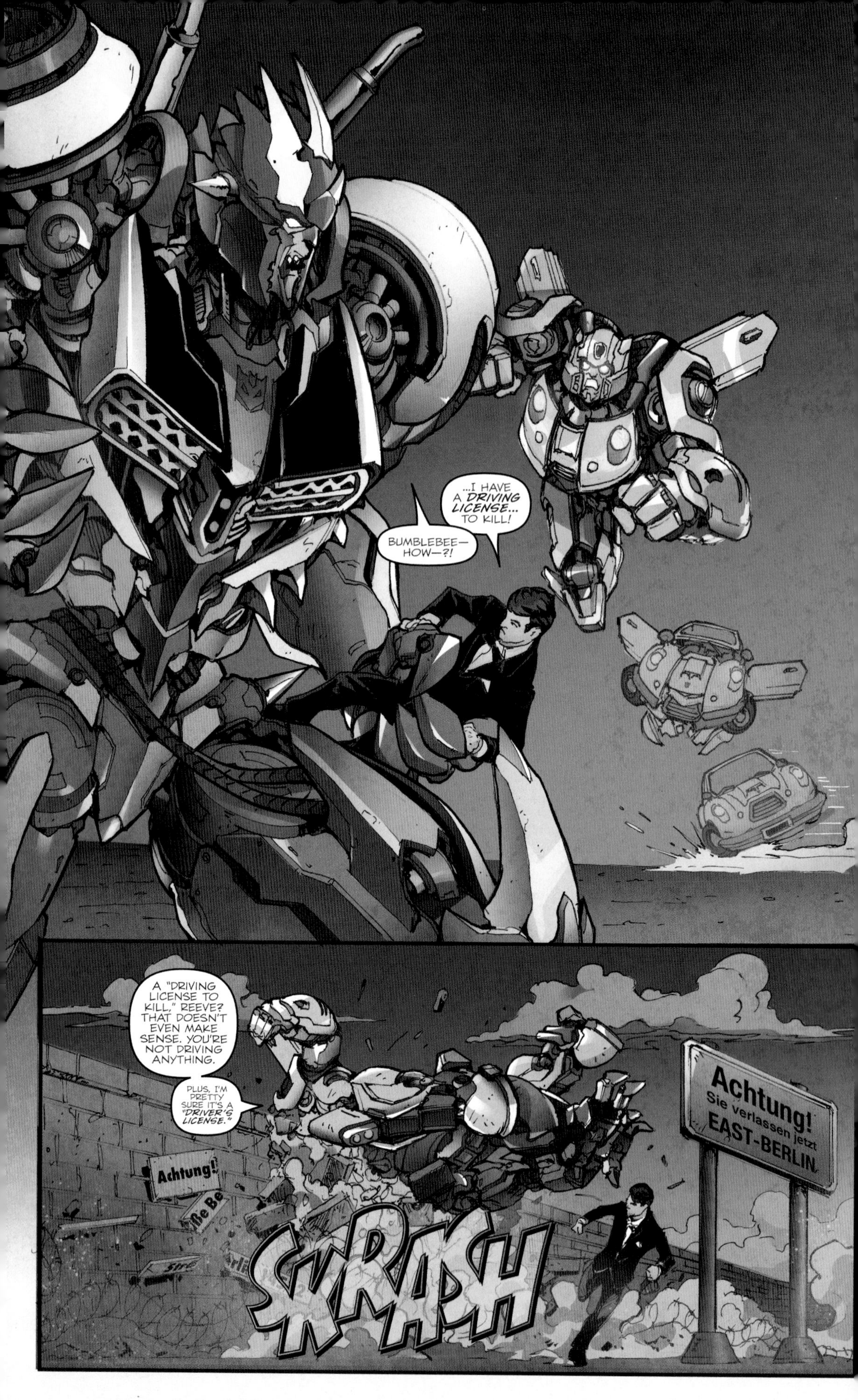
BUMBLEBEE— HOW—?!
...I HAVE A *DRIVING LICENSE*... TO KILL!
A "DRIVING LICENSE TO KILL," REEVE? THAT DOESN'T EVEN MAKE SENSE. YOU'RE NOT DRIVING ANYTHING.
PLUS, I'M PRETTY SURE IT'S A *"DRIVER'S LICENSE."*
Achtung!
Achtung! Sie verlassen jetzt EAST-BERLIN.
SKRASH

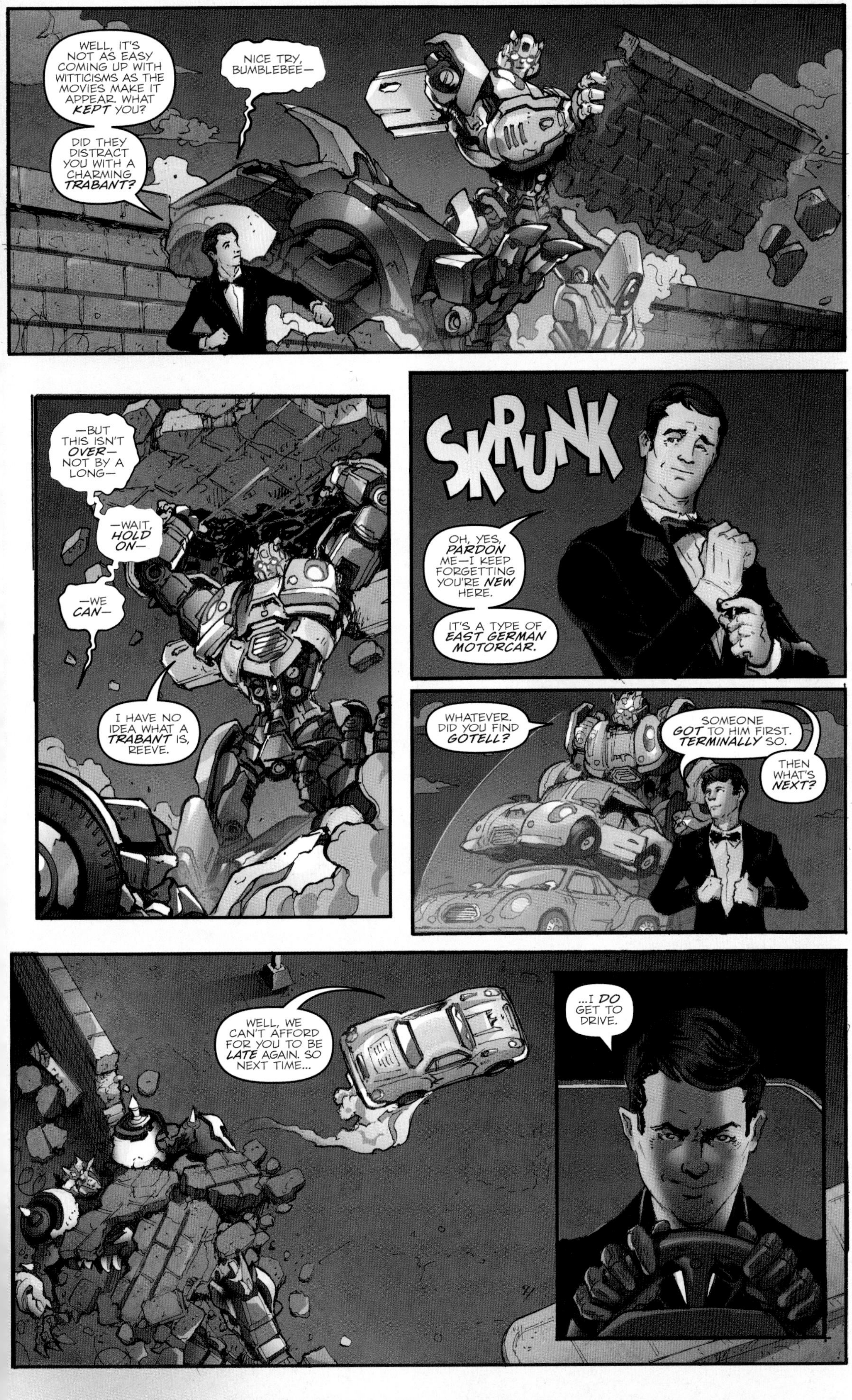
WELL, IT'S NOT AS EASY COMING UP WITH WITTICISMS AS THE MOVIES MAKE IT APPEAR. WHAT KEPT YOU?
DID THEY DISTRACT YOU WITH A CHARMING TRABANT?
NICE TRY, BUMBLEBEE—
—BUT THIS ISN'T OVER— NOT BY A LONG—
—WAIT, HOLD ON—
—WE CAN—
I HAVE NO IDEA WHAT A TRABANT IS, REEVE.
SKRUNK
OH, YES, PARDON ME—I KEEP FORGETTING YOU'RE NEW HERE.
IT'S A TYPE OF EAST GERMAN MOTORCAR.
WHATEVER. DID YOU FIND GOTELL?
SOMEONE GOT TO HIM FIRST. TERMINALLY SO.
THEN WHAT'S NEXT?
WELL, WE CAN'T AFFORD FOR YOU TO BE LATE AGAIN. SO NEXT TIME...
...I DO GET TO DRIVE.

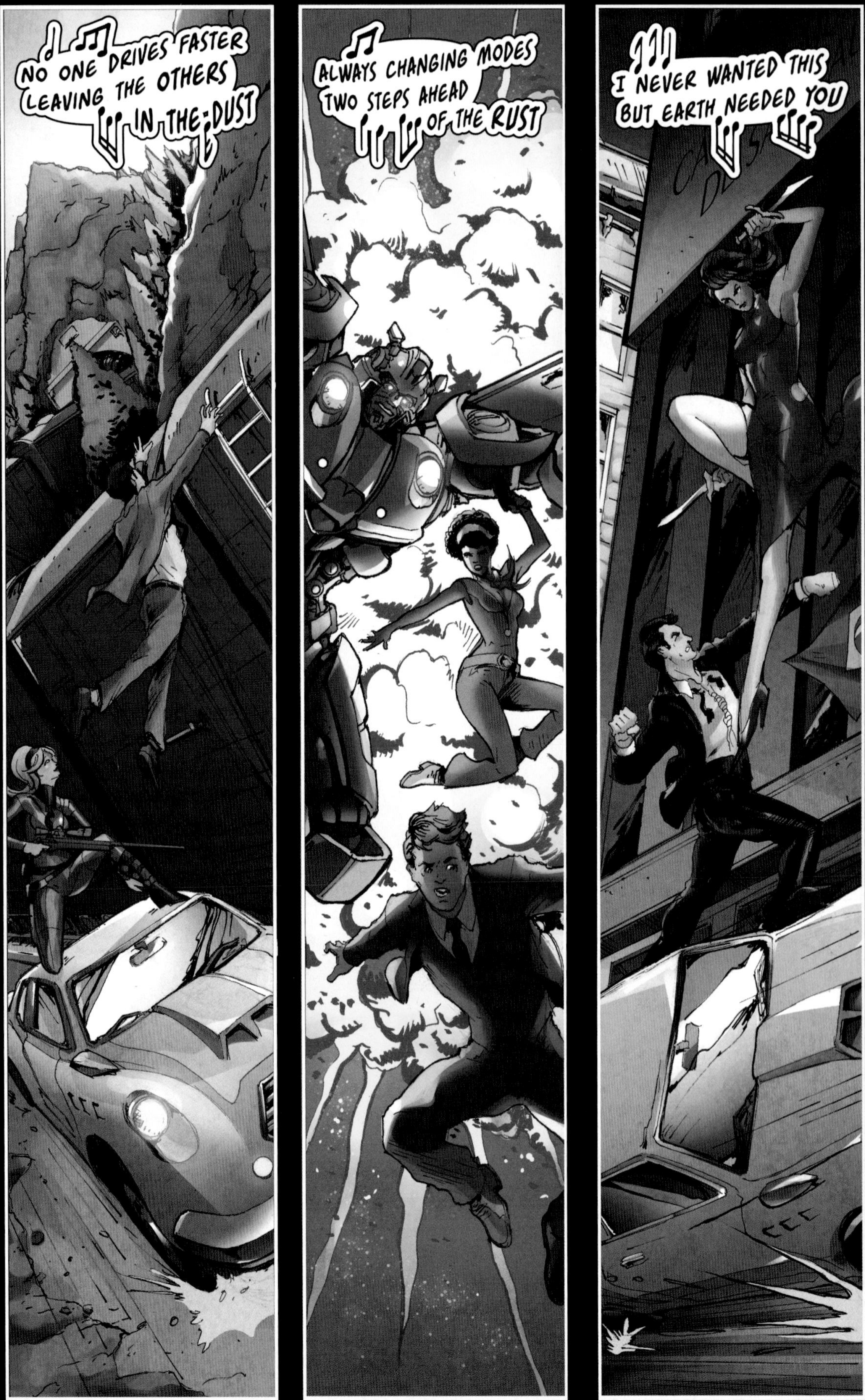
NO ONE DRIVES FASTER LEAVING THE OTHERS IN THE DUST
ALWAYS CHANGING MODES TWO STEPS AHEAD OF THE RUST
I NEVER WANTED THIS BUT EARTH NEEDED YOU

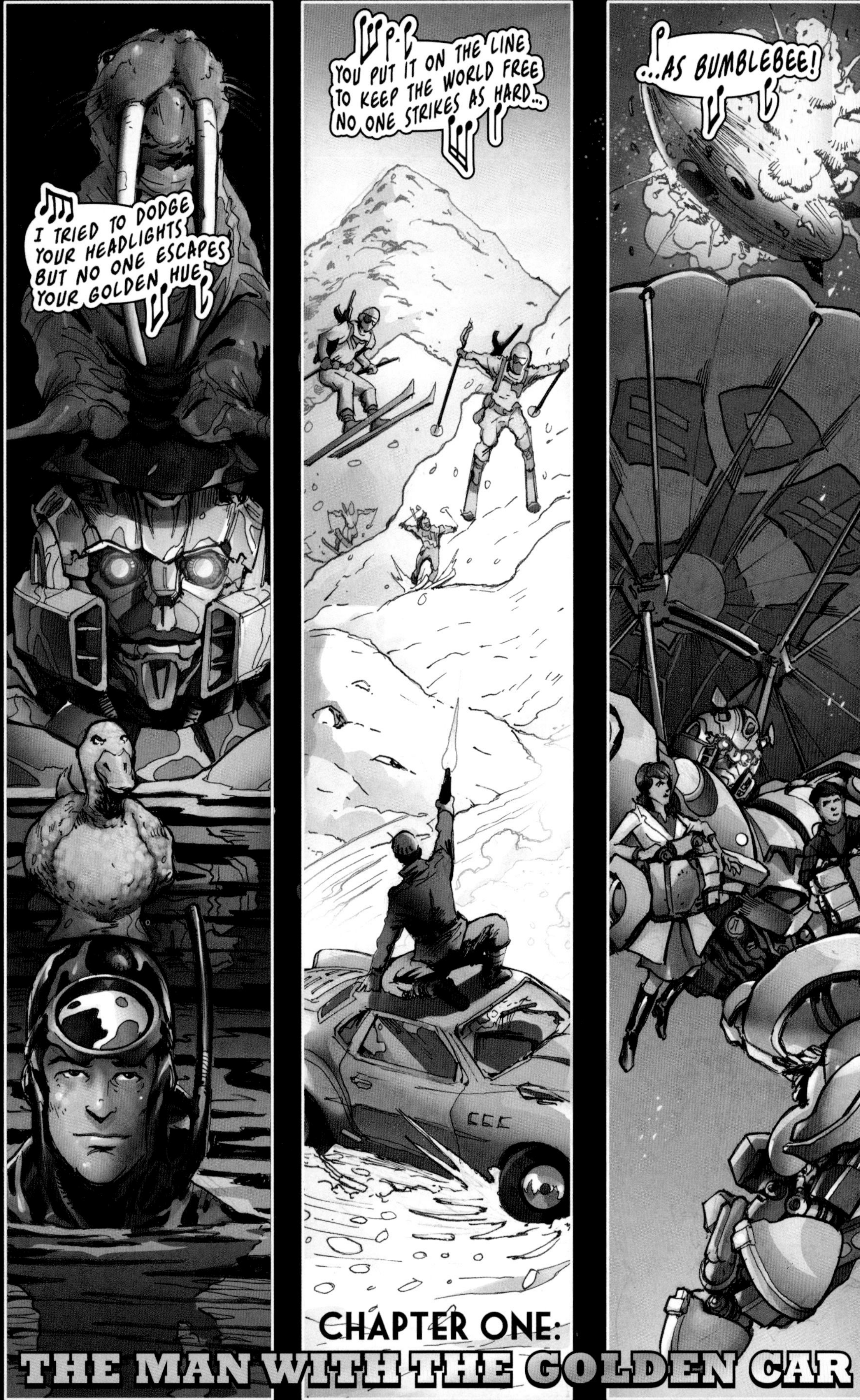
I TRIED TO DODGE YOUR HEADLIGHTS BUT NO ONE ESCAPES YOUR GOLDEN HUE
YOU PUT IT ON THE LINE TO KEEP THE WORLD FREE NO ONE STRIKES AS HARD...
...AS BUMBLEBEE!
CHAPTER ONE:
THE MAN WITH THE GOLDEN CAR

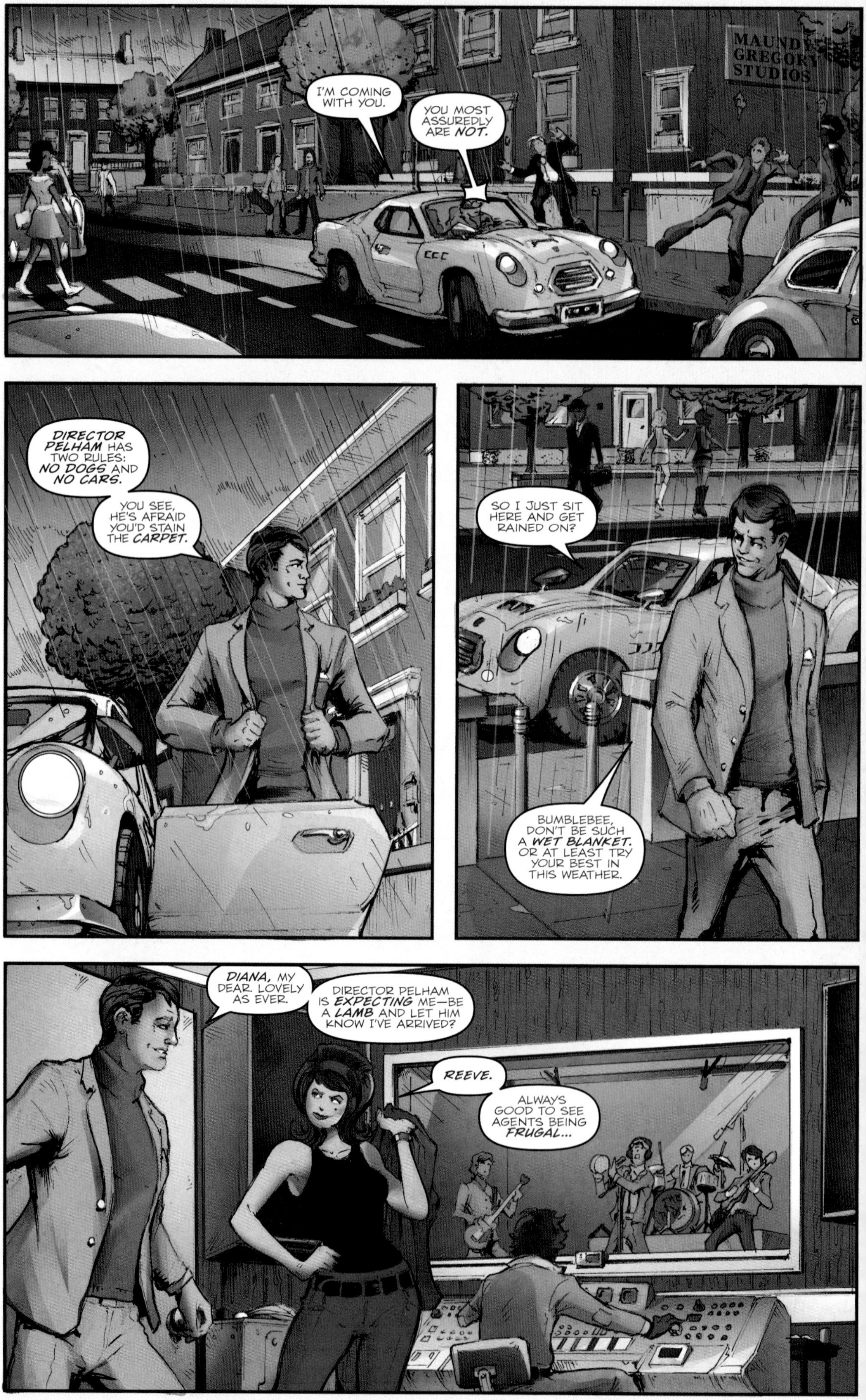
MAUNDY GREGORY STUDIOS
I'M COMING WITH YOU.
YOU MOST ASSUREDLY ARE NOT.
DIRECTOR PELHAM HAS TWO RULES: NO DOGS AND NO CARS.
YOU SEE, HE'S AFRAID YOU'D STAIN THE CARPET.
SO I JUST SIT HERE AND GET RAINED ON?
BUMBLEBEE, DON'T BE SUCH A WET BLANKET. OR AT LEAST TRY YOUR BEST IN THIS WEATHER.
DIANA, MY DEAR. LOVELY AS EVER.
DIRECTOR PELHAM IS EXPECTING ME—BE A LAMB AND LET HIM KNOW I'VE ARRIVED?
REEVE.
ALWAYS GOOD TO SEE AGENTS BEING FRUGAL...

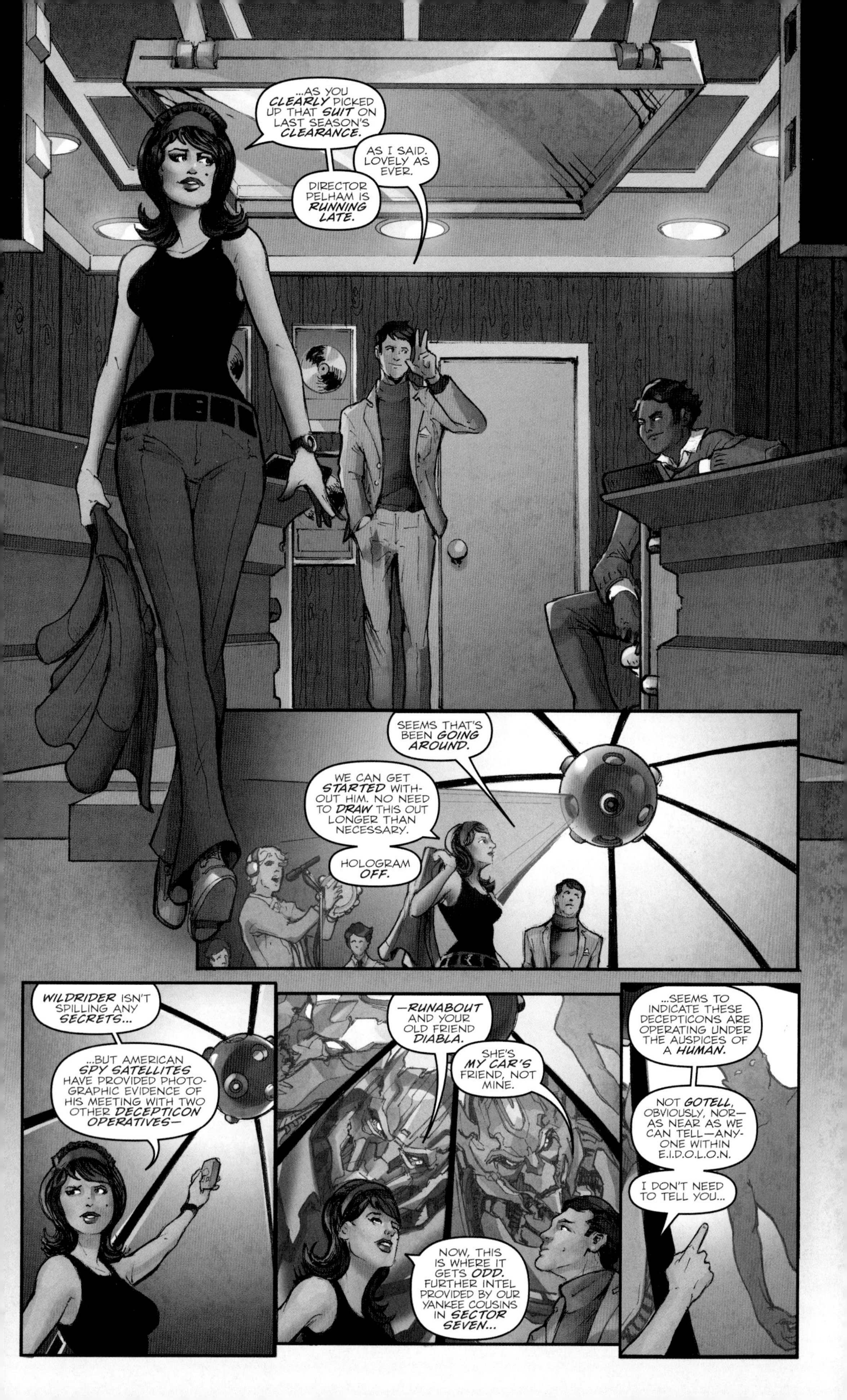
...AS YOU CLEARLY PICKED UP THAT SUIT ON LAST SEASON'S CLEARANCE.
AS I SAID. LOVELY AS EVER.
DIRECTOR PELHAM IS RUNNING LATE.
SEEMS THAT'S BEEN GOING AROUND.
WE CAN GET STARTED WITHOUT HIM. NO NEED TO DRAW THIS OUT LONGER THAN NECESSARY.
HOLOGRAM OFF.
WILDRIDER ISN'T SPILLING ANY SECRETS...
...BUT AMERICAN SPY SATELLITES HAVE PROVIDED PHOTOGRAPHIC EVIDENCE OF HIS MEETING WITH TWO OTHER DECEPTICON OPERATIVES—
—RUNABOUT AND YOUR OLD FRIEND DIABLA.
SHE'S MY CAR'S FRIEND, NOT MINE.
NOW, THIS IS WHERE IT GETS ODD. FURTHER INTEL PROVIDED BY OUR YANKEE COUSINS IN SECTOR SEVEN...
...SEEMS TO INDICATE THESE DECEPTICONS ARE OPERATING UNDER THE AUSPICES OF A HUMAN.
NOT GOTELL, OBVIOUSLY, NOR—AS NEAR AS WE CAN TELL—ANYONE WITHIN E.I.D.O.L.O.N.
I DON'T NEED TO TELL YOU...

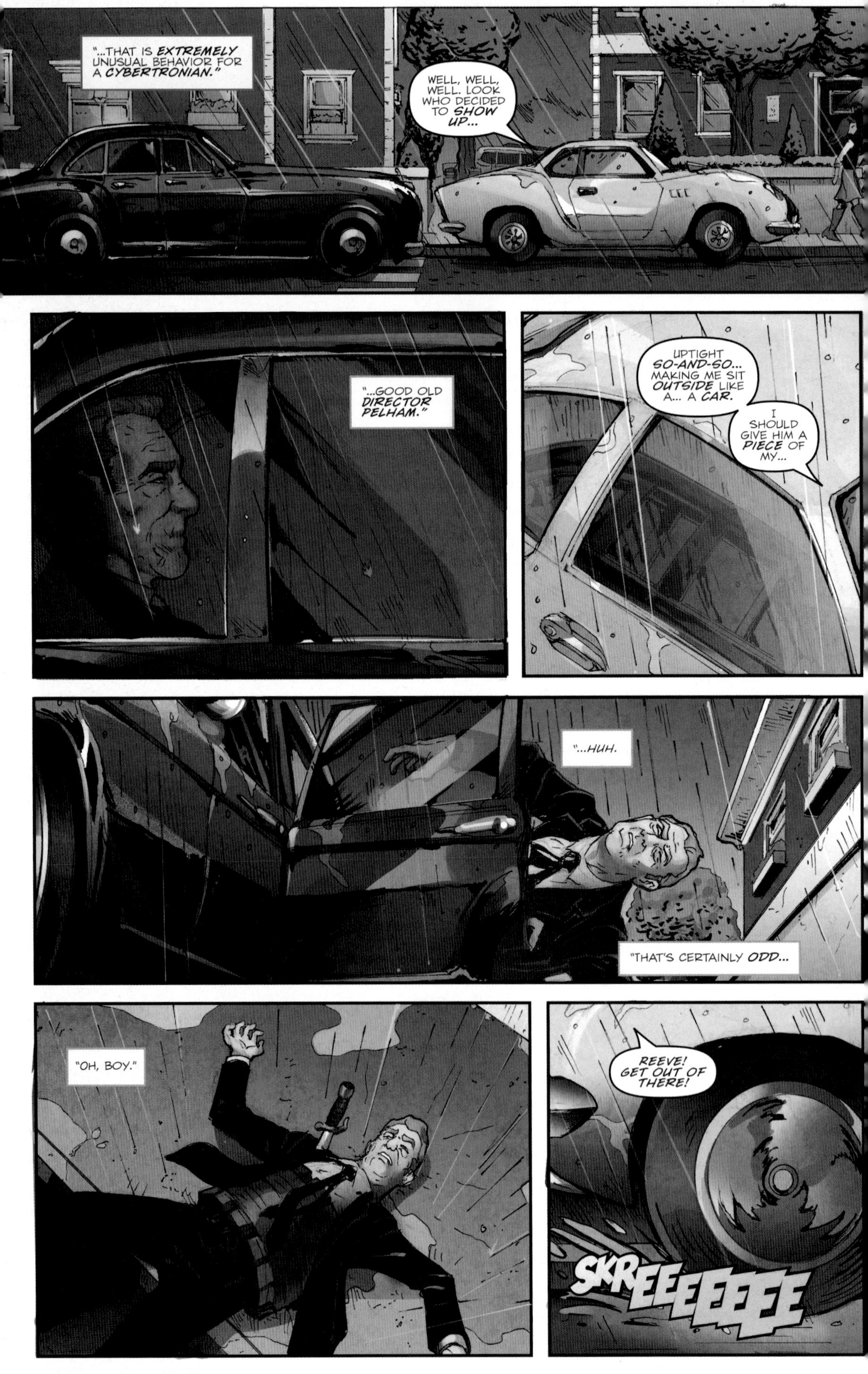
"...THAT IS EXTREMELY UNUSUAL BEHAVIOR FOR A CYBERTRONIAN."
WELL, WELL, WELL. LOOK WHO DECIDED TO SHOW UP...
"...GOOD OLD DIRECTOR PELHAM."
UPTIGHT SO-AND-SO... MAKING ME SIT OUTSIDE LIKE A... A CAR.
I SHOULD GIVE HIM A PIECE OF MY...
"...HUH.
"THAT'S CERTAINLY ODD...
"OH, BOY."
REEVE! GET OUT OF THERE!
SKREEEEEEEE

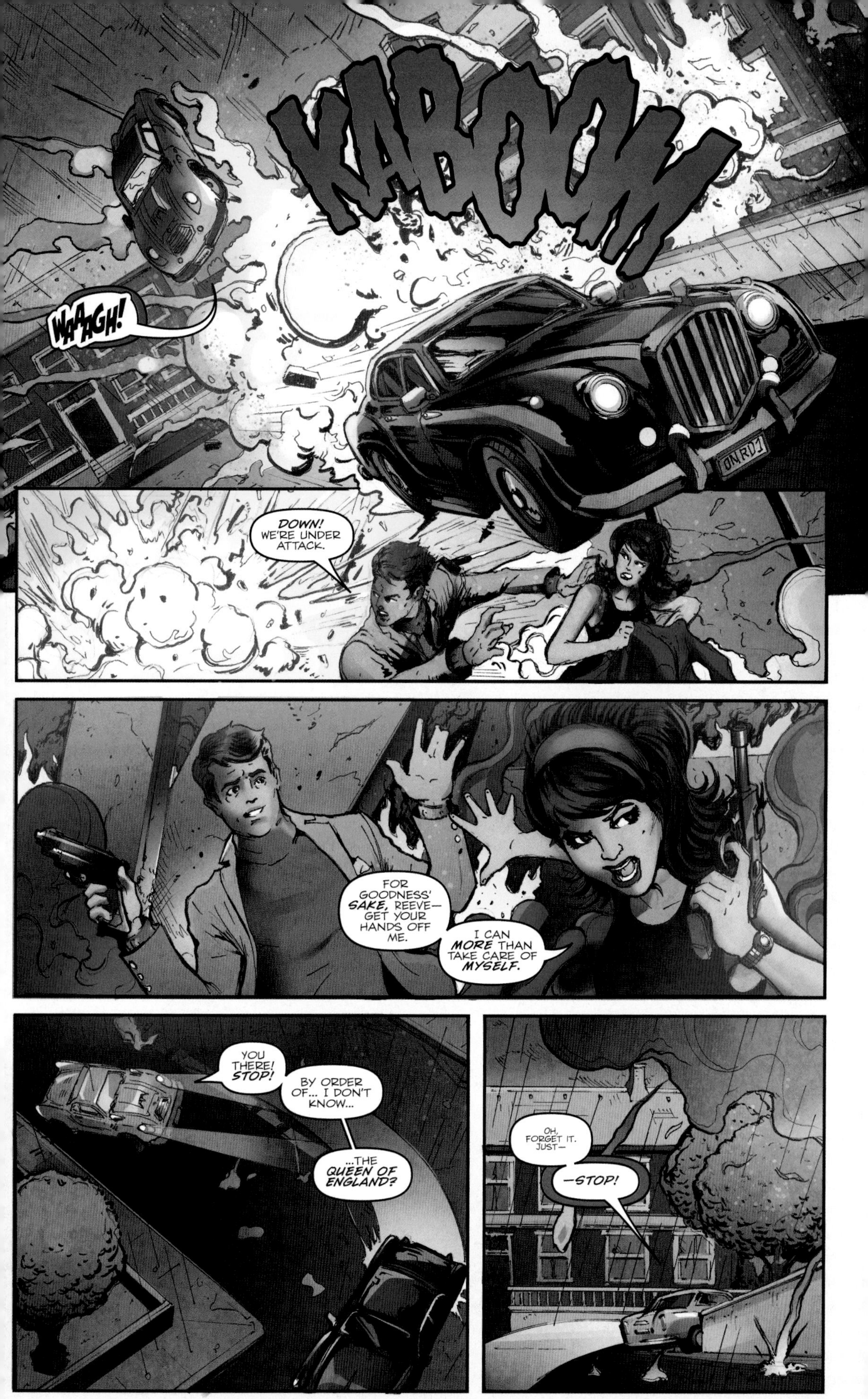
KABOOM
WAAAGH!
DOWN! WE'RE UNDER ATTACK.
FOR GOODNESS' SAKE, REEVE—GET YOUR HANDS OFF ME.
I CAN MORE THAN TAKE CARE OF MYSELF.
YOU THERE! STOP!
BY ORDER OF... I DON'T KNOW...
...THE QUEEN OF ENGLAND?
OH, FORGET IT. JUST—
—STOP!

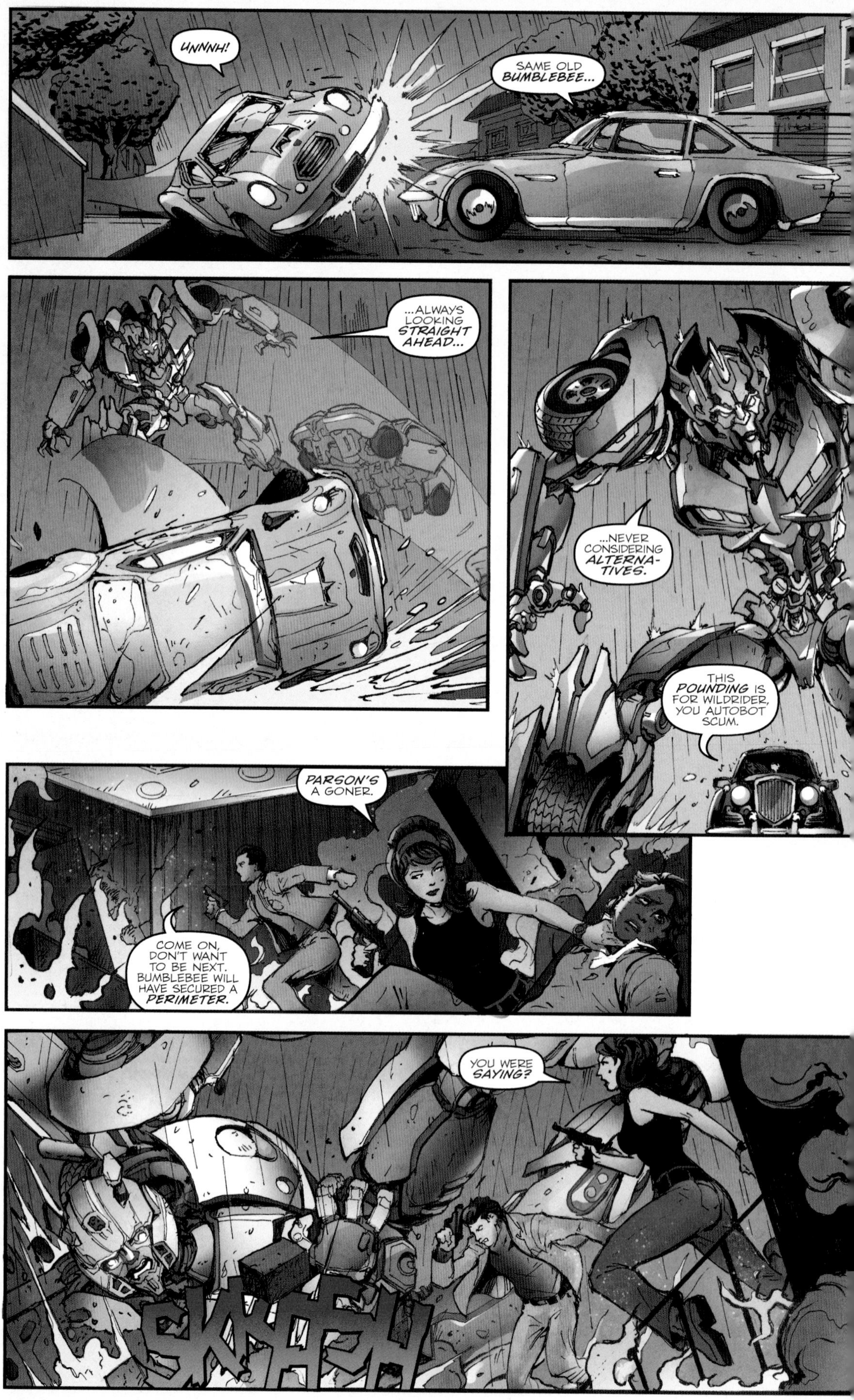
UNNNH!
SAME OLD BUMBLEBEE...
...ALWAYS LOOKING STRAIGHT AHEAD...
...NEVER CONSIDERING ALTERNATIVES.
THIS POUNDING IS FOR WILDRIDER, YOU AUTOBOT SCUM.
PARSON'S A GONER.
COME ON, DON'T WANT TO BE NEXT. BUMBLEBEE WILL HAVE SECURED A PERIMETER.
YOU WERE SAYING?

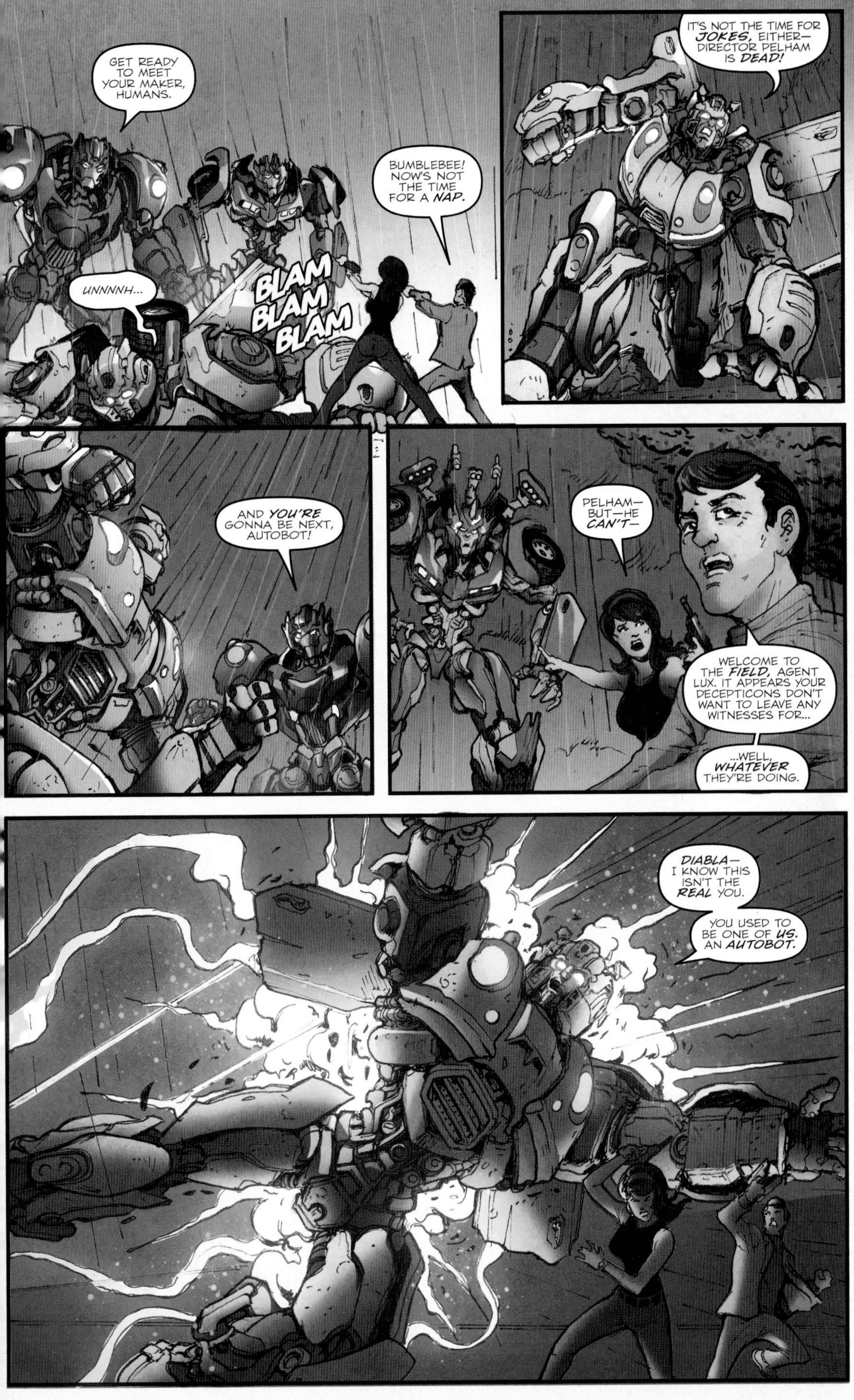
GET READY TO MEET YOUR MAKER, HUMANS.
UNNNNH...
BLAM BLAM BLAM
BUMBLEBEE! NOW'S NOT THE TIME FOR A NAP.
IT'S NOT THE TIME FOR JOKES, EITHER—DIRECTOR PELHAM IS DEAD!
AND YOU'RE GONNA BE NEXT, AUTOBOT!
PELHAM—BUT—HE CAN'T—
WELCOME TO THE FIELD, AGENT LUX. IT APPEARS YOUR DECEPTICONS DON'T WANT TO LEAVE ANY WITNESSES FOR...
...WELL, WHATEVER THEY'RE DOING.
DIABLA—I KNOW THIS ISN'T THE REAL YOU.
YOU USED TO BE ONE OF US. AN AUTOBOT.

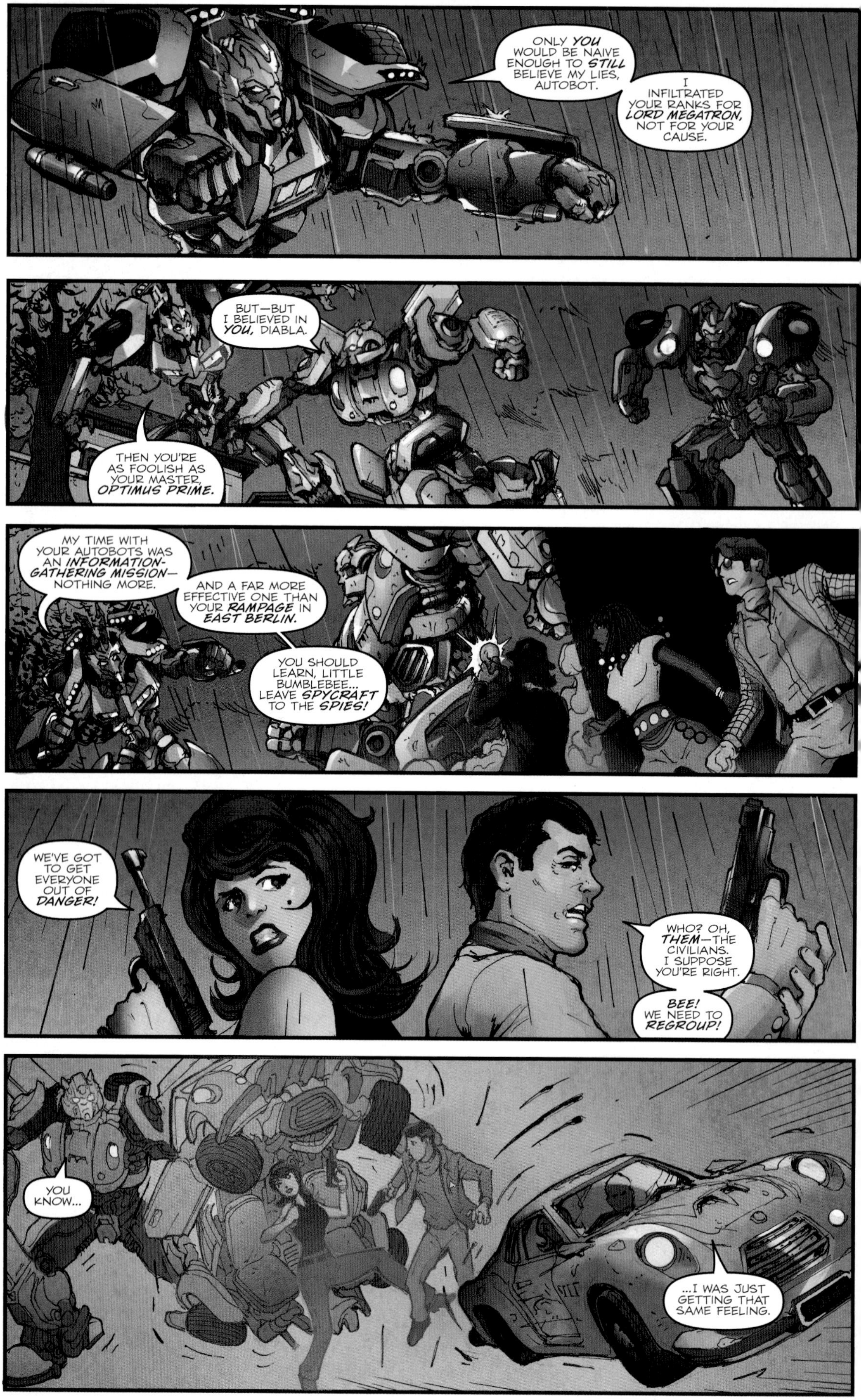
ONLY *YOU* WOULD BE NAIVE ENOUGH TO *STILL* BELIEVE MY LIES, AUTOBOT.
I INFILTRATED YOUR RANKS FOR *LORD MEGATRON,* NOT FOR YOUR CAUSE.
BUT—BUT I BELIEVED IN *YOU,* DIABLA.
THEN YOU'RE AS FOOLISH AS YOUR MASTER, *OPTIMUS PRIME.*
MY TIME WITH YOUR AUTOBOTS WAS AN *INFORMATION-GATHERING MISSION*—NOTHING MORE.
AND A FAR MORE EFFECTIVE ONE THAN YOUR *RAMPAGE* IN *EAST BERLIN.*
YOU SHOULD LEARN, LITTLE BUMBLEBEE... LEAVE *SPYCRAFT* TO THE *SPIES!*
WE'VE GOT TO GET EVERYONE OUT OF *DANGER!*
WHO? OH, *THEM*—THE CIVILIANS. I SUPPOSE YOU'RE RIGHT.
BEE! WE NEED TO *REGROUP!*
YOU KNOW...
...I WAS JUST GETTING THAT SAME FEELING.

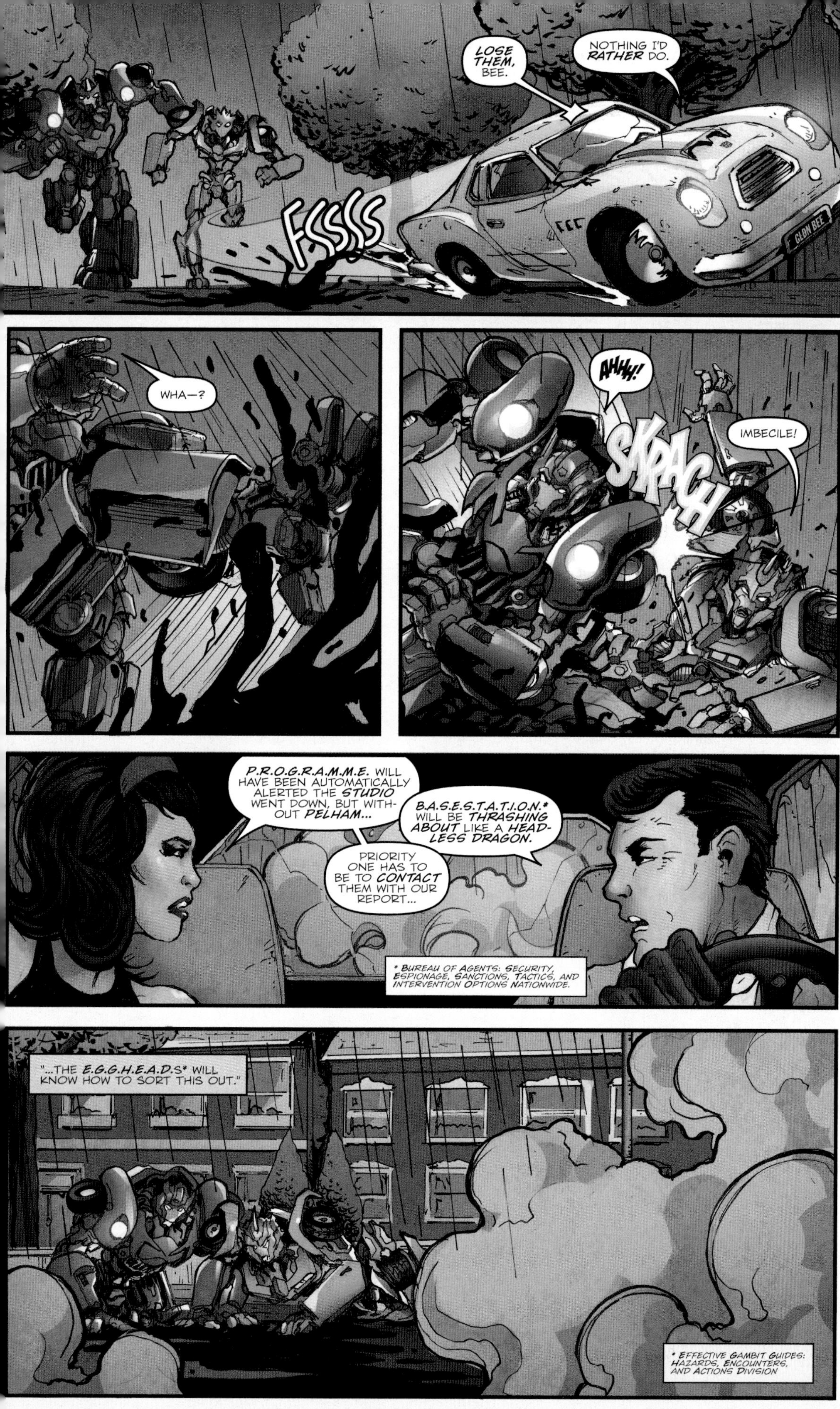
LOSE THEM, BEE.
NOTHING I'D RATHER DO.
FSSSS
GLDN BEE
WHA—?
AHHH!
SKRACH
IMBECILE!
P.R.O.G.R.A.M.M.E. WILL HAVE BEEN AUTOMATICALLY ALERTED THE STUDIO WENT DOWN, BUT WITHOUT PELHAM...
B.A.S.E.S.T.A.T.I.O.N.* WILL BE THRASHING ABOUT LIKE A HEADLESS DRAGON.
PRIORITY ONE HAS TO BE TO CONTACT THEM WITH OUR REPORT...
* BUREAU OF AGENTS: SECURITY, ESPIONAGE, SANCTIONS, TACTICS, AND INTERVENTION OPTIONS NATIONWIDE.
"...THE E.G.G.H.E.A.D.S* WILL KNOW HOW TO SORT THIS OUT."
* EFFECTIVE GAMBIT GUIDES: HAZARDS, ENCOUNTERS, AND ACTIONS DIVISION

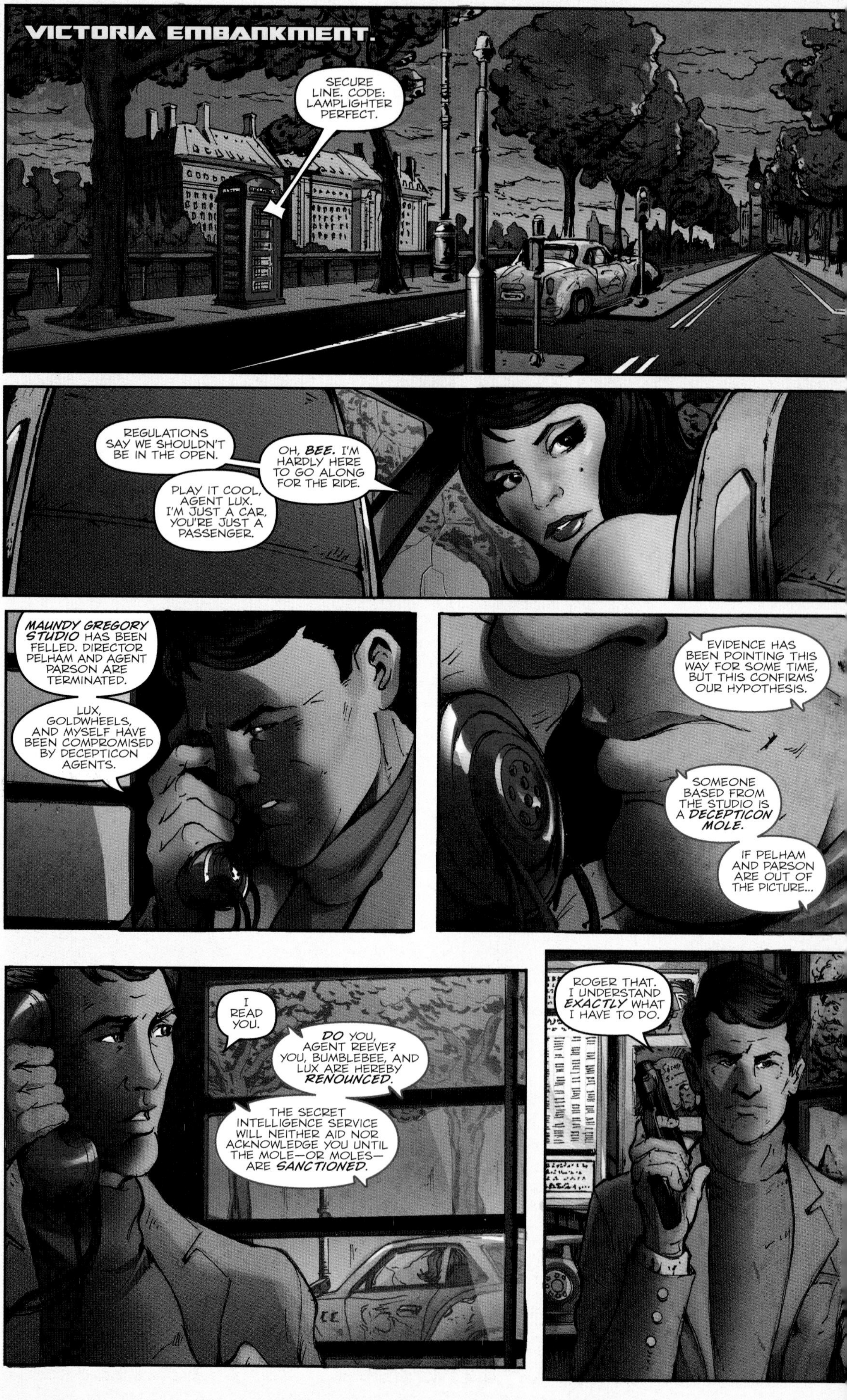
VICTORIA EMBANKMENT.
SECURE LINE. CODE: LAMPLIGHTER PERFECT.
REGULATIONS SAY WE SHOULDN'T BE IN THE OPEN.
OH, BEE. I'M HARDLY HERE TO GO ALONG FOR THE RIDE.
PLAY IT COOL, AGENT LUX. I'M JUST A CAR, YOU'RE JUST A PASSENGER.
MAUNDY GREGORY STUDIO HAS BEEN FELLED. DIRECTOR PELHAM AND AGENT PARSON ARE TERMINATED.
LUX, GOLDWHEELS, AND MYSELF HAVE BEEN COMPROMISED BY DECEPTICON AGENTS.
EVIDENCE HAS BEEN POINTING THIS WAY FOR SOME TIME, BUT THIS CONFIRMS OUR HYPOTHESIS.
SOMEONE BASED FROM THE STUDIO IS A DECEPTICON MOLE.
IF PELHAM AND PARSON ARE OUT OF THE PICTURE...
I READ YOU.
DO YOU, AGENT REEVE? YOU, BUMBLEBEE, AND LUX ARE HEREBY RENOUNCED.
THE SECRET INTELLIGENCE SERVICE WILL NEITHER AID NOR ACKNOWLEDGE YOU UNTIL THE MOLE—OR MOLES—ARE SANCTIONED.
ROGER THAT. I UNDERSTAND EXACTLY WHAT I HAVE TO DO.

TRANSFORMERS

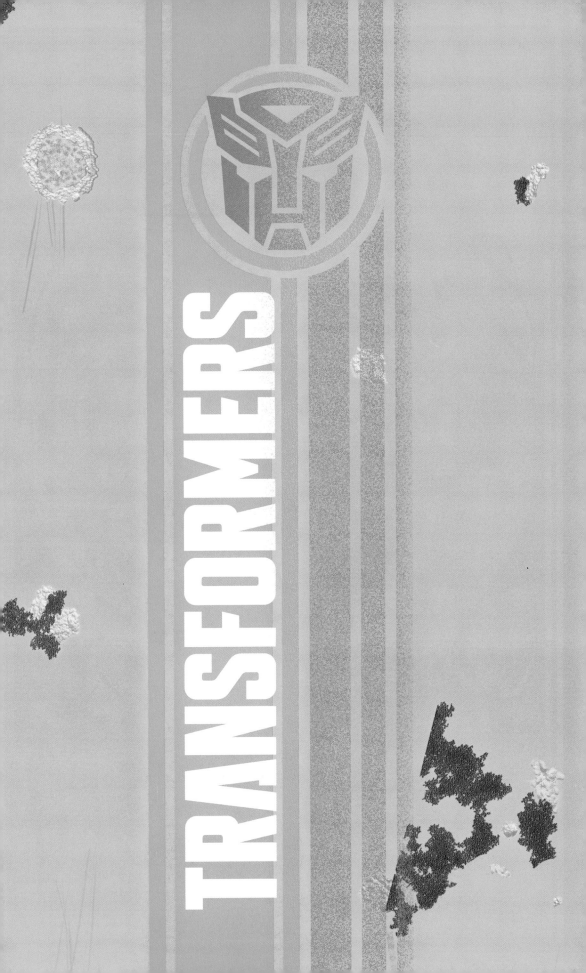

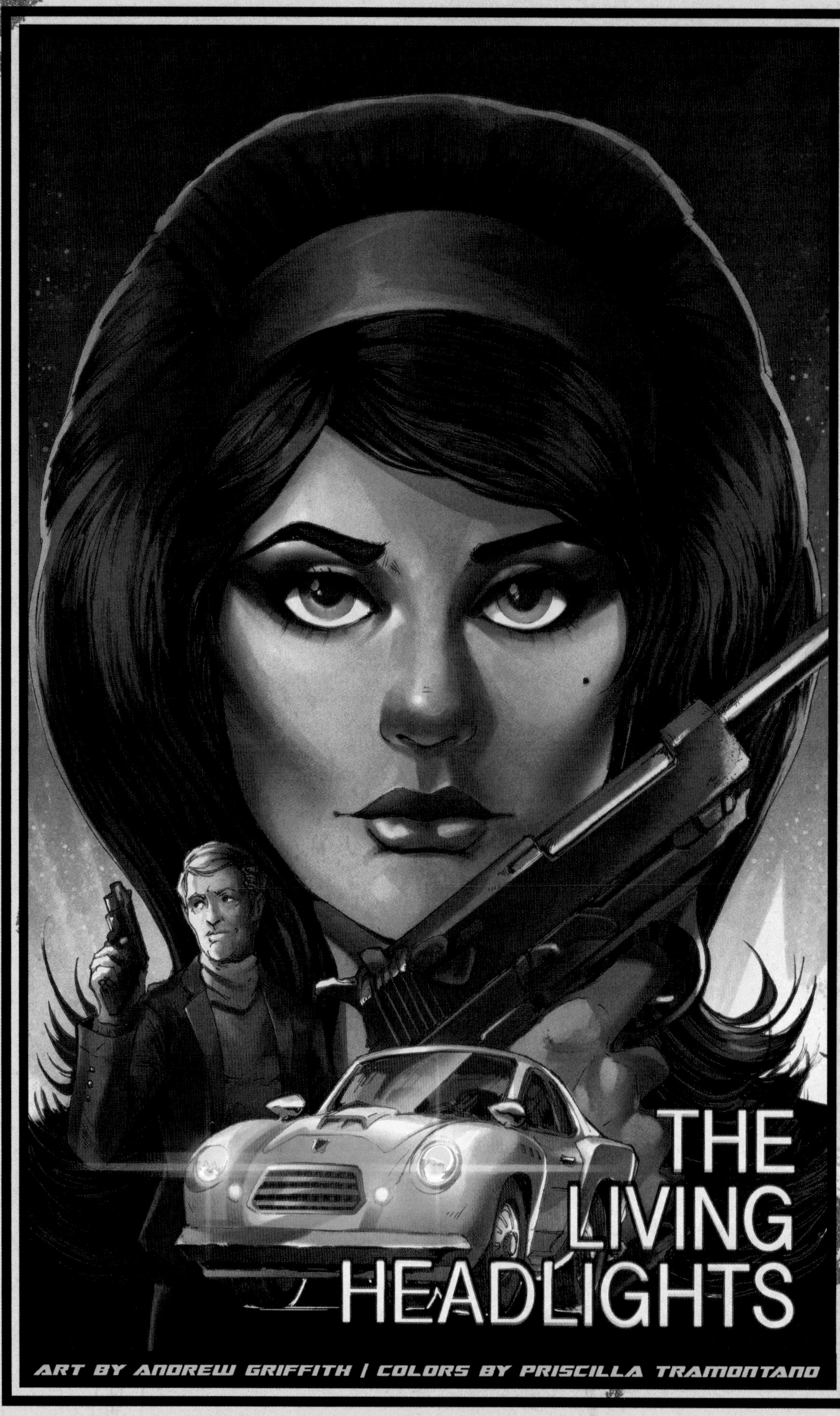
THE
LIVING
HEADLIGHTS
ART BY ANDREW GRIFFITH | COLORS BY PRISCILLA TRAMONTANO

VICTORIA EMBANKMENT.
WESTMINSTER, LONDON.

UH... WHAT ARE YOU DOING, DIANA?

THAT'S *AGENT LUX* TO YOU. YOU'RE AS BAD AS *REEVE*.

AND I'VE *INTERCEPTED* HIS CALL.

"YOU DON'T *TRUST* HIM?"

DIRECTOR *PELHAM* HAS BEEN *MURDERED*, OUR COVER IS *BLOWN*, AND THE *STUDIO* IS IN *RUINS*.

I'M NOT IN A *TRUSTING* MOOD TODAY.

FZZTTS PECIALIN TELLIGENZ ZZTTTTFF FFAIDFFF

"WHAT DO YOU THINK YOU'RE GONNA *HEAR?* REEVE'S JUST GETTING *ORDERS* FROM *B.A.S.E.S.T.A.T.I.O.N.**"

CHAK

*BUREAU OF AGENTS: SECURITY, ESPIONAGE, SANCTIONS, TACTICS, AND INTERVENTION OPTIONS NATIONWIDE.

FGGHSSS EREBY RENOUNCED.

THE SECRET INTELLIGENCE SERVICE WILL NEITHER *AID* NOR *ACKNOWLEDGE* YOU UNTIL THE MOLE— OR MOLES—ARE *SANCTIONED*.

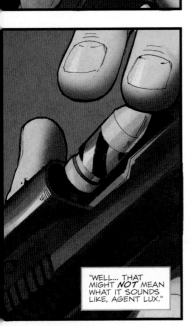

"WELL... THAT MIGHT *NOT* MEAN WHAT IT SOUNDS LIKE, AGENT LUX."

ROGER THAT. I UNDERSTAND *EXACTLY* WHAT I HAVE TO DO.

SORRY, BUMBLEBEE, DIANA...

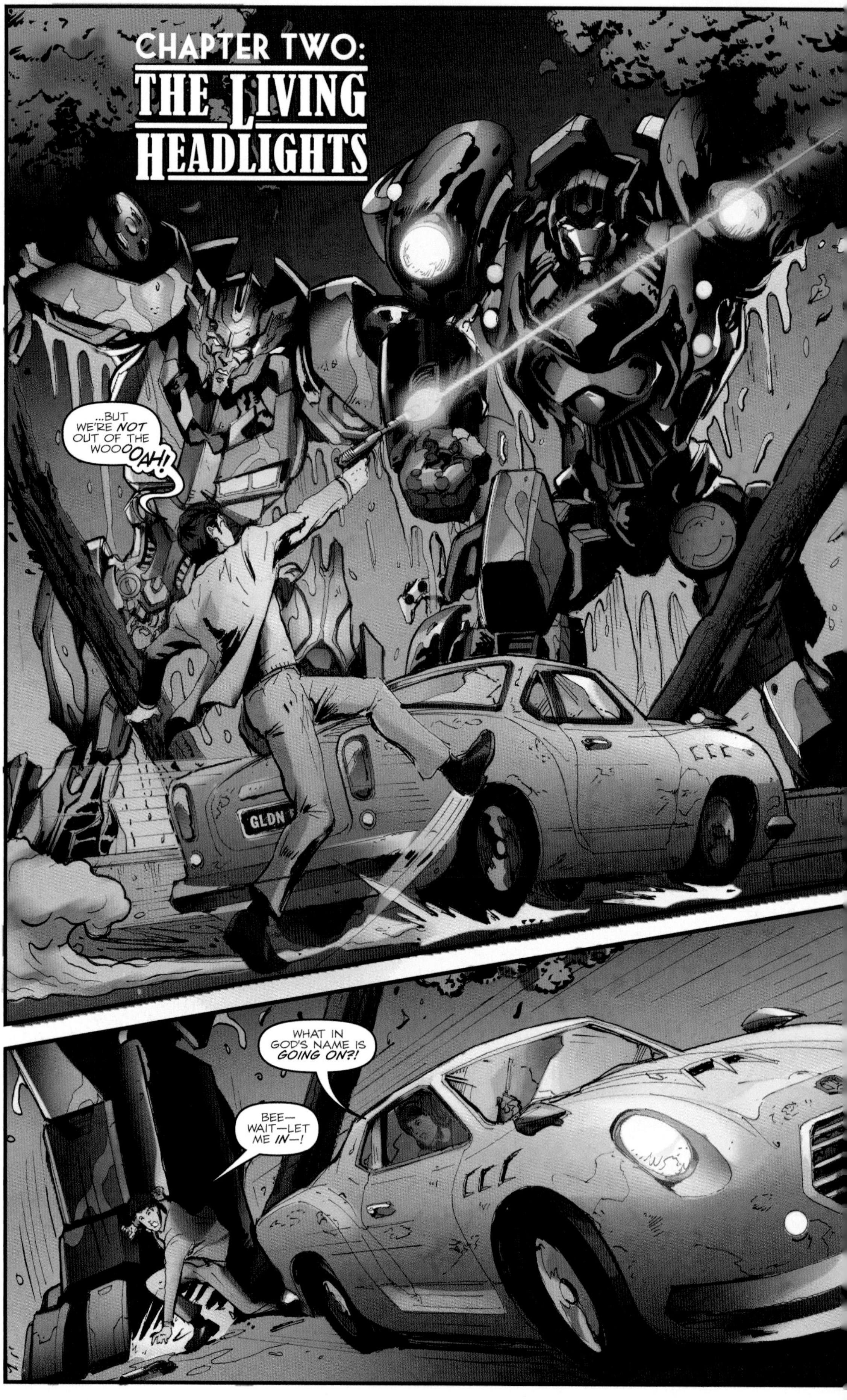
CHAPTER TWO:
THE LIVING HEADLIGHTS
...BUT WE'RE NOT OUT OF THE WOOOOAH!
GLDN
WHAT IN GOD'S NAME IS GOING ON?!
BEE— WAIT—LET ME IN—!

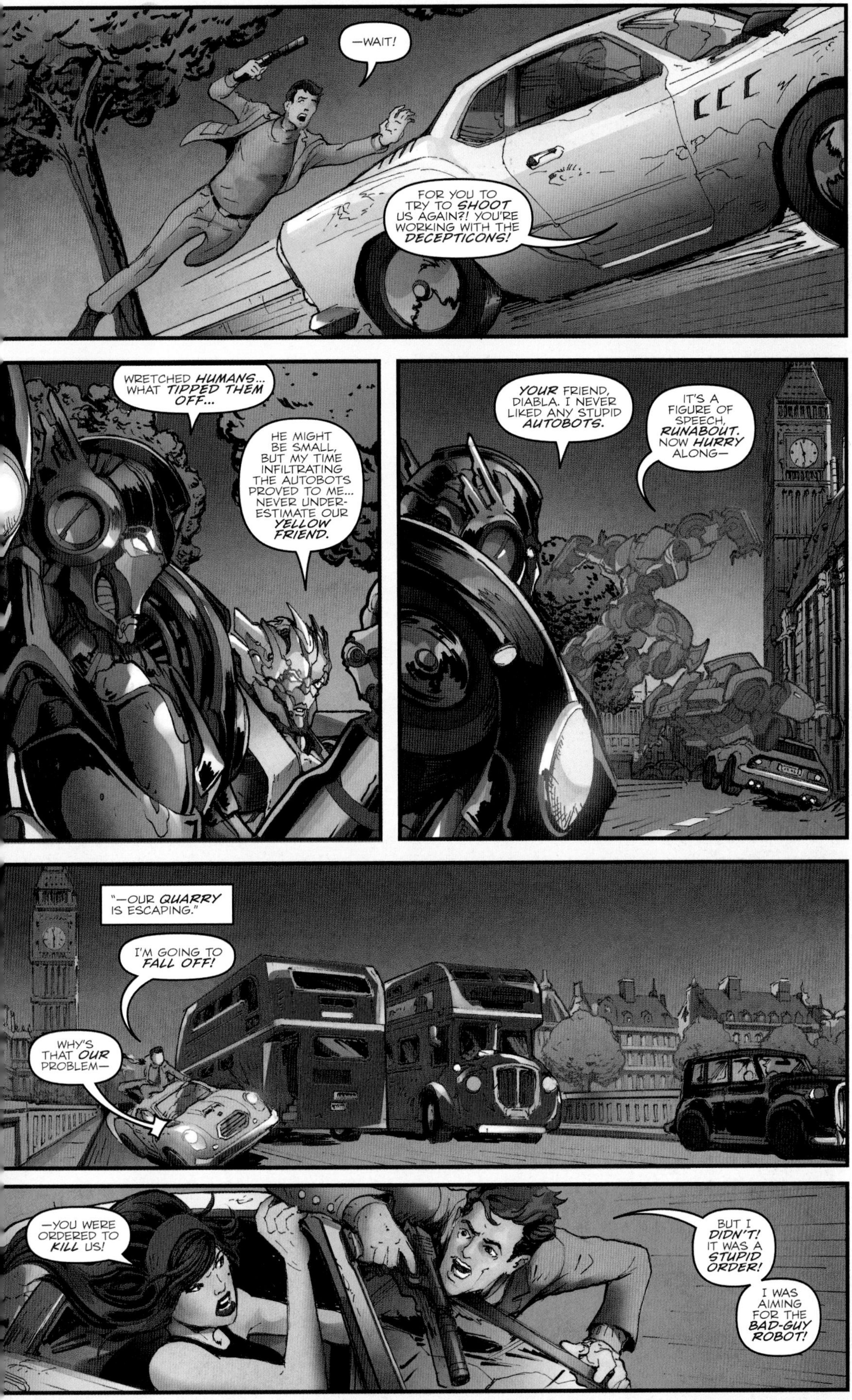
—WAIT!
FOR YOU TO TRY TO SHOOT US AGAIN?! YOU'RE WORKING WITH THE DECEPTICONS!
WRETCHED HUMANS... WHAT TIPPED THEM OFF...
HE MIGHT BE SMALL, BUT MY TIME INFILTRATING THE AUTOBOTS PROVED TO ME... NEVER UNDER-ESTIMATE OUR YELLOW FRIEND.
YOUR FRIEND, DIABLA. I NEVER LIKED ANY STUPID AUTOBOTS.
IT'S A FIGURE OF SPEECH, RUNABOUT. NOW HURRY ALONG—
"—OUR QUARRY IS ESCAPING."
I'M GOING TO FALL OFF!
WHY'S THAT OUR PROBLEM—
—YOU WERE ORDERED TO KILL US!
BUT I DIDN'T! IT WAS A STUPID ORDER!
I WAS AIMING FOR THE BAD-GUY ROBOT!

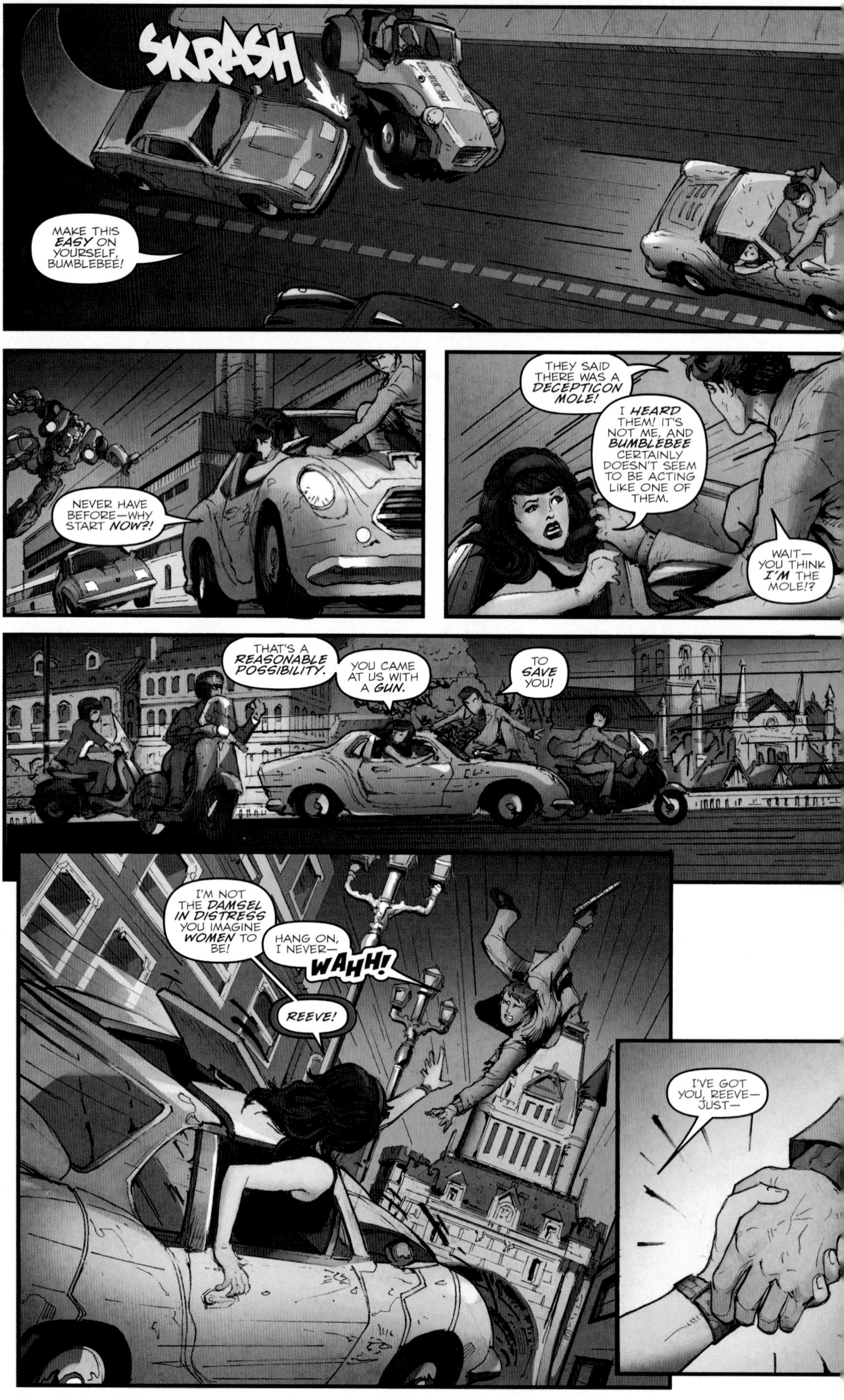
SKRASH
MAKE THIS EASY ON YOURSELF, BUMBLEBEE!
NEVER HAVE BEFORE—WHY START NOW?!
THEY SAID THERE WAS A DECEPTICON MOLE!
I HEARD THEM! IT'S NOT ME, AND BUMBLEBEE CERTAINLY DOESN'T SEEM TO BE ACTING LIKE ONE OF THEM.
WAIT—YOU THINK I'M THE MOLE!?
THAT'S A REASONABLE POSSIBILITY.
YOU CAME AT US WITH A GUN.
TO SAVE YOU!
I'M NOT THE DAMSEL IN DISTRESS YOU IMAGINE WOMEN TO BE!
HANG ON, I NEVER—
WAHH!
REEVE!
I'VE GOT YOU, REEVE—JUST—

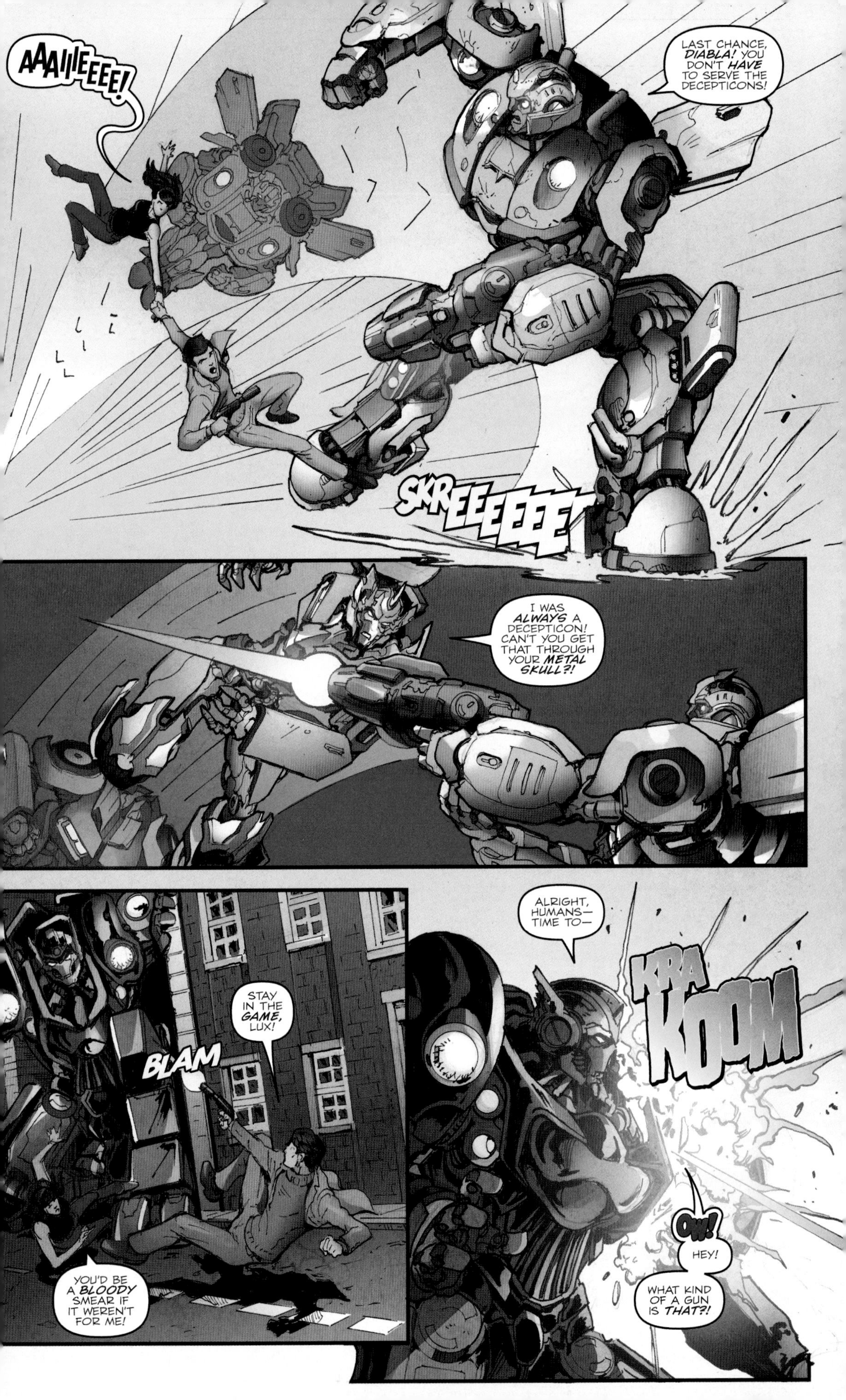
AAAIIIEEEE!
LAST CHANCE, DIABLA! YOU DON'T HAVE TO SERVE THE DECEPTICONS!
SKREEEEEEET
I WAS ALWAYS A DECEPTICON! CAN'T YOU GET THAT THROUGH YOUR METAL SKULL?!
STAY IN THE GAME, LUX!
BLAM
YOU'D BE A BLOODY SMEAR IF IT WEREN'T FOR ME!
ALRIGHT, HUMANS— TIME TO—
KRA KOOM
OW!
HEY!
WHAT KIND OF A GUN IS THAT?!

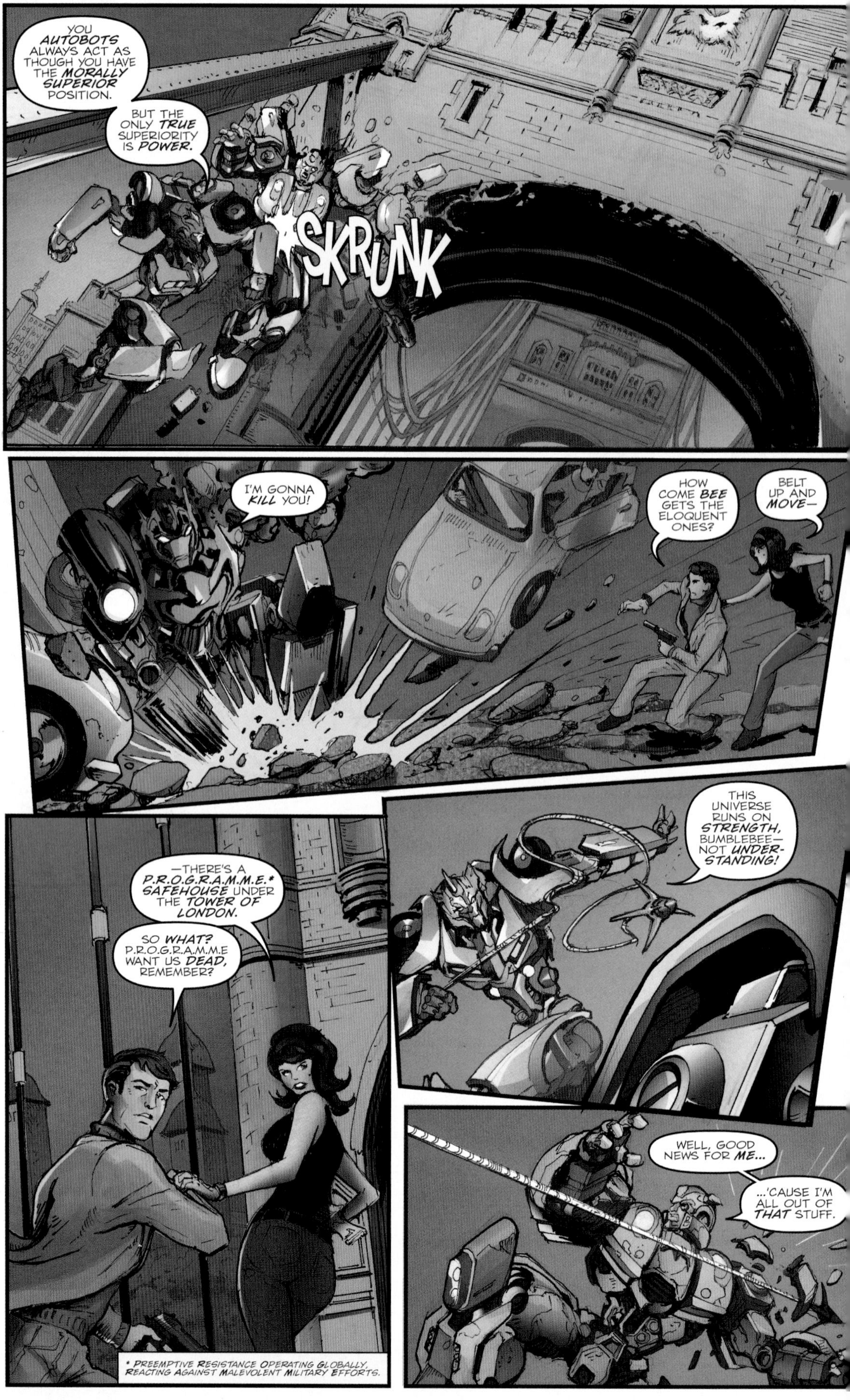
YOU AUTOBOTS ALWAYS ACT AS THOUGH YOU HAVE THE MORALLY SUPERIOR POSITION.
BUT THE ONLY TRUE SUPERIORITY IS POWER.
SKRUNK
I'M GONNA KILL YOU!
HOW COME BEE GETS THE ELOQUENT ONES?
BELT UP AND MOVE—
—THERE'S A P.R.O.G.R.A.M.M.E.* SAFEHOUSE UNDER THE TOWER OF LONDON.
SO WHAT? P.R.O.G.R.A.M.M.E WANT US DEAD, REMEMBER?
* PREEMPTIVE RESISTANCE OPERATING GLOBALLY, REACTING AGAINST MALEVOLENT MILITARY EFFORTS.
THIS UNIVERSE RUNS ON STRENGTH, BUMBLEBEE— NOT UNDER-STANDING!
WELL, GOOD NEWS FOR ME...
...'CAUSE I'M ALL OUT OF THAT STUFF.

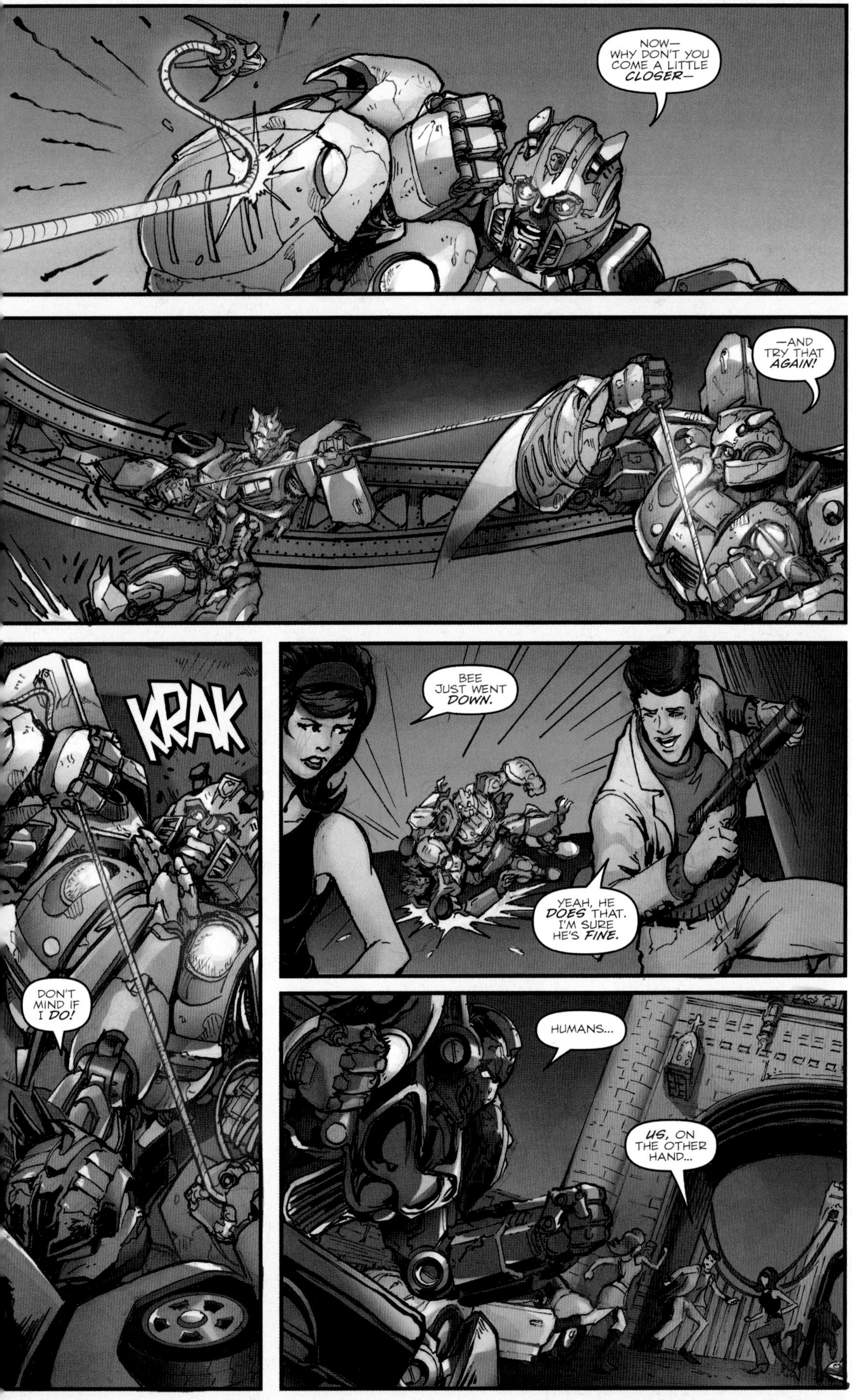
NOW— WHY DON'T YOU COME A LITTLE CLOSER—
—AND TRY THAT AGAIN!
KRAK
DON'T MIND IF I DO!
BEE JUST WENT DOWN.
YEAH, HE DOES THAT. I'M SURE HE'S FINE.
HUMANS...
US, ON THE OTHER HAND...

I'VE GOT AN *IDEA*.

OKAY, BUT DID I EVER TELL YOU MY THING ABOUT *DYING*?

I'D RATHER *NOT*.

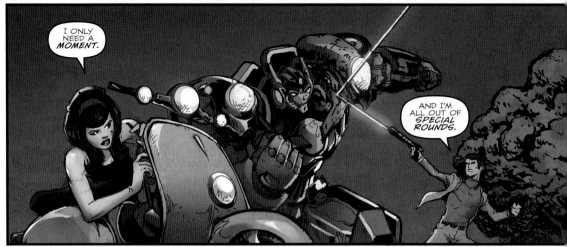

I ONLY NEED A *MOMENT*.

AND I'M ALL OUT OF *SPECIAL ROUNDS*.

BEST THING ABOUT THE YOUTH OF *TODAY*—

—THEY DON'T MIND *SHARING*. NOW GET ON.

VROOM

REEVE— I COULD USE SOME OF THOSE *SPECIAL ROUNDS* OF YOURS, RIGHT ABOUT NOW.

REEVE? *REEVE?!*

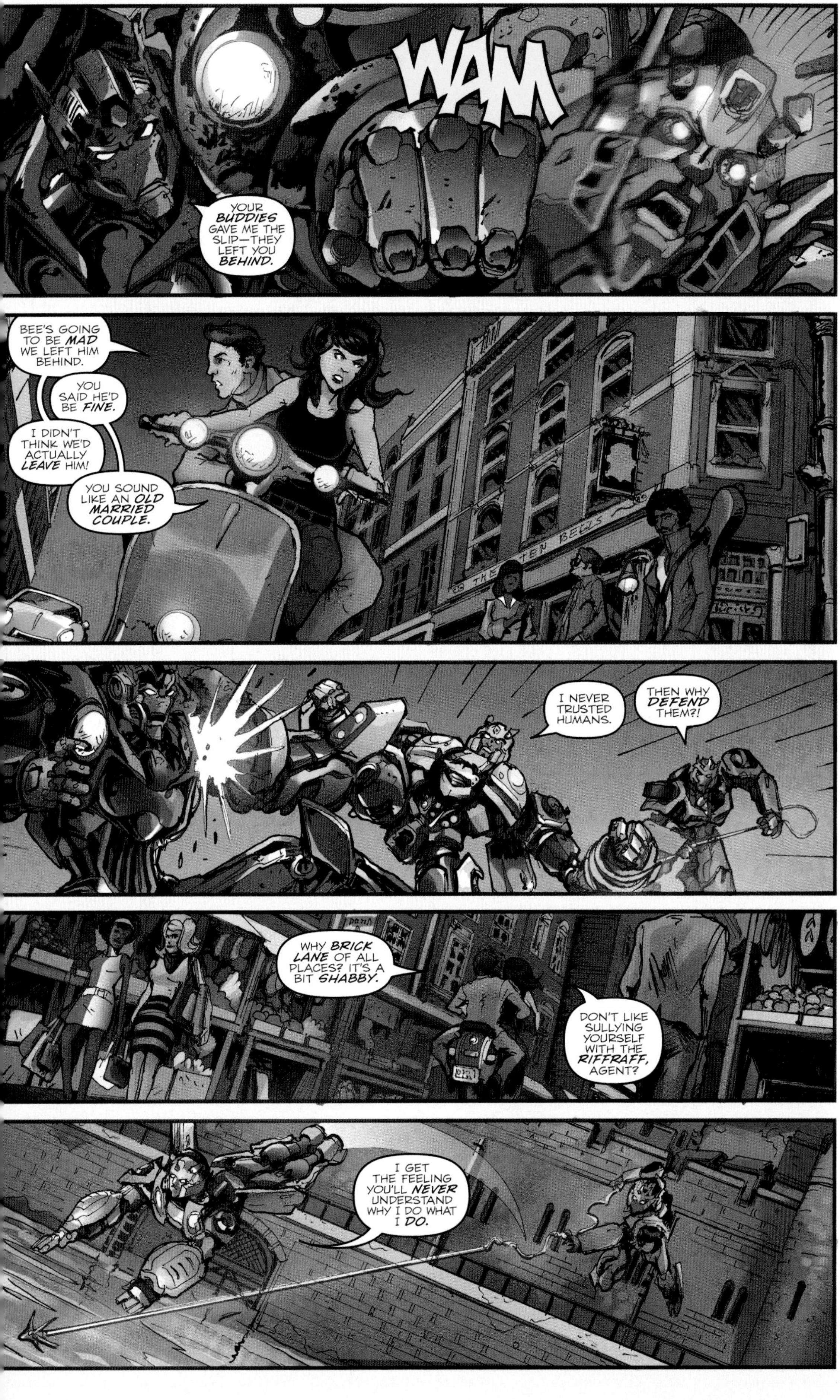
WAM
YOUR BUDDIES GAVE ME THE SLIP—THEY LEFT YOU BEHIND.
BEE'S GOING TO BE MAD WE LEFT HIM BEHIND.
YOU SAID HE'D BE FINE.
I DIDN'T THINK WE'D ACTUALLY LEAVE HIM!
YOU SOUND LIKE AN OLD MARRIED COUPLE.
I NEVER TRUSTED HUMANS.
THEN WHY DEFEND THEM?!
WHY BRICK LANE OF ALL PLACES? IT'S A BIT SHABBY.
DON'T LIKE SULLYING YOURSELF WITH THE RIFFRAFF, AGENT?
I GET THE FEELING YOU'LL NEVER UNDERSTAND WHY I DO WHAT I DO.

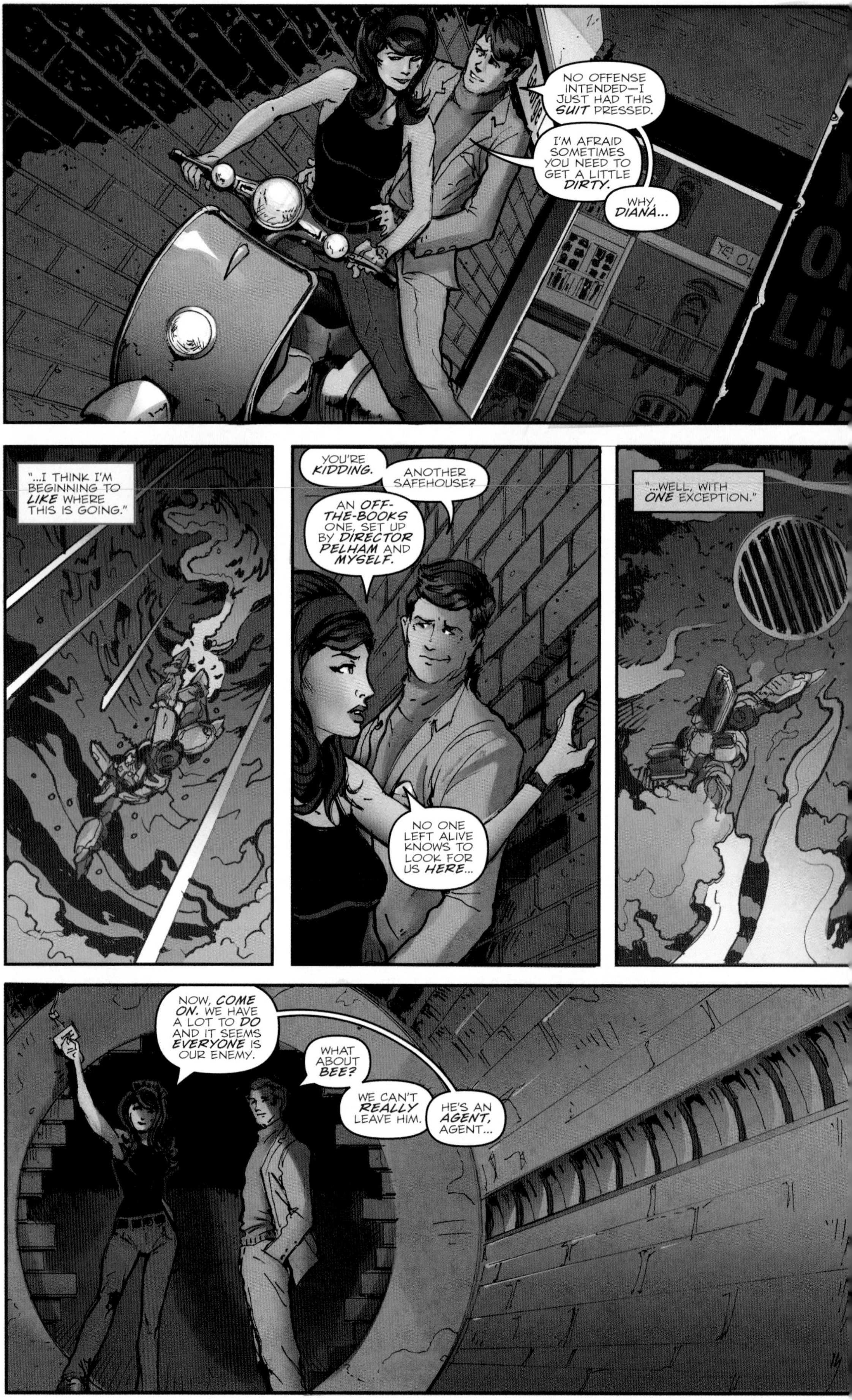
NO OFFENSE INTENDED—I JUST HAD THIS SUIT PRESSED.
I'M AFRAID SOMETIMES YOU NEED TO GET A LITTLE DIRTY.
WHY, DIANA...
"...I THINK I'M BEGINNING TO LIKE WHERE THIS IS GOING."
YOU'RE KIDDING.
ANOTHER SAFEHOUSE?
AN OFF-THE-BOOKS ONE, SET UP BY DIRECTOR PELHAM AND MYSELF.
NO ONE LEFT ALIVE KNOWS TO LOOK FOR US HERE...
"...WELL, WITH ONE EXCEPTION."
NOW, COME ON. WE HAVE A LOT TO DO AND IT SEEMS EVERYONE IS OUR ENEMY.
WHAT ABOUT BEE?
WE CAN'T REALLY LEAVE HIM.
HE'S AN AGENT, AGENT...

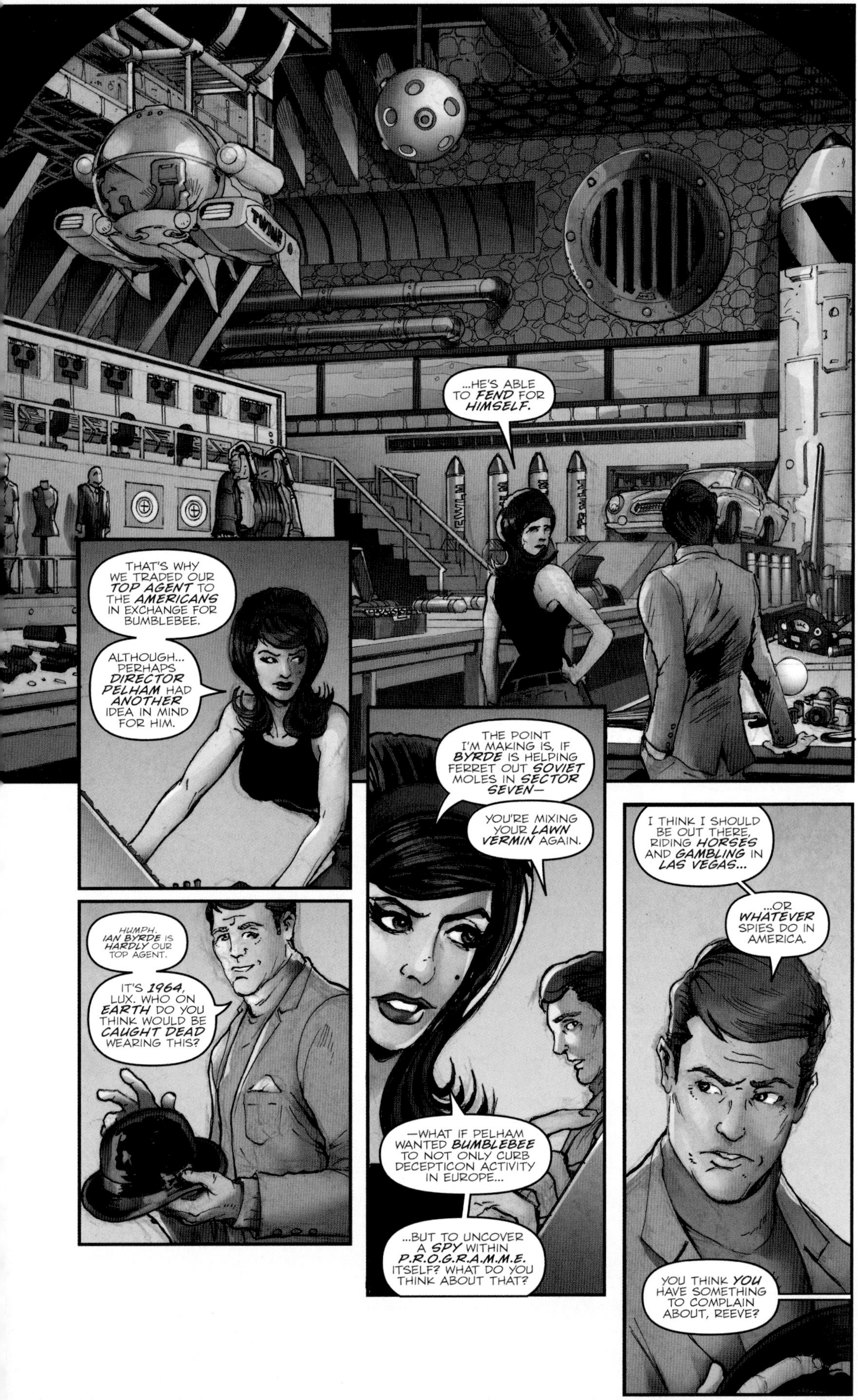

...HE'S ABLE TO FEND FOR HIMSELF.
THAT'S WHY WE TRADED OUR TOP AGENT TO THE AMERICANS IN EXCHANGE FOR BUMBLEBEE.
ALTHOUGH... PERHAPS DIRECTOR PELHAM HAD ANOTHER IDEA IN MIND FOR HIM.
HUMPH. IAN BYRDE IS HARDLY OUR TOP AGENT.
IT'S 1964, LUX. WHO ON EARTH DO YOU THINK WOULD BE CAUGHT DEAD WEARING THIS?
THE POINT I'M MAKING IS, IF BYRDE IS HELPING FERRET OUT SOVIET MOLES IN SECTOR SEVEN—
YOU'RE MIXING YOUR LAWN VERMIN AGAIN.
—WHAT IF PELHAM WANTED BUMBLEBEE TO NOT ONLY CURB DECEPTICON ACTIVITY IN EUROPE...
...BUT TO UNCOVER A SPY WITHIN P.R.O.G.R.A.M.M.E. ITSELF? WHAT DO YOU THINK ABOUT THAT?
I THINK I SHOULD BE OUT THERE, RIDING HORSES AND GAMBLING IN LAS VEGAS...
...OR WHATEVER SPIES DO IN AMERICA.
YOU THINK YOU HAVE SOMETHING TO COMPLAIN ABOUT, REEVE?

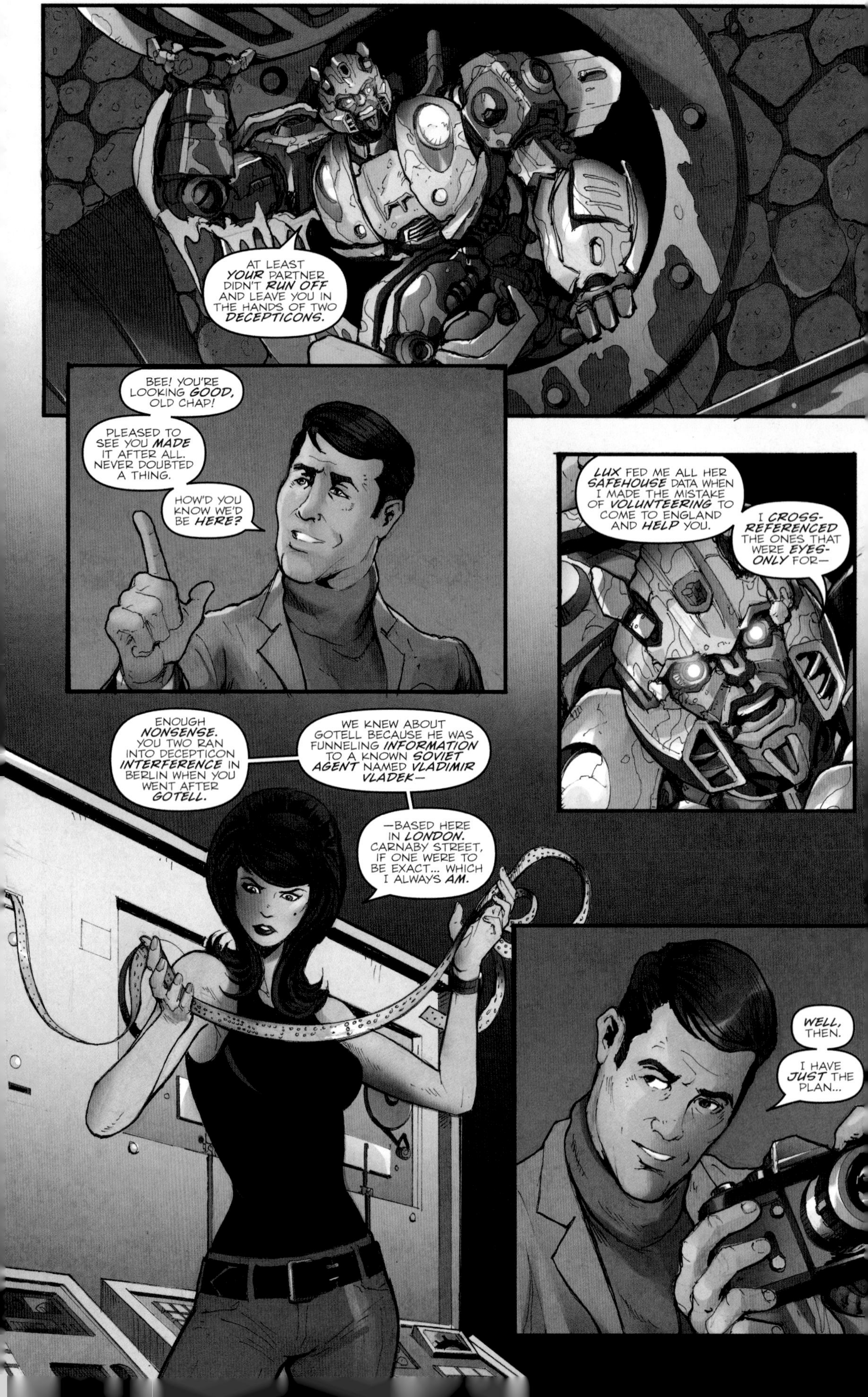
AT LEAST YOUR PARTNER DIDN'T RUN OFF AND LEAVE YOU IN THE HANDS OF TWO DECEPTICONS.
BEE! YOU'RE LOOKING GOOD, OLD CHAP!
PLEASED TO SEE YOU MADE IT AFTER ALL. NEVER DOUBTED A THING.
HOW'D YOU KNOW WE'D BE HERE?
LUX FED ME ALL HER SAFEHOUSE DATA WHEN I MADE THE MISTAKE OF VOLUNTEERING TO COME TO ENGLAND AND HELP YOU.
I CROSS-REFERENCED THE ONES THAT WERE EYES-ONLY FOR—
ENOUGH NONSENSE. YOU TWO RAN INTO DECEPTICON INTERFERENCE IN BERLIN WHEN YOU WENT AFTER GOTELL.
WE KNEW ABOUT GOTELL BECAUSE HE WAS FUNNELING INFORMATION TO A KNOWN SOVIET AGENT NAMED VLADIMIR VLADEK—
—BASED HERE IN LONDON. CARNABY STREET, IF ONE WERE TO BE EXACT... WHICH I ALWAYS AM.
WELL, THEN.
I HAVE JUST THE PLAN...

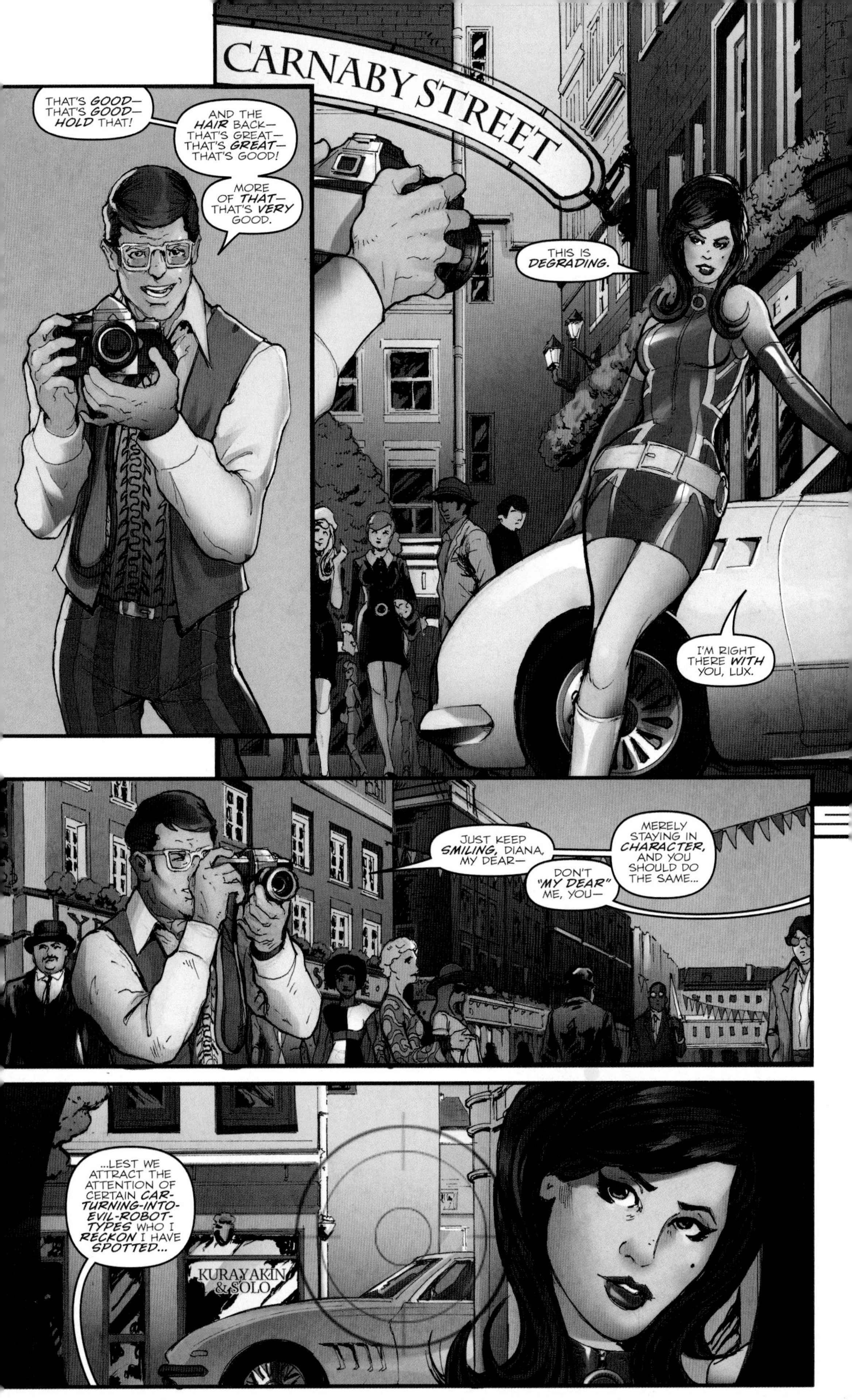

CARNABY STREET
THAT'S GOOD— THAT'S GOOD— HOLD THAT!
AND THE HAIR BACK— THAT'S GREAT— THAT'S GREAT— THAT'S GOOD!
MORE OF THAT— THAT'S VERY GOOD.
THIS IS DEGRADING.
I'M RIGHT THERE WITH YOU, LUX.
JUST KEEP SMILING, DIANA, MY DEAR—
DON'T "MY DEAR" ME, YOU—
MERELY STAYING IN CHARACTER, AND YOU SHOULD DO THE SAME...
...LEST WE ATTRACT THE ATTENTION OF CERTAIN CAR-TURNING-INTO-EVIL-ROBOT-TYPES WHO I RECKON I HAVE SPOTTED...
KURAYAKIN & SOLO

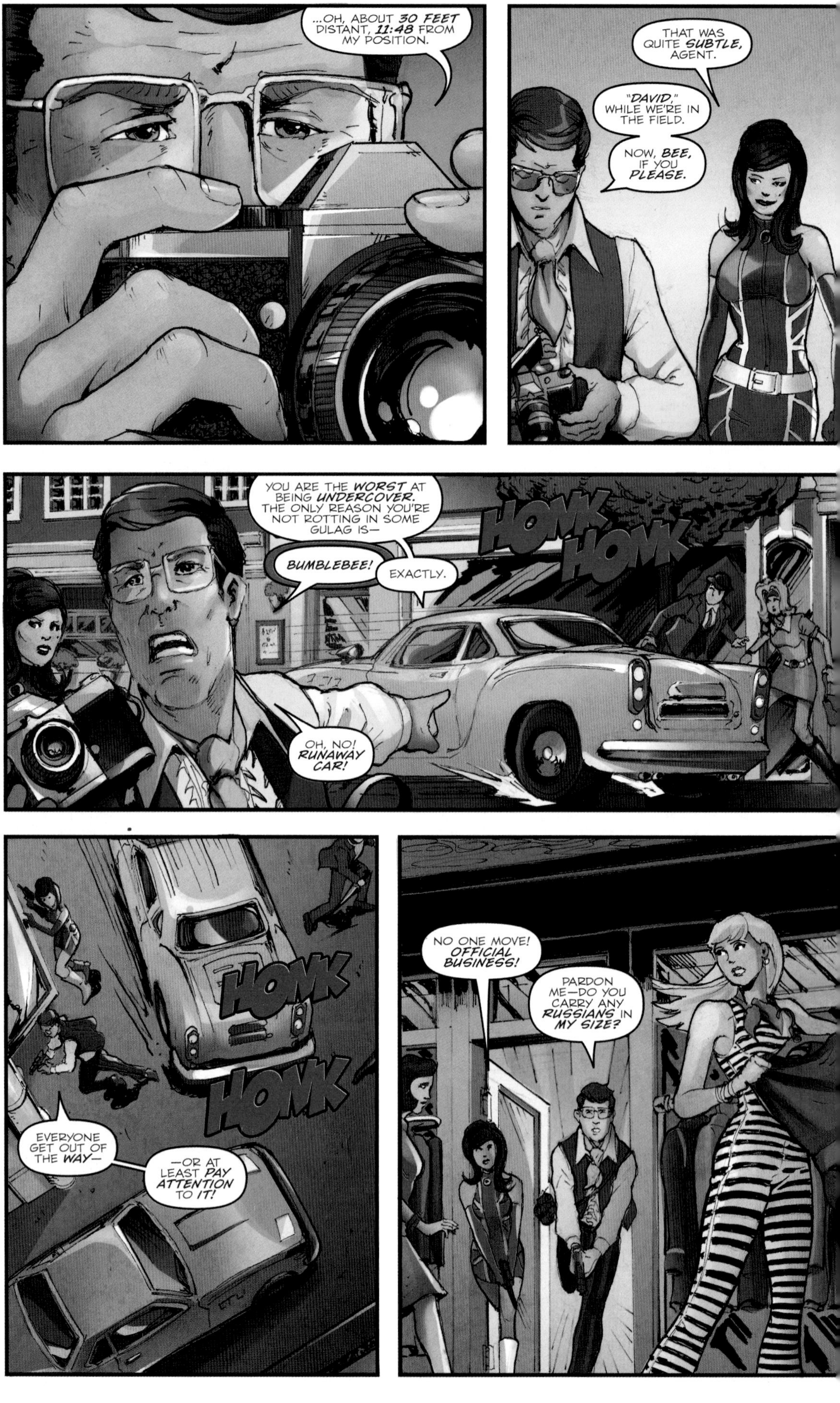

...OH, ABOUT 30 FEET DISTANT, 11:48 FROM MY POSITION.
THAT WAS QUITE SUBTLE, AGENT.
"DAVID," WHILE WE'RE IN THE FIELD.
NOW, BEE, IF YOU PLEASE.
YOU ARE THE WORST AT BEING UNDERCOVER. THE ONLY REASON YOU'RE NOT ROTTING IN SOME GULAG IS—
BUMBLEBEE!
EXACTLY.
HONK HONK
OH, NO! RUNAWAY CAR!
HONK
HONK
EVERYONE GET OUT OF THE WAY—
—OR AT LEAST PAY ATTENTION TO IT!
NO ONE MOVE! OFFICIAL BUSINESS!
PARDON ME—DO YOU CARRY ANY RUSSIANS IN MY SIZE?

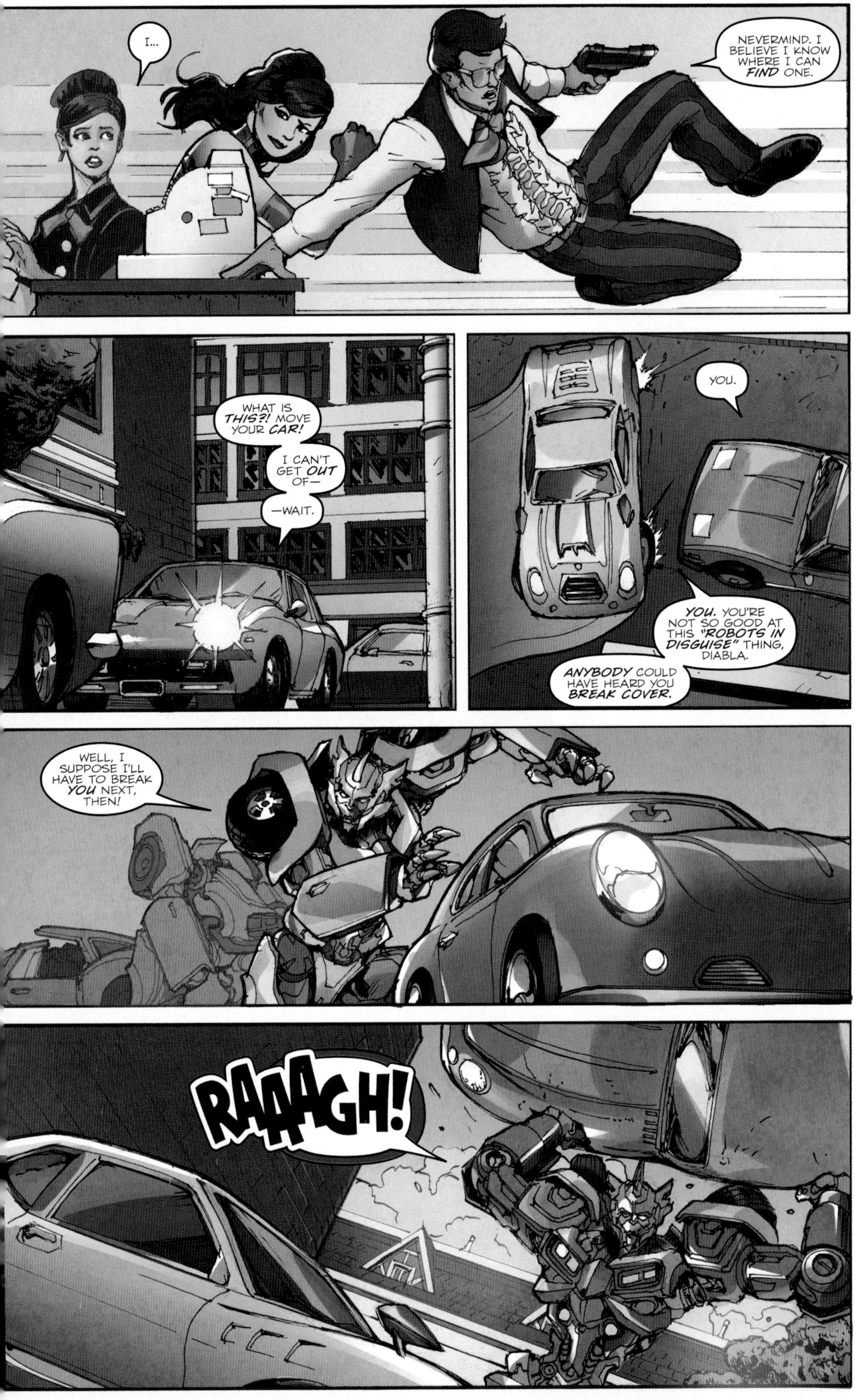
I...
NEVERMIND. I BELIEVE I KNOW WHERE I CAN FIND ONE.
WHAT IS THIS?! MOVE YOUR CAR!
I CAN'T GET OUT OF—
—WAIT.
YOU.
YOU. YOU'RE NOT SO GOOD AT THIS "ROBOTS IN DISGUISE" THING, DIABLA.
ANYBODY COULD HAVE HEARD YOU BREAK COVER.
WELL, I SUPPOSE I'LL HAVE TO BREAK YOU NEXT, THEN!
RAAAGH!

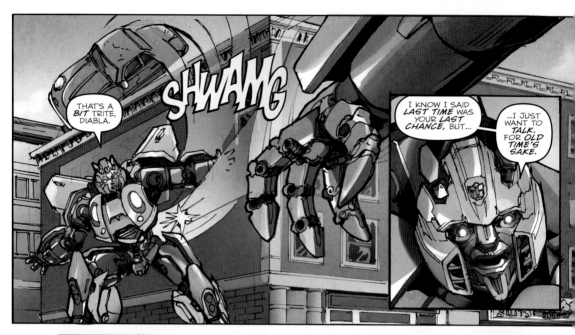

SHWAMG

THAT'S A *BIT* TRITE, DIABLA.

I KNOW I SAID *LAST TIME* WAS YOUR *LAST CHANCE*, BUT... ...I JUST WANT TO *TALK*. FOR *OLD TIME'S SAKE*.

... MAKE IT *FAST*.

I NEED A MINUTE.

THIS IS A *HAMILTON SPG 2131* LOCK—

—*QUAD CHAMBERED*, SO THE *PICKS* WON'T DO IT—

—PLUS IT'S *HEAT RESISTANT*, AND GIVING THE *LASER* A RUN FOR ITS MONEY.

I'M *WELL FAMILIAR* WITH THE SPG 2131, REEVE.

IF YOU'D PAY ATTENTION AT *BRIEFINGS*, YOU'D KNOW I *LITERALLY* WROTE THE *BOOK* ON ITS WEAKNESSES.

LIKE EVERYTHING, IT COMES DOWN TO PLAYING THE PROPER *ANGLES*.

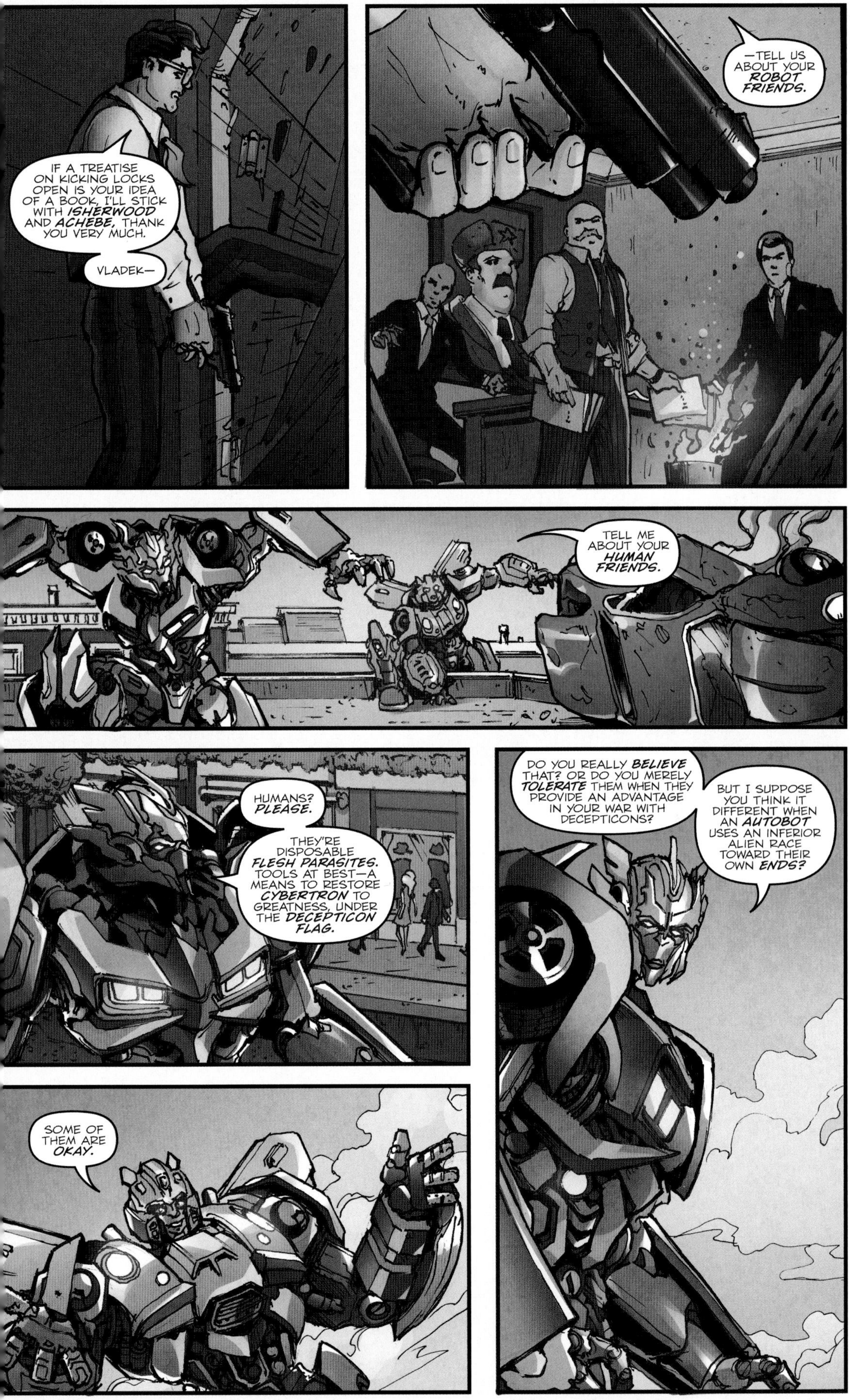
IF A TREATISE ON KICKING LOCKS OPEN IS YOUR IDEA OF A BOOK, I'LL STICK WITH *ISHERWOOD* AND *ACHEBE,* THANK YOU VERY MUCH.
VLADEK—
—TELL US ABOUT YOUR *ROBOT FRIENDS.*
TELL ME ABOUT YOUR *HUMAN FRIENDS.*
HUMANS? *PLEASE.*
THEY'RE DISPOSABLE *FLESH PARASITES.* TOOLS AT BEST—A MEANS TO RESTORE *CYBERTRON* TO GREATNESS, UNDER THE *DECEPTICON FLAG.*
SOME OF THEM ARE *OKAY.*
DO YOU REALLY *BELIEVE* THAT? OR DO YOU MERELY *TOLERATE* THEM WHEN THEY PROVIDE AN ADVANTAGE IN YOUR WAR WITH DECEPTICONS?
BUT I SUPPOSE YOU THINK IT DIFFERENT WHEN AN *AUTOBOT* USES AN INFERIOR ALIEN RACE TOWARD THEIR OWN *ENDS?*

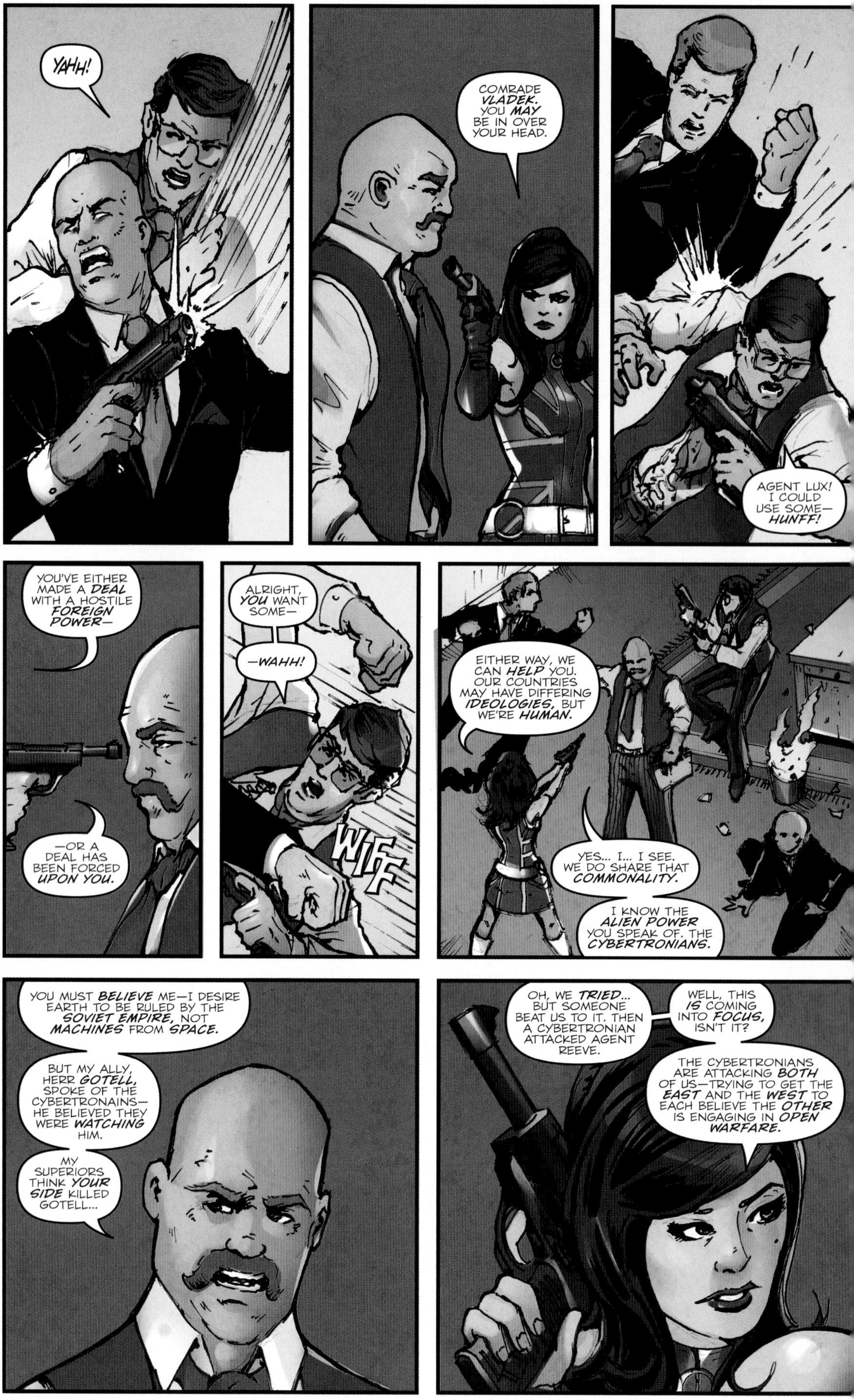
YAHH!
COMRADE VLADEK. YOU MAY BE IN OVER YOUR HEAD.
AGENT LUX! I COULD USE SOME— HUNFF!
YOU'VE EITHER MADE A DEAL WITH A HOSTILE FOREIGN POWER—
—OR A DEAL HAS BEEN FORCED UPON YOU.
ALRIGHT, YOU WANT SOME—
—WAHH!
WIFF
EITHER WAY, WE CAN HELP YOU. OUR COUNTRIES MAY HAVE DIFFERING IDEOLOGIES, BUT WE'RE HUMAN.
YES... I... I SEE. WE DO SHARE THAT COMMONALITY.
I KNOW THE ALIEN POWER YOU SPEAK OF. THE CYBERTRONIANS.
YOU MUST BELIEVE ME—I DESIRE EARTH TO BE RULED BY THE SOVIET EMPIRE, NOT MACHINES FROM SPACE.
BUT MY ALLY, HERR GOTELL, SPOKE OF THE CYBERTRONAINS—HE BELIEVED THEY WERE WATCHING HIM.
MY SUPERIORS THINK YOUR SIDE KILLED GOTELL...
OH, WE TRIED... BUT SOMEONE BEAT US TO IT. THEN A CYBERTRONIAN ATTACKED AGENT REEVE.
WELL, THIS IS COMING INTO FOCUS, ISN'T IT?
THE CYBERTRONIANS ARE ATTACKING BOTH OF US—TRYING TO GET THE EAST AND THE WEST TO EACH BELIEVE THE OTHER IS ENGAGING IN OPEN WARFARE.

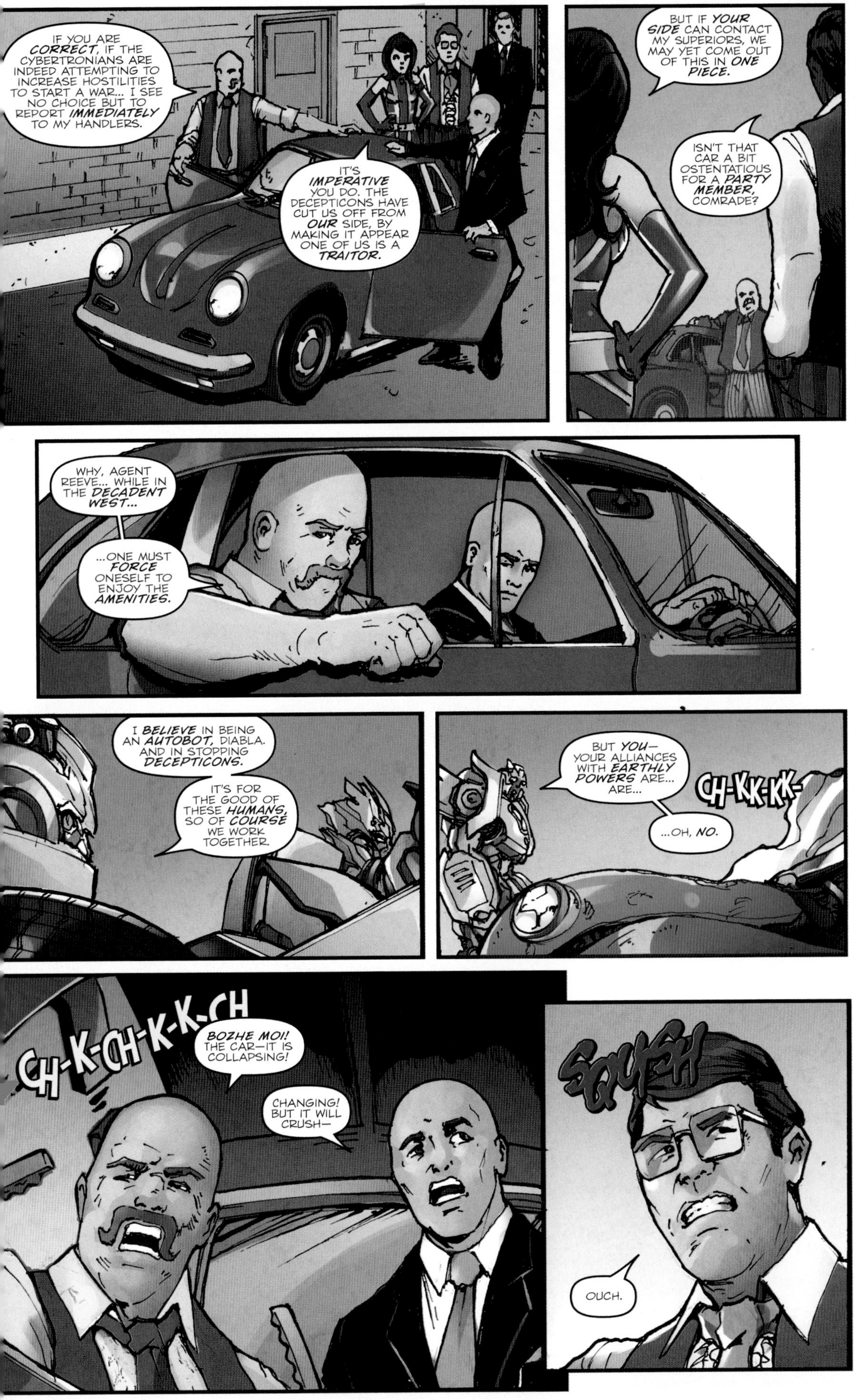
IF YOU ARE CORRECT, IF THE CYBERTRONIANS ARE INDEED ATTEMPTING TO INCREASE HOSTILITIES TO START A WAR... I SEE NO CHOICE BUT TO REPORT IMMEDIATELY TO MY HANDLERS.
IT'S IMPERATIVE YOU DO. THE DECEPTICONS HAVE CUT US OFF FROM OUR SIDE, BY MAKING IT APPEAR ONE OF US IS A TRAITOR.
BUT IF YOUR SIDE CAN CONTACT MY SUPERIORS, WE MAY YET COME OUT OF THIS IN ONE PIECE.
ISN'T THAT CAR A BIT OSTENTATIOUS FOR A PARTY MEMBER, COMRADE?
WHY, AGENT REEVE... WHILE IN THE DECADENT WEST...
...ONE MUST FORCE ONESELF TO ENJOY THE AMENITIES.
I BELIEVE IN BEING AN AUTOBOT, DIABLA. AND IN STOPPING DECEPTICONS.
IT'S FOR THE GOOD OF THESE HUMANS, SO OF COURSE WE WORK TOGETHER.
BUT YOU— YOUR ALLIANCES WITH EARTHLY POWERS ARE... ARE...
CH-KK-KK-
...OH, NO.
CH-K-CH-K-K-CH
BOZHE MOI! THE CAR—IT IS COLLAPSING!
CHANGING! BUT IT WILL CRUSH—
SQUISH
OUCH.

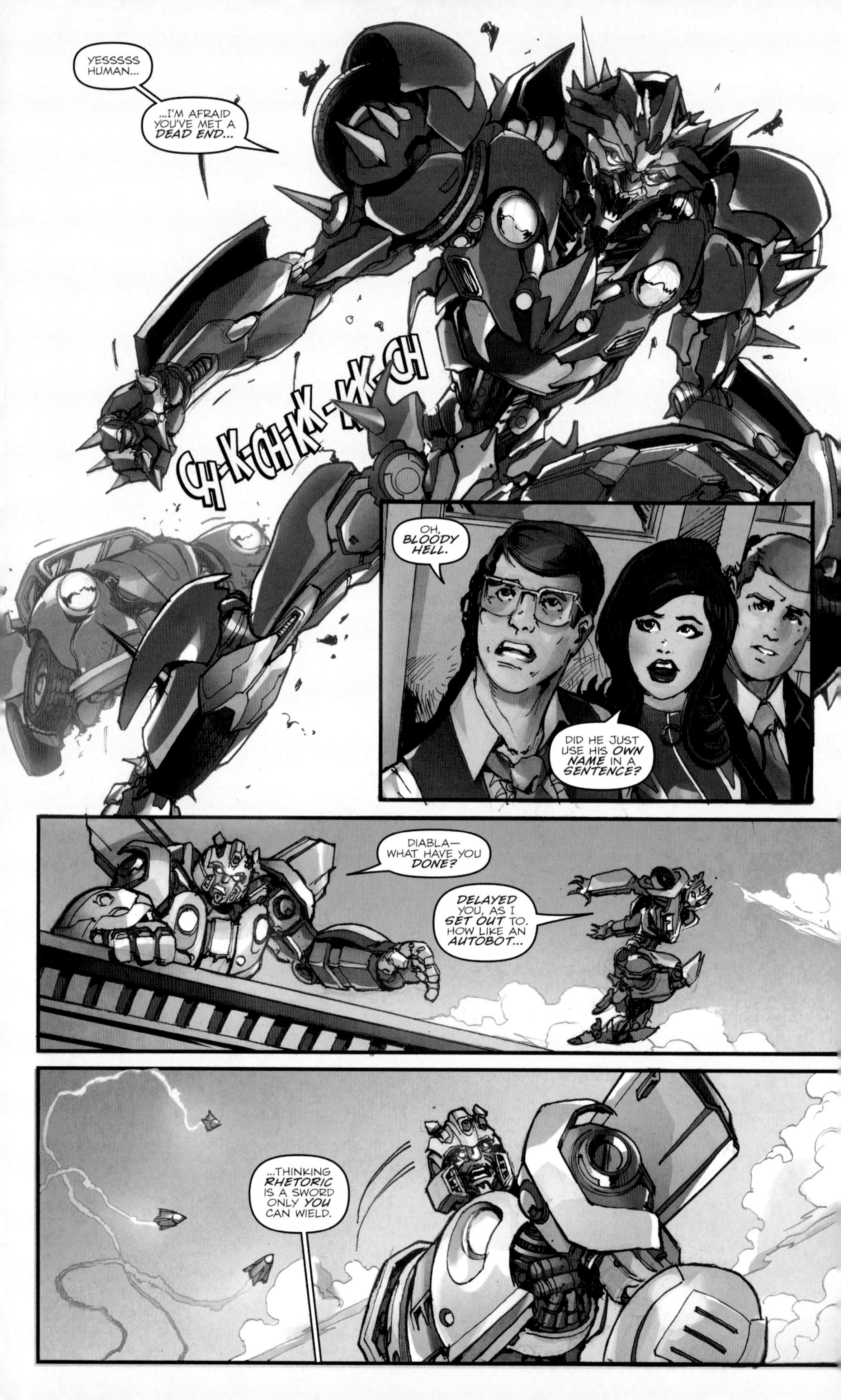
YESSSSS HUMAN...
...I'M AFRAID YOU'VE MET A DEAD END...
CH-K-CH-K-K-KK-CH
OH, BLOODY HELL.
DID HE JUST USE HIS OWN NAME IN A SENTENCE?
DIABLA— WHAT HAVE YOU DONE?
DELAYED YOU, AS I SET OUT TO. HOW LIKE AN AUTOBOT...
...THINKING RHETORIC IS A SWORD ONLY YOU CAN WIELD.

TRANSFORMERS®

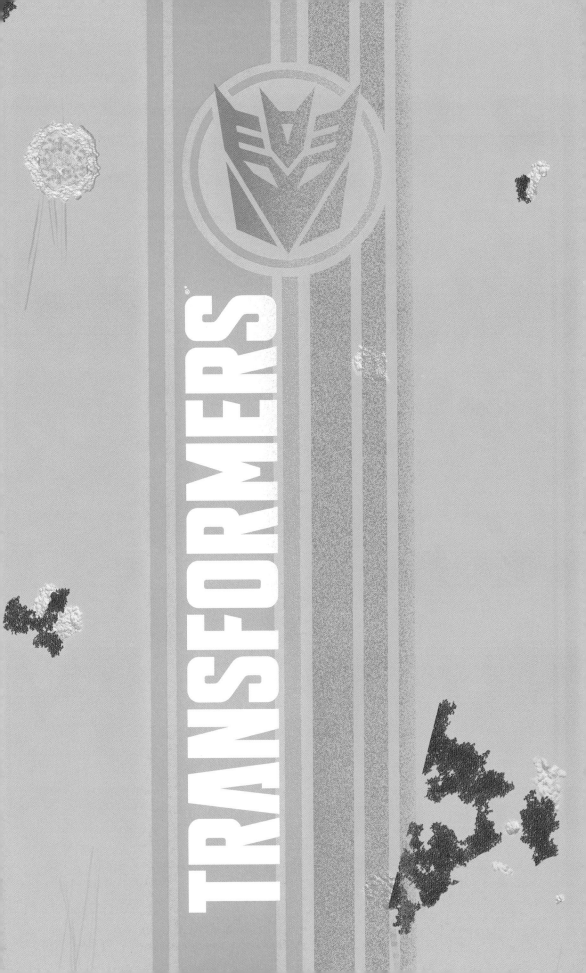

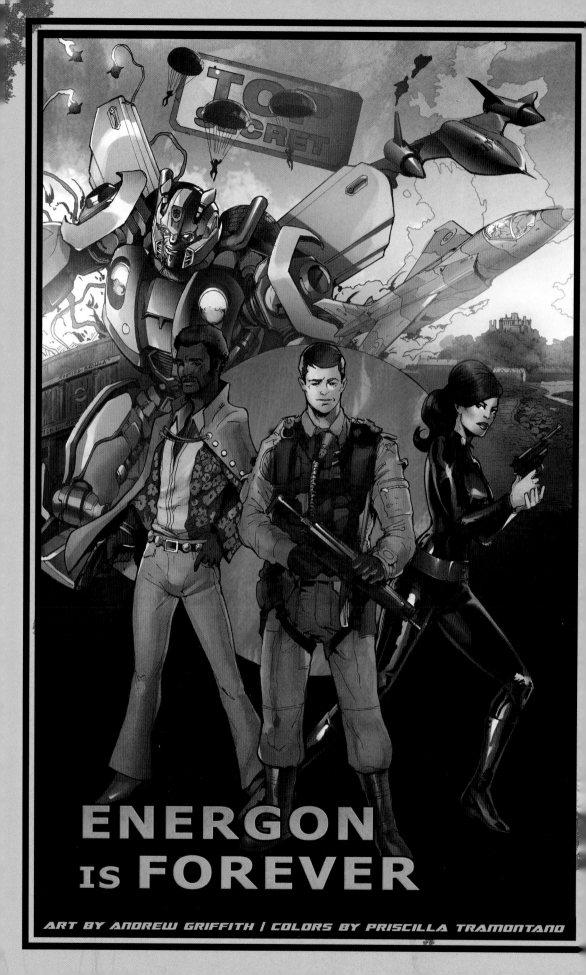

ENERGON IS FOREVER

ART BY ANDREW GRIFFITH | COLORS BY PRISCILLA TRAMONTANO

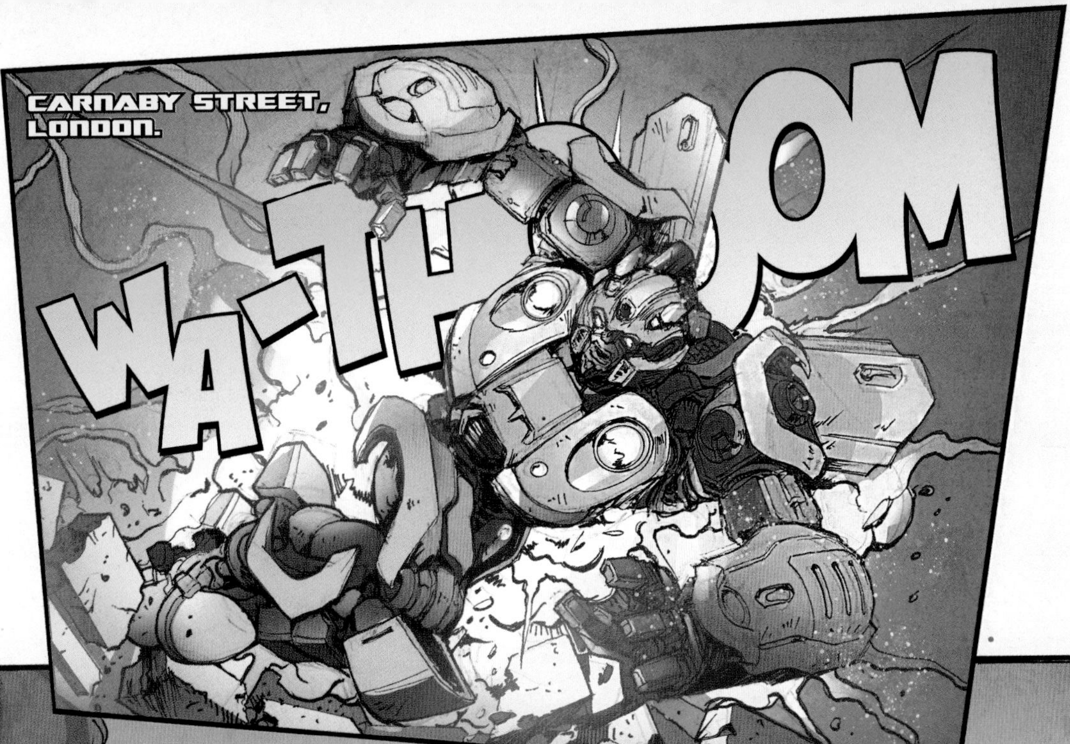
CARNABY STREET, LONDON.
WA-THOOM

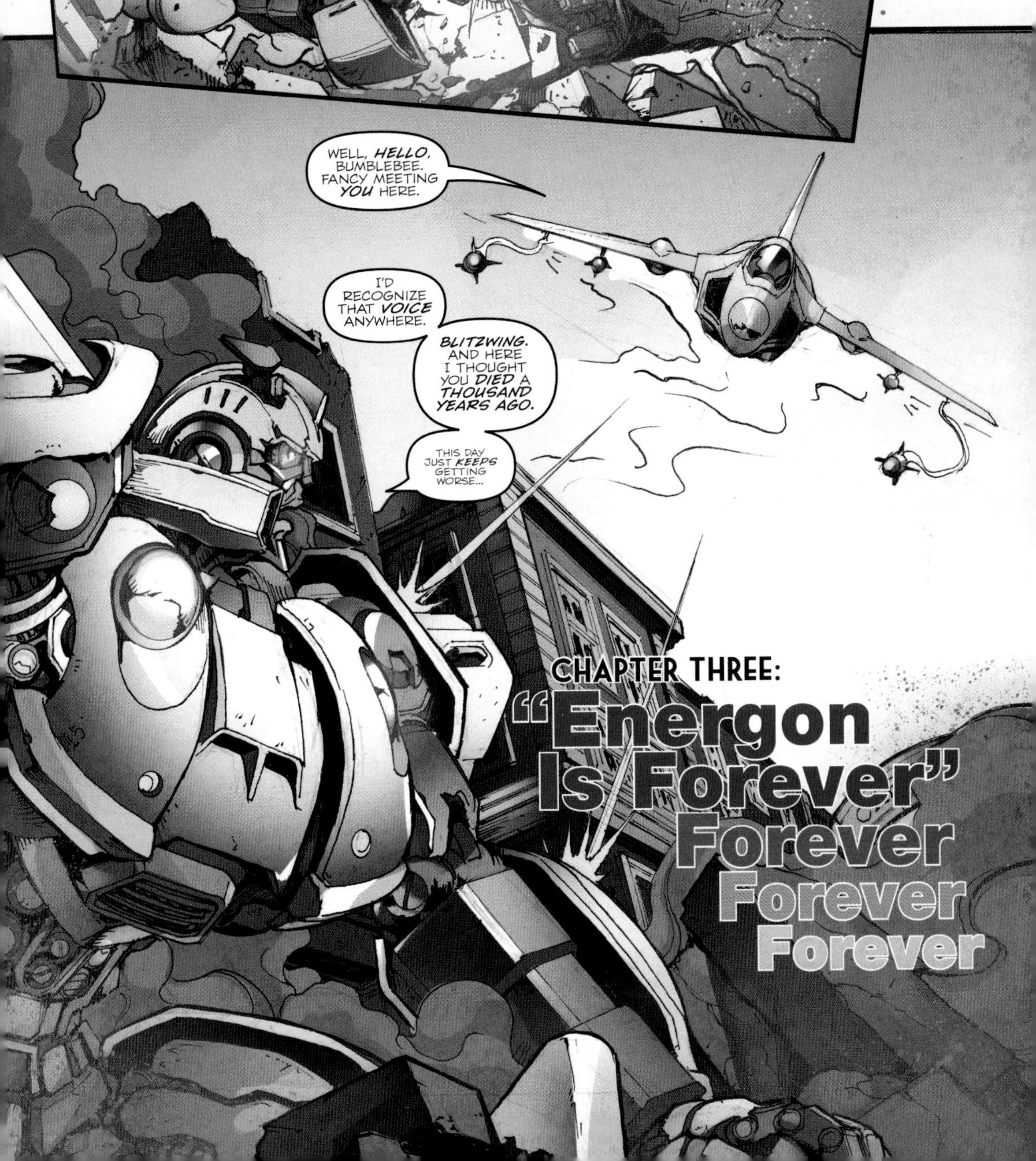
WELL, HELLO, BUMBLEBEE. FANCY MEETING YOU HERE.
I'D RECOGNIZE THAT VOICE ANYWHERE.
BLITZWING. AND HERE I THOUGHT YOU DIED A THOUSAND YEARS AGO.
THIS DAY JUST KEEPS GETTING WORSE...
CHAPTER THREE:
"Energon Is Forever"
Forever
Forever
Forever

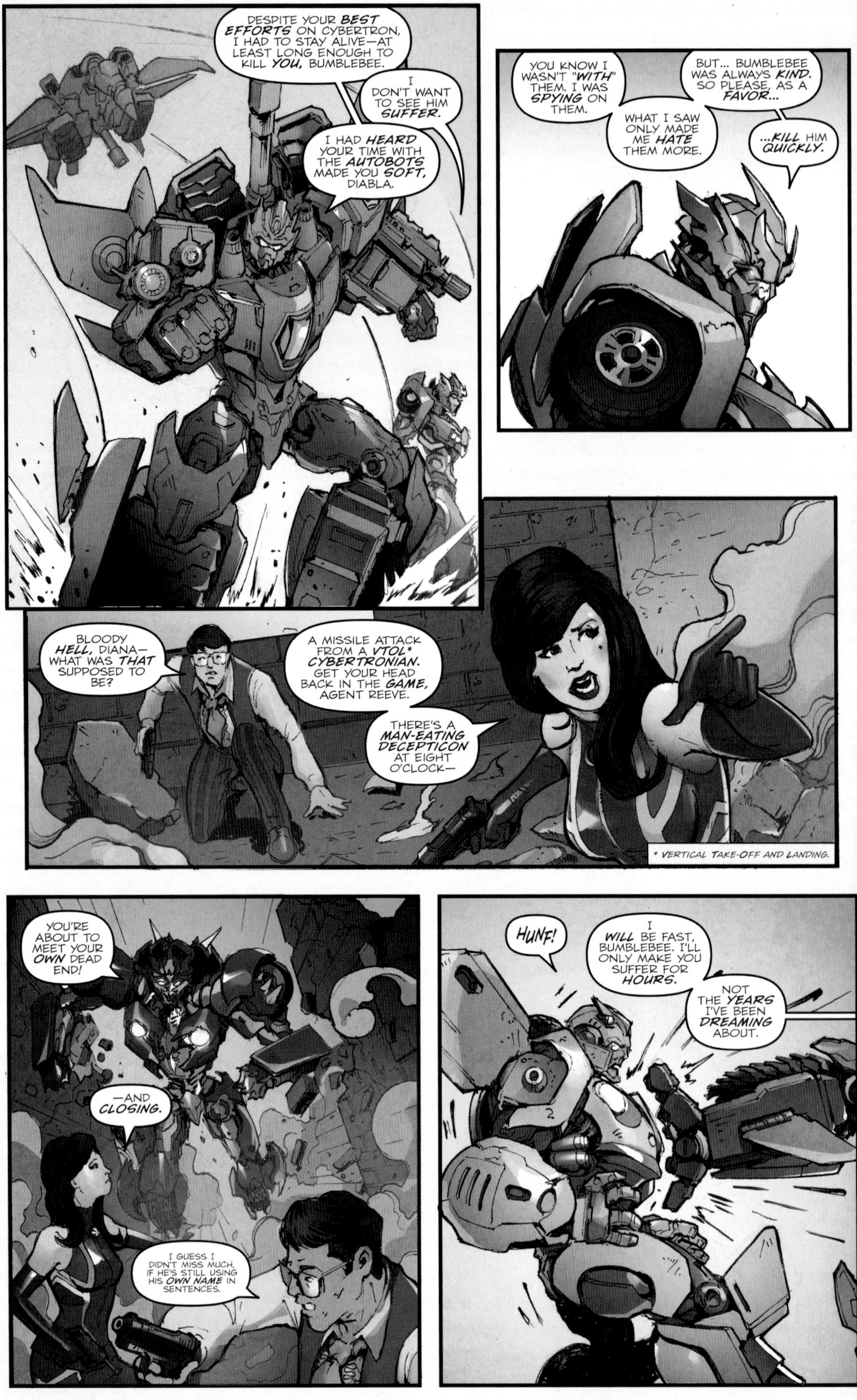

DESPITE YOUR BEST EFFORTS ON CYBERTRON, I HAD TO STAY ALIVE—AT LEAST LONG ENOUGH TO KILL YOU, BUMBLEBEE.
I DON'T WANT TO SEE HIM SUFFER.
I HAD HEARD YOUR TIME WITH THE AUTOBOTS MADE YOU SOFT, DIABLA.
YOU KNOW I WASN'T "WITH" THEM. I WAS SPYING ON THEM.
WHAT I SAW ONLY MADE ME HATE THEM MORE.
BUT... BUMBLEBEE WAS ALWAYS KIND. SO PLEASE, AS A FAVOR...
...KILL HIM QUICKLY.
BLOODY HELL, DIANA—WHAT WAS THAT SUPPOSED TO BE?
A MISSILE ATTACK FROM A VTOL* CYBERTRONIAN. GET YOUR HEAD BACK IN THE GAME, AGENT REEVE.
THERE'S A MAN-EATING DECEPTICON AT EIGHT O'CLOCK—
* VERTICAL TAKE-OFF AND LANDING.
YOU'RE ABOUT TO MEET YOUR OWN DEAD END!
—AND CLOSING.
I GUESS I DIDN'T MISS MUCH, IF HE'S STILL USING HIS OWN NAME IN SENTENCES.
HUNF!
I WILL BE FAST, BUMBLEBEE. I'LL ONLY MAKE YOU SUFFER FOR HOURS.
NOT THE YEARS I'VE BEEN DREAMING ABOUT.

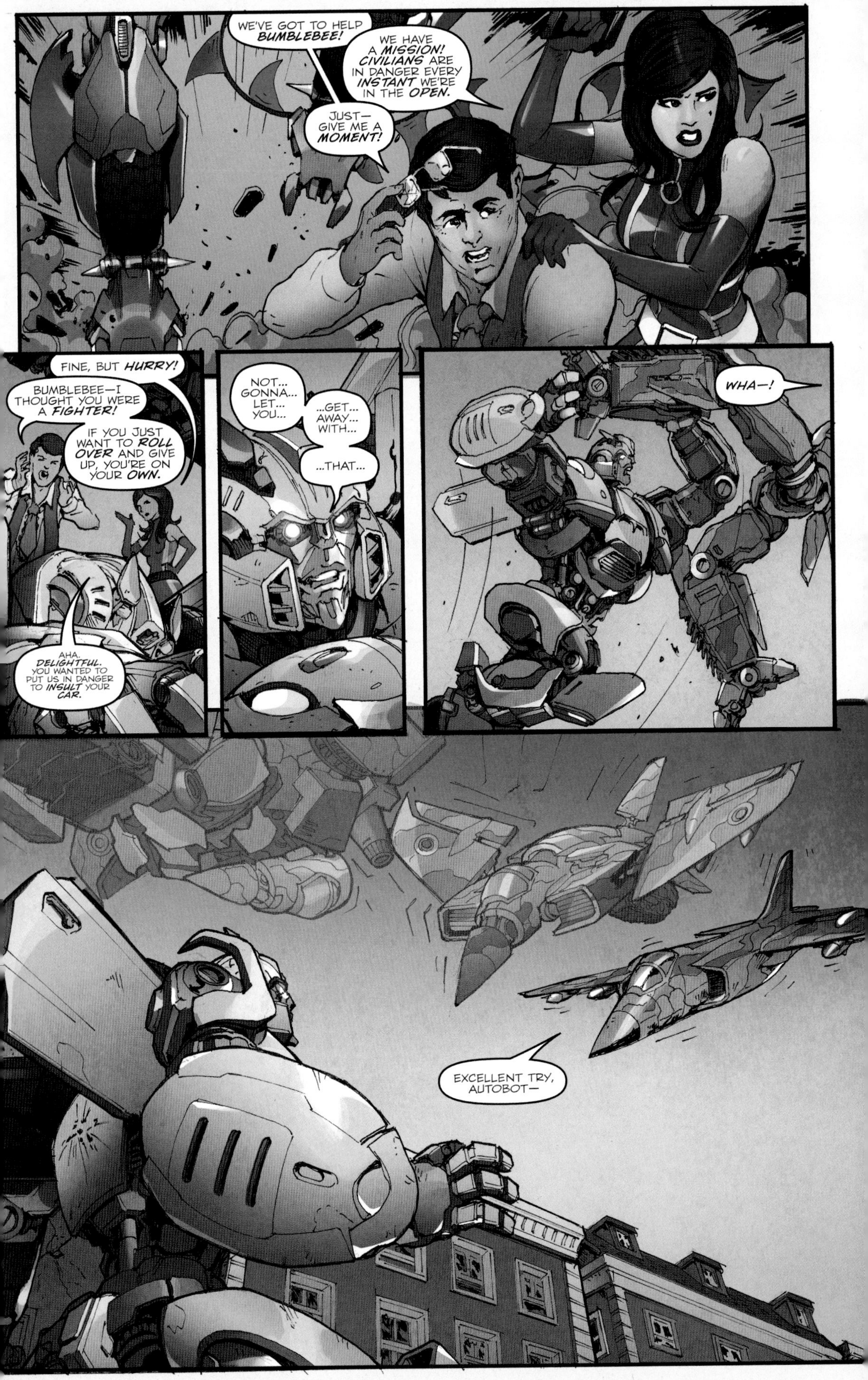

WE'VE GOT TO HELP BUMBLEBEE!
WE HAVE A MISSION! CIVILIANS ARE IN DANGER EVERY INSTANT WE'RE IN THE OPEN.
JUST— GIVE ME A MOMENT!
FINE, BUT HURRY!
BUMBLEBEE—I THOUGHT YOU WERE A FIGHTER!
IF YOU JUST WANT TO ROLL OVER AND GIVE UP, YOU'RE ON YOUR OWN.
AHA. DELIGHTFUL. YOU WANTED TO PUT US IN DANGER TO INSULT YOUR CAR.
NOT... GONNA... LET... YOU...
...GET... AWAY... WITH...
...THAT...
WHA—!
EXCELLENT TRY, AUTOBOT—

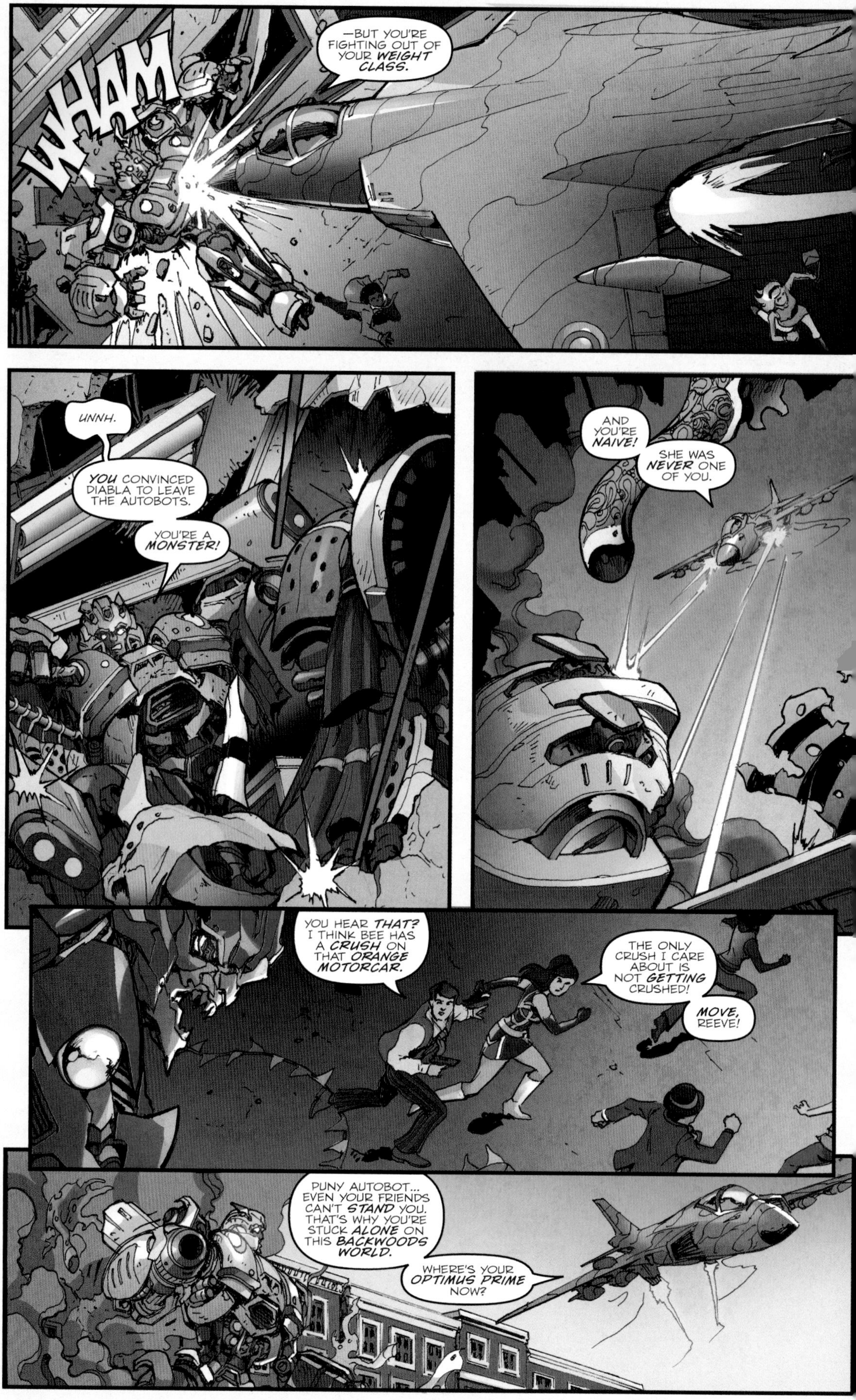
WHAM
—BUT YOU'RE FIGHTING OUT OF YOUR WEIGHT CLASS.
UNNH.
YOU CONVINCED DIABLA TO LEAVE THE AUTOBOTS.
YOU'RE A MONSTER!
AND YOU'RE NAIVE!
SHE WAS NEVER ONE OF YOU.
YOU HEAR THAT? I THINK BEE HAS A CRUSH ON THAT ORANGE MOTORCAR.
THE ONLY CRUSH I CARE ABOUT IS NOT GETTING CRUSHED!
MOVE, REEVE!
PUNY AUTOBOT... EVEN YOUR FRIENDS CAN'T STAND YOU. THAT'S WHY YOU'RE STUCK ALONE ON THIS BACKWOODS WORLD.
WHERE'S YOUR OPTIMUS PRIME NOW?

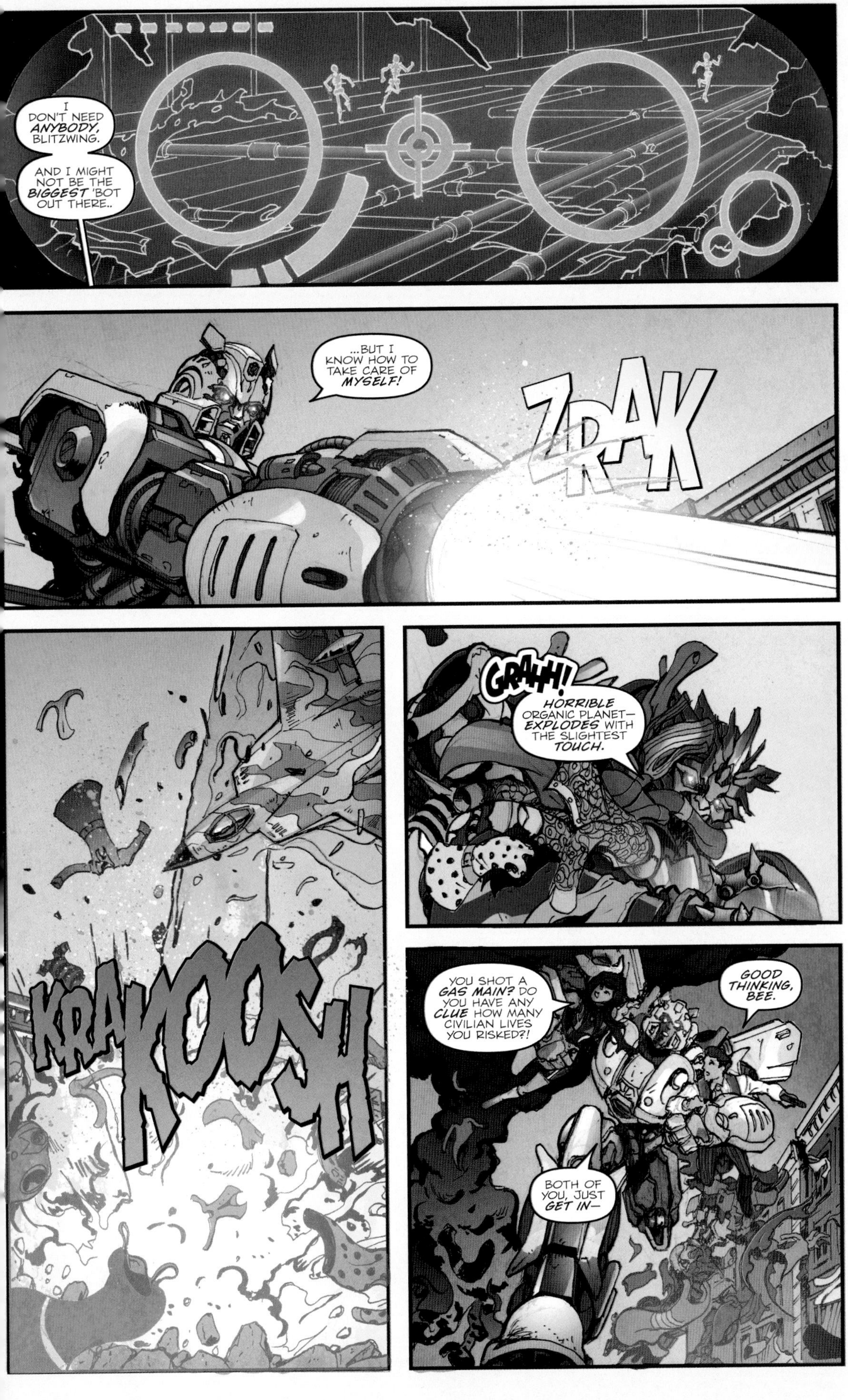
I DON'T NEED ANYBODY, BLITZWING.
AND I MIGHT NOT BE THE BIGGEST 'BOT OUT THERE..
...BUT I KNOW HOW TO TAKE CARE OF MYSELF!
ZRAK
KRAKOOSH
GRAHH!
HORRIBLE ORGANIC PLANET— EXPLODES WITH THE SLIGHTEST TOUCH.
YOU SHOT A GAS MAIN? DO YOU HAVE ANY CLUE HOW MANY CIVILIAN LIVES YOU RISKED?!
GOOD THINKING, BEE.
BOTH OF YOU, JUST GET IN—

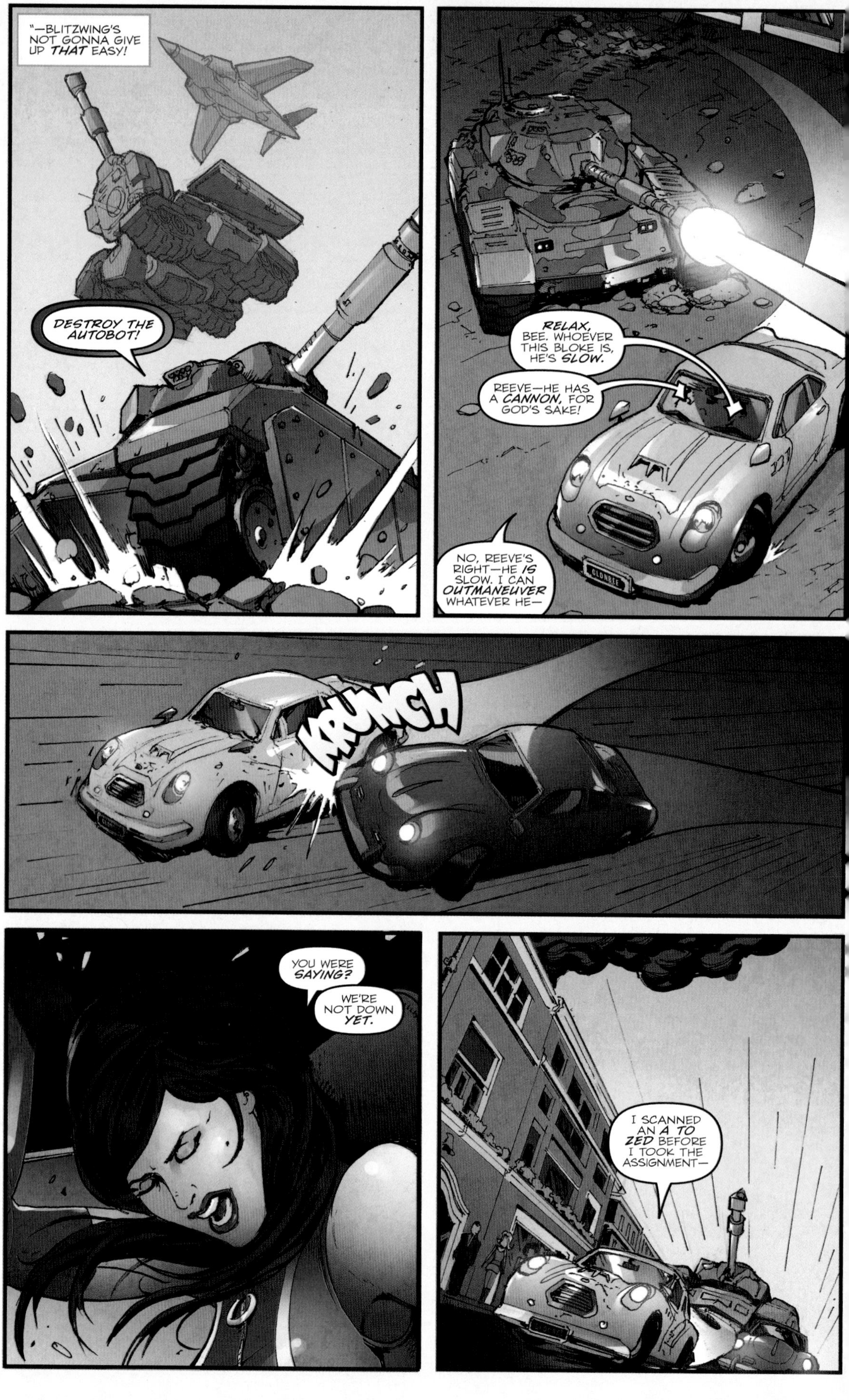
"—BLITZWING'S NOT GONNA GIVE UP THAT EASY!
DESTROY THE AUTOBOT!
RELAX, BEE. WHOEVER THIS BLOKE IS, HE'S SLOW.
REEVE—HE HAS A CANNON, FOR GOD'S SAKE!
NO, REEVE'S RIGHT—HE IS SLOW. I CAN OUTMANEUVER WHATEVER HE—
KRUNCH
YOU WERE SAYING?
WE'RE NOT DOWN YET.
I SCANNED AN A TO ZED BEFORE I TOOK THE ASSIGNMENT—

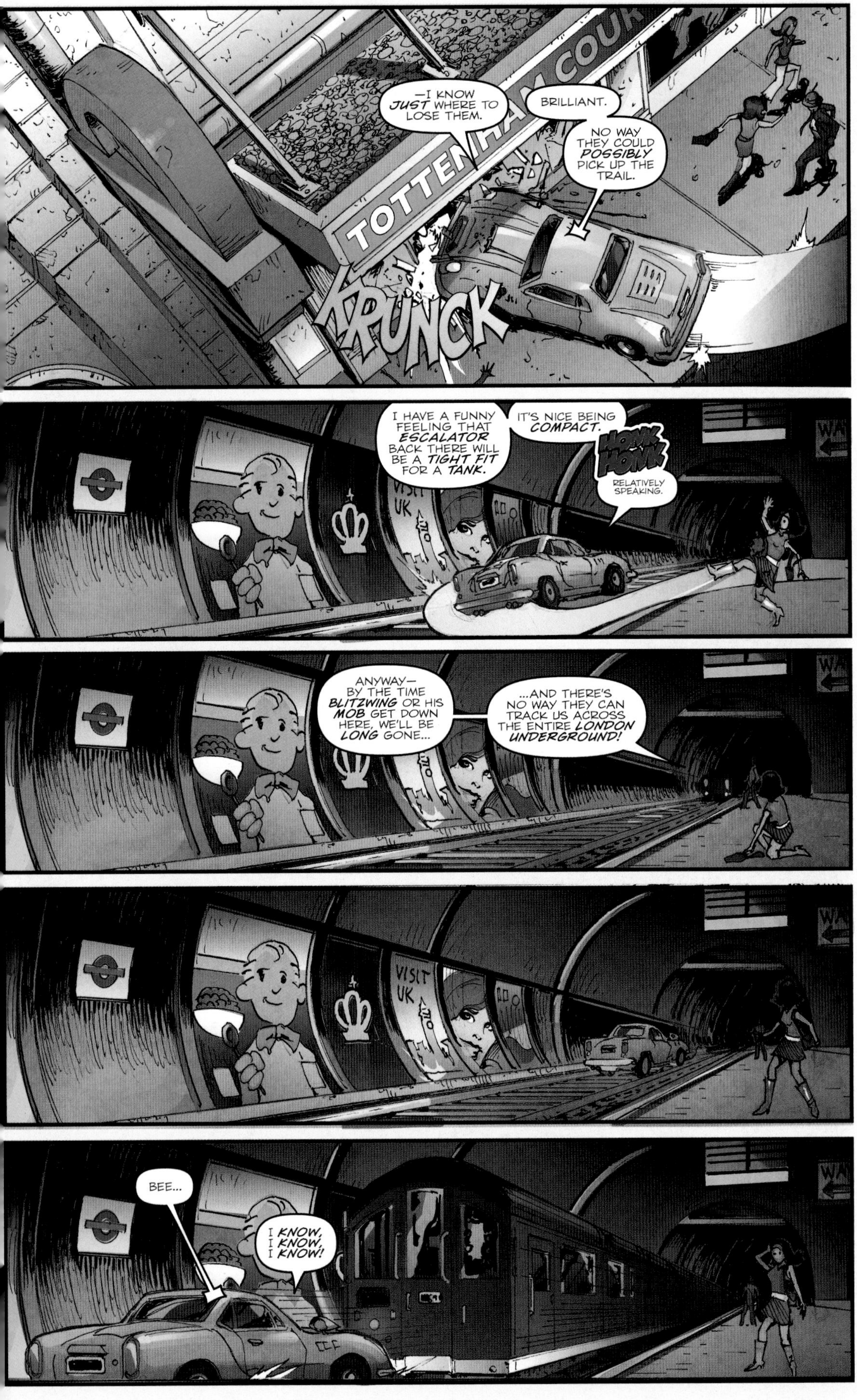
—I KNOW JUST WHERE TO LOSE THEM.
BRILLIANT.
NO WAY THEY COULD POSSIBLY PICK UP THE TRAIL.
TOTTENHAM COUR
KRUNCK
I HAVE A FUNNY FEELING THAT ESCALATOR BACK THERE WILL BE A TIGHT FIT FOR A TANK.
IT'S NICE BEING COMPACT.
HONK HONK
RELATIVELY SPEAKING.
VISIT UK
ANYWAY— BY THE TIME BLITZWING OR HIS MOB GET DOWN HERE, WE'LL BE LONG GONE...
...AND THERE'S NO WAY THEY CAN TRACK US ACROSS THE ENTIRE LONDON UNDERGROUND!
VISIT UK
BEE...
I KNOW, I KNOW, I KNOW!

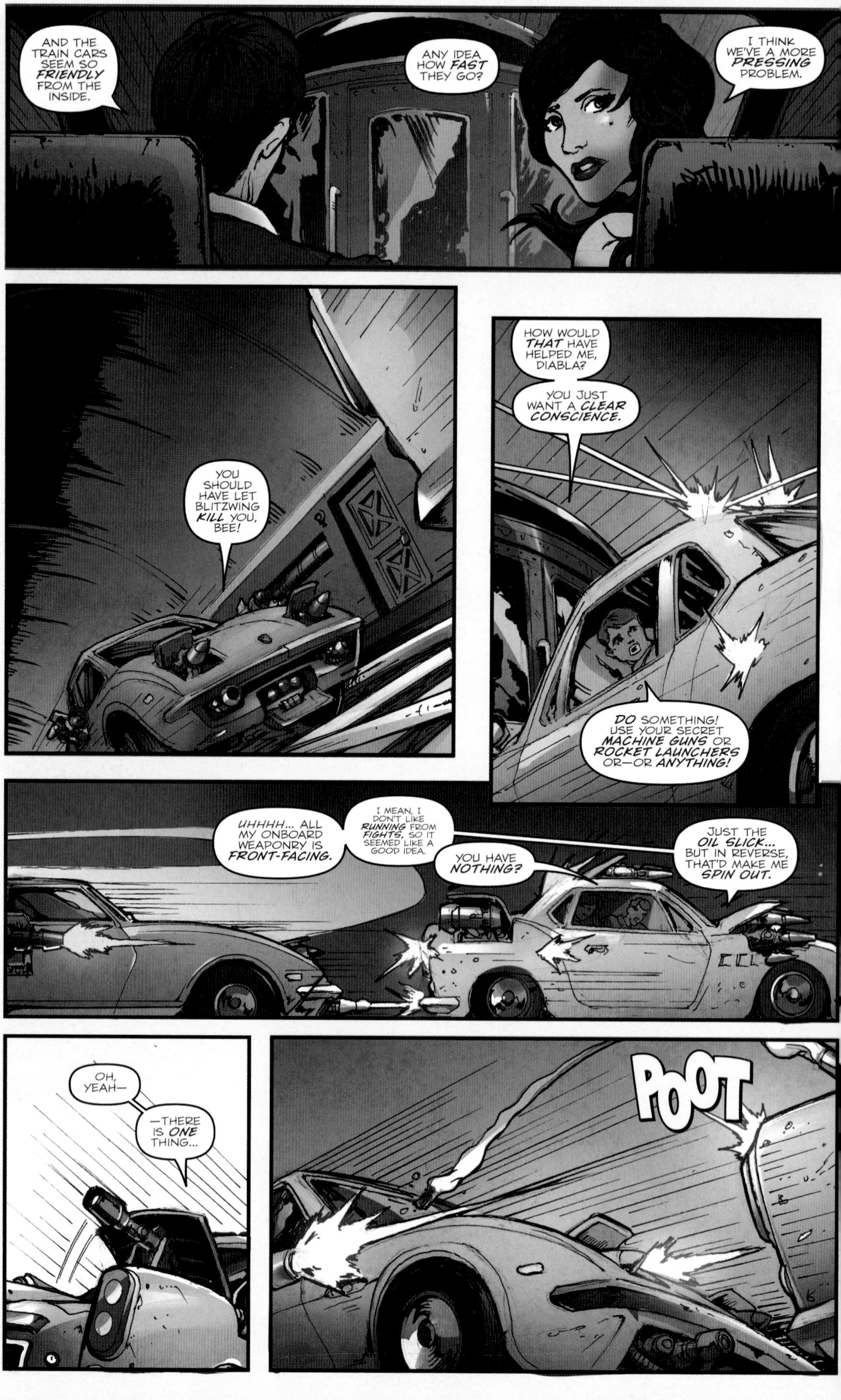
AND THE TRAIN CARS SEEM SO *FRIENDLY* FROM THE INSIDE.
ANY IDEA HOW *FAST* THEY GO?
I THINK WE'VE A MORE *PRESSING* PROBLEM.
YOU SHOULD HAVE LET BLITZWING *KILL* YOU, BEE!
HOW WOULD *THAT* HAVE HELPED ME, DIABLA?
YOU JUST WANT A *CLEAR CONSCIENCE.*
DO SOMETHING! USE YOUR SECRET *MACHINE GUNS* OR *ROCKET LAUNCHERS* OR—OR *ANYTHING!*
UHHHH... ALL MY ONBOARD WEAPONRY IS *FRONT-FACING.*
I MEAN, I DON'T LIKE *RUNNING* FROM *FIGHTS,* SO IT SEEMED LIKE A GOOD IDEA.
YOU HAVE *NOTHING?*
JUST THE *OIL SLICK...* BUT IN REVERSE, THAT'D MAKE ME *SPIN OUT.*
OH, YEAH—
—THERE IS *ONE* THING...
POOT

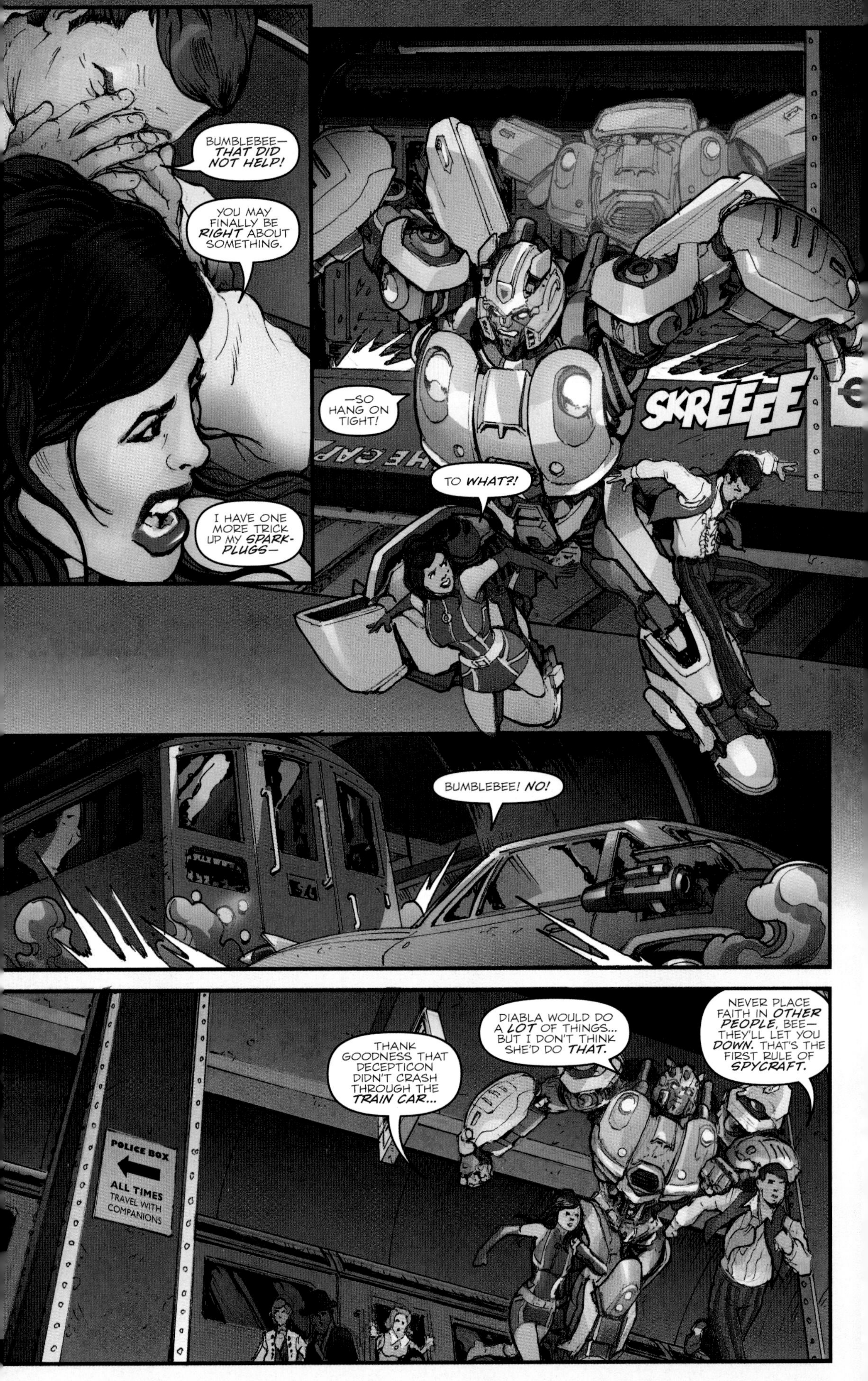

BUMBLEBEE— THAT DID NOT HELP!
YOU MAY FINALLY BE RIGHT ABOUT SOMETHING.
I HAVE ONE MORE TRICK UP MY SPARK-PLUGS—
—SO HANG ON TIGHT!
SKREEEE
TO WHAT?!
BUMBLEBEE! NO!
POLICE BOX
ALL TIMES TRAVEL WITH COMPANIONS
THANK GOODNESS THAT DECEPTICON DIDN'T CRASH THROUGH THE TRAIN CAR...
DIABLA WOULD DO A LOT OF THINGS... BUT I DON'T THINK SHE'D DO THAT.
NEVER PLACE FAITH IN OTHER PEOPLE, BEE— THEY'LL LET YOU DOWN. THAT'S THE FIRST RULE OF SPYCRAFT.

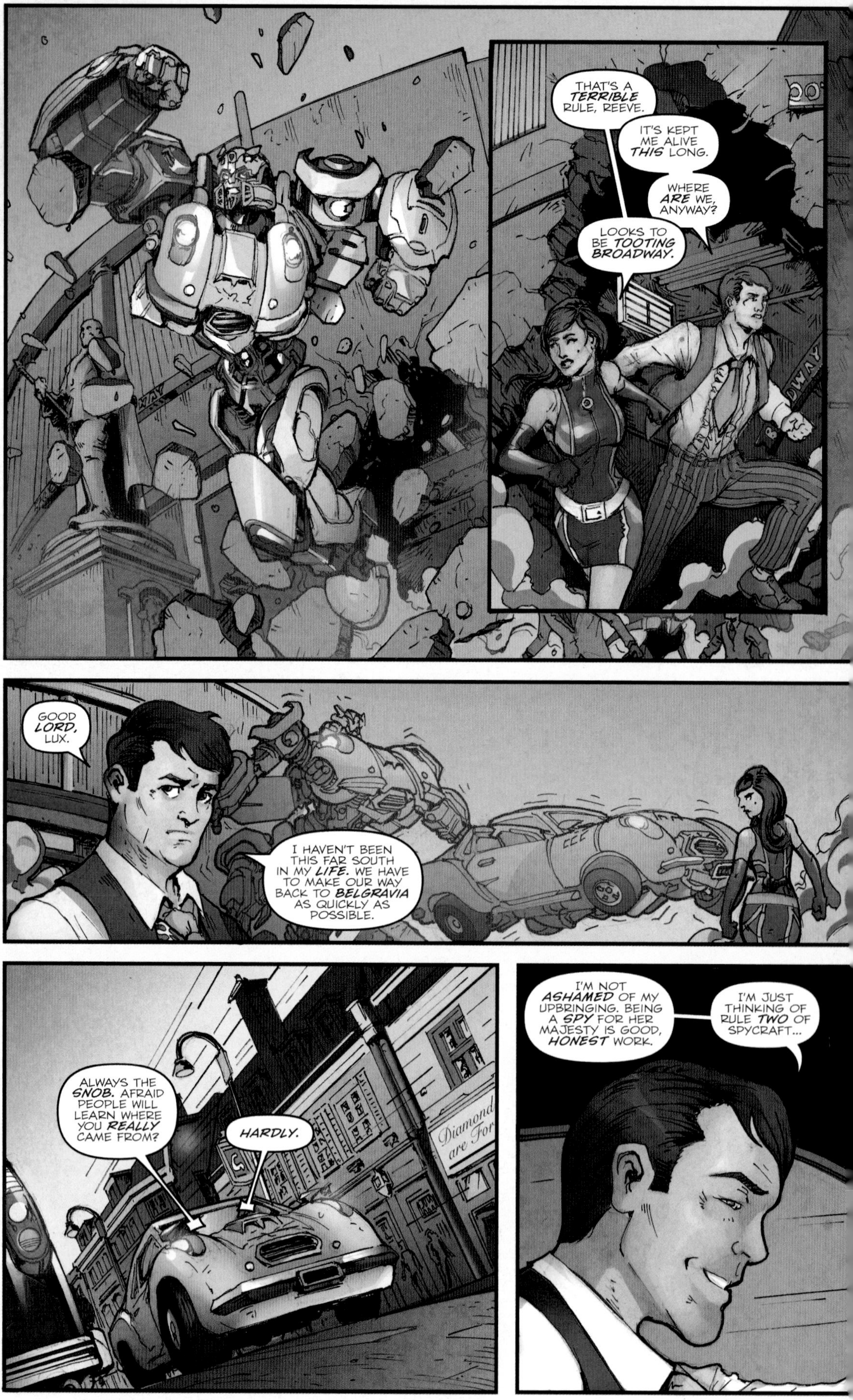
THAT'S A TERRIBLE RULE, REEVE.
IT'S KEPT ME ALIVE THIS LONG.
WHERE ARE WE, ANYWAY?
LOOKS TO BE TOOTING BROADWAY.
GOOD LORD, LUX.
I HAVEN'T BEEN THIS FAR SOUTH IN MY LIFE. WE HAVE TO MAKE OUR WAY BACK TO BELGRAVIA AS QUICKLY AS POSSIBLE.
ALWAYS THE SNOB. AFRAID PEOPLE WILL LEARN WHERE YOU REALLY CAME FROM?
HARDLY.
I'M NOT ASHAMED OF MY UPBRINGING. BEING A SPY FOR HER MAJESTY IS GOOD, HONEST WORK.
I'M JUST THINKING OF RULE TWO OF SPYCRAFT...

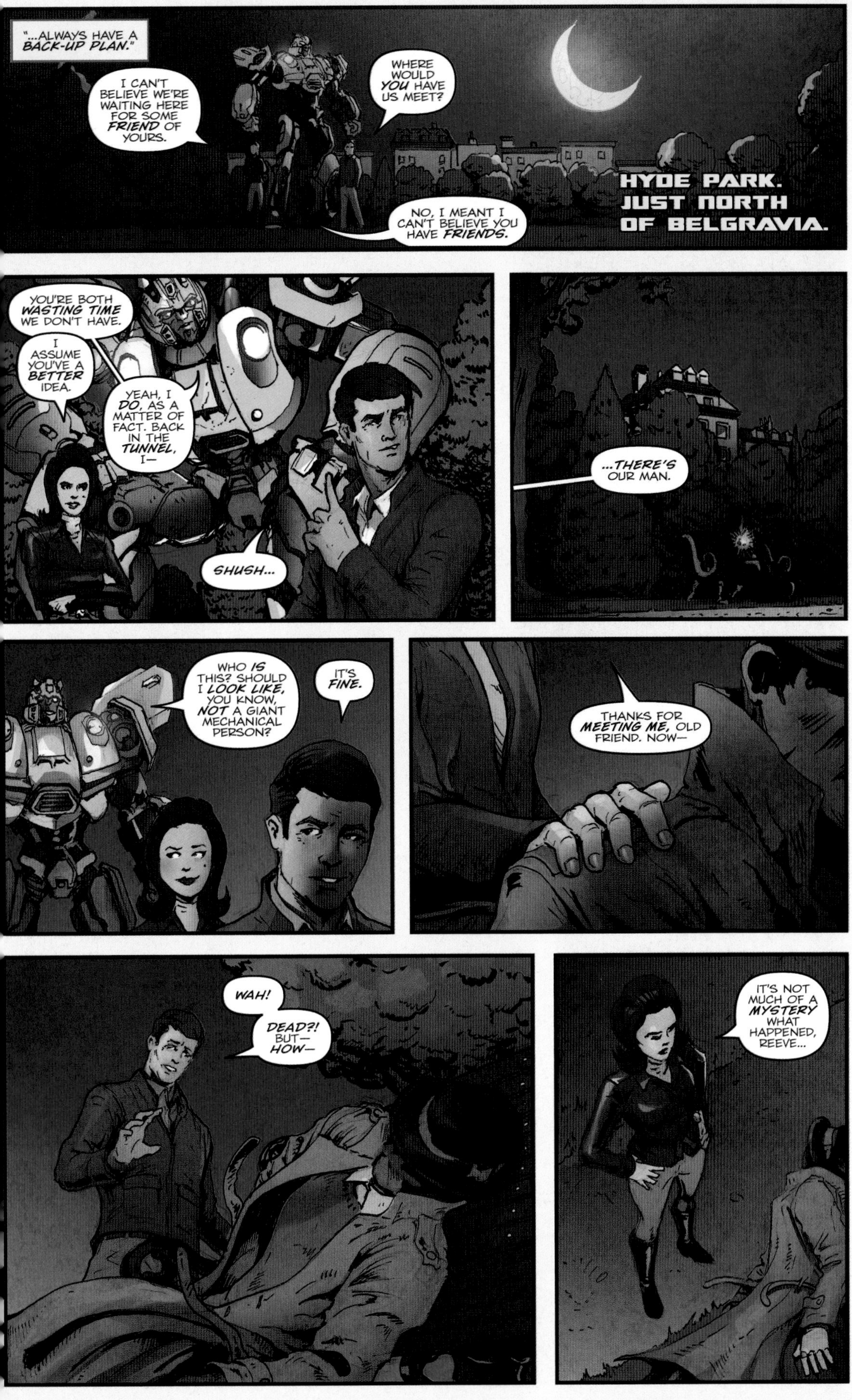
"...ALWAYS HAVE A BACK-UP PLAN."
I CAN'T BELIEVE WE'RE WAITING HERE FOR SOME FRIEND OF YOURS.
WHERE WOULD YOU HAVE US MEET?
HYDE PARK. JUST NORTH OF BELGRAVIA.
NO, I MEANT I CAN'T BELIEVE YOU HAVE FRIENDS.
YOU'RE BOTH WASTING TIME WE DON'T HAVE.
I ASSUME YOU'VE A BETTER IDEA.
YEAH, I DO, AS A MATTER OF FACT. BACK IN THE TUNNEL, I—
SHUSH...
...THERE'S OUR MAN.
WHO IS THIS? SHOULD I LOOK LIKE, YOU KNOW, NOT A GIANT MECHANICAL PERSON?
IT'S FINE.
THANKS FOR MEETING ME, OLD FRIEND. NOW—
WAH!
DEAD?! BUT— HOW—
IT'S NOT MUCH OF A MYSTERY WHAT HAPPENED, REEVE...

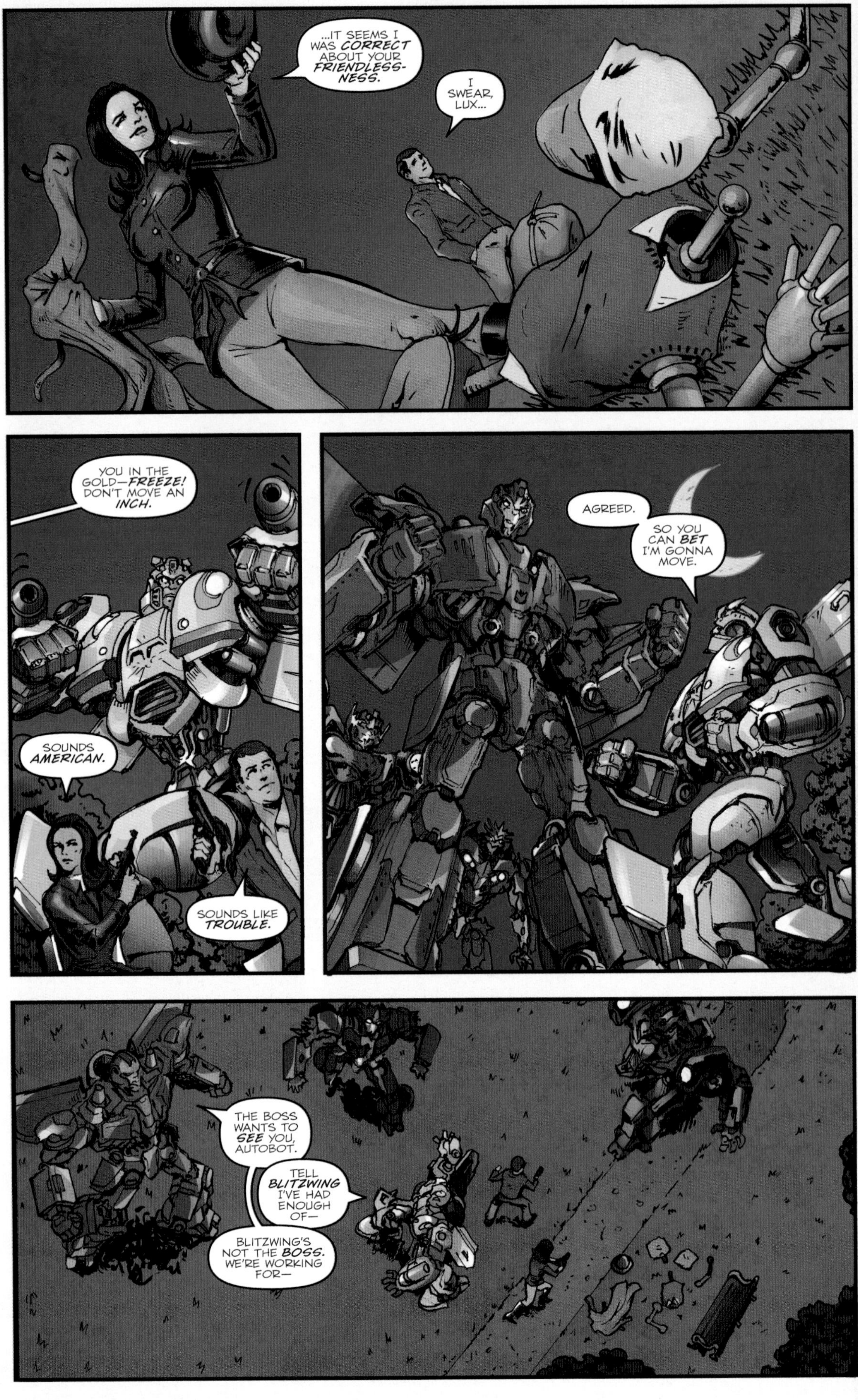
...IT SEEMS I WAS CORRECT ABOUT YOUR FRIENDLESS-NESS.
I SWEAR, LUX...
YOU IN THE GOLD—FREEZE! DON'T MOVE AN INCH.
SOUNDS AMERICAN.
SOUNDS LIKE TROUBLE.
AGREED.
SO YOU CAN BET I'M GONNA MOVE.
THE BOSS WANTS TO SEE YOU, AUTOBOT.
TELL BLITZWING I'VE HAD ENOUGH OF—
BLITZWING'S NOT THE BOSS. WE'RE WORKING FOR—

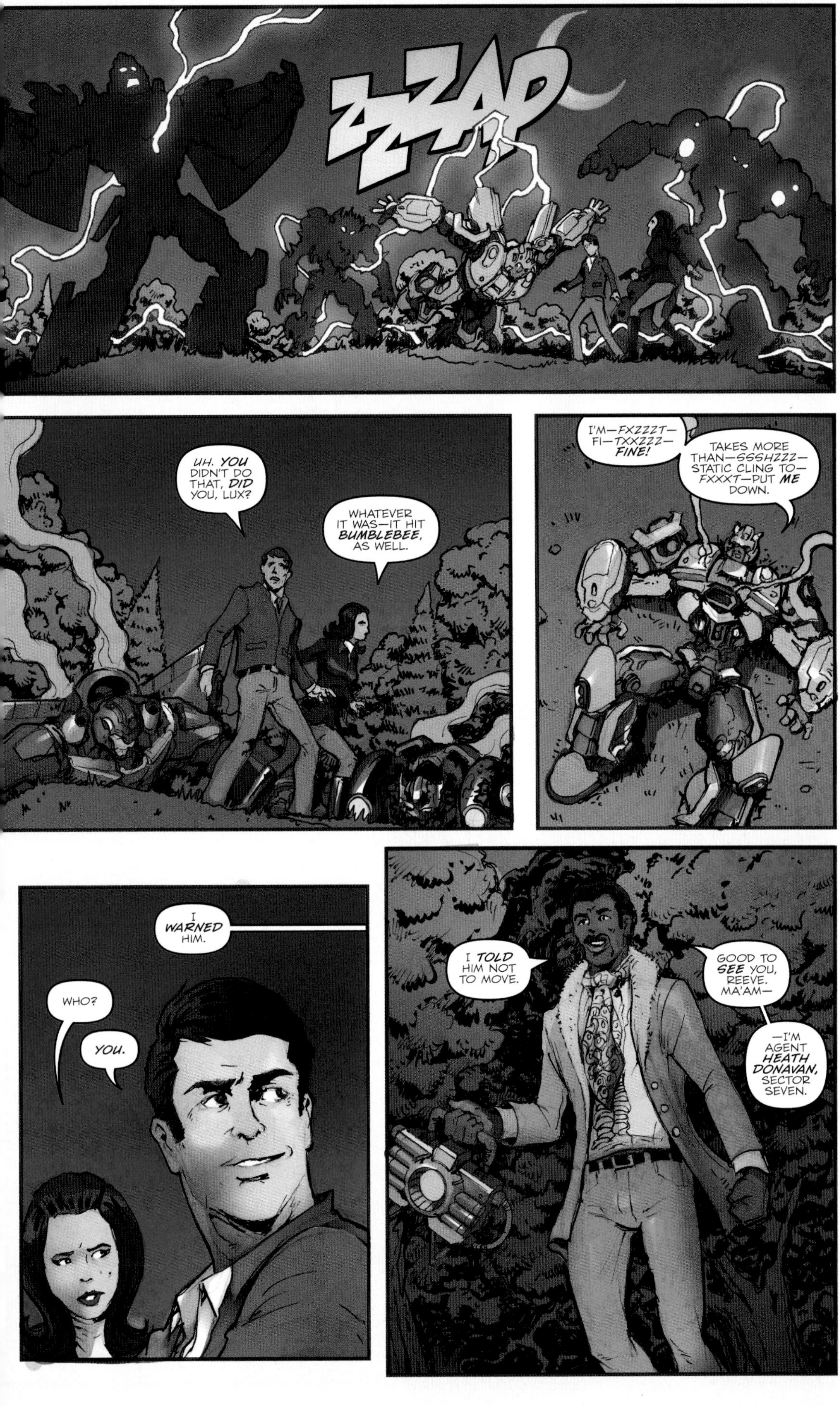
ZZZAP
UH. YOU DIDN'T DO THAT, DID YOU, LUX?
WHATEVER IT WAS—IT HIT BUMBLEBEE, AS WELL.
I'M—FXZZZT—FI—TXXZZZ—FINE!
TAKES MORE THAN—SSSHZZZ—STATIC CLING TO—FXXXT—PUT ME DOWN.
I WARNED HIM.
WHO?
YOU.
I TOLD HIM NOT TO MOVE.
GOOD TO SEE YOU, REEVE. MA'AM—
—I'M AGENT HEATH DONAVAN, SECTOR SEVEN.

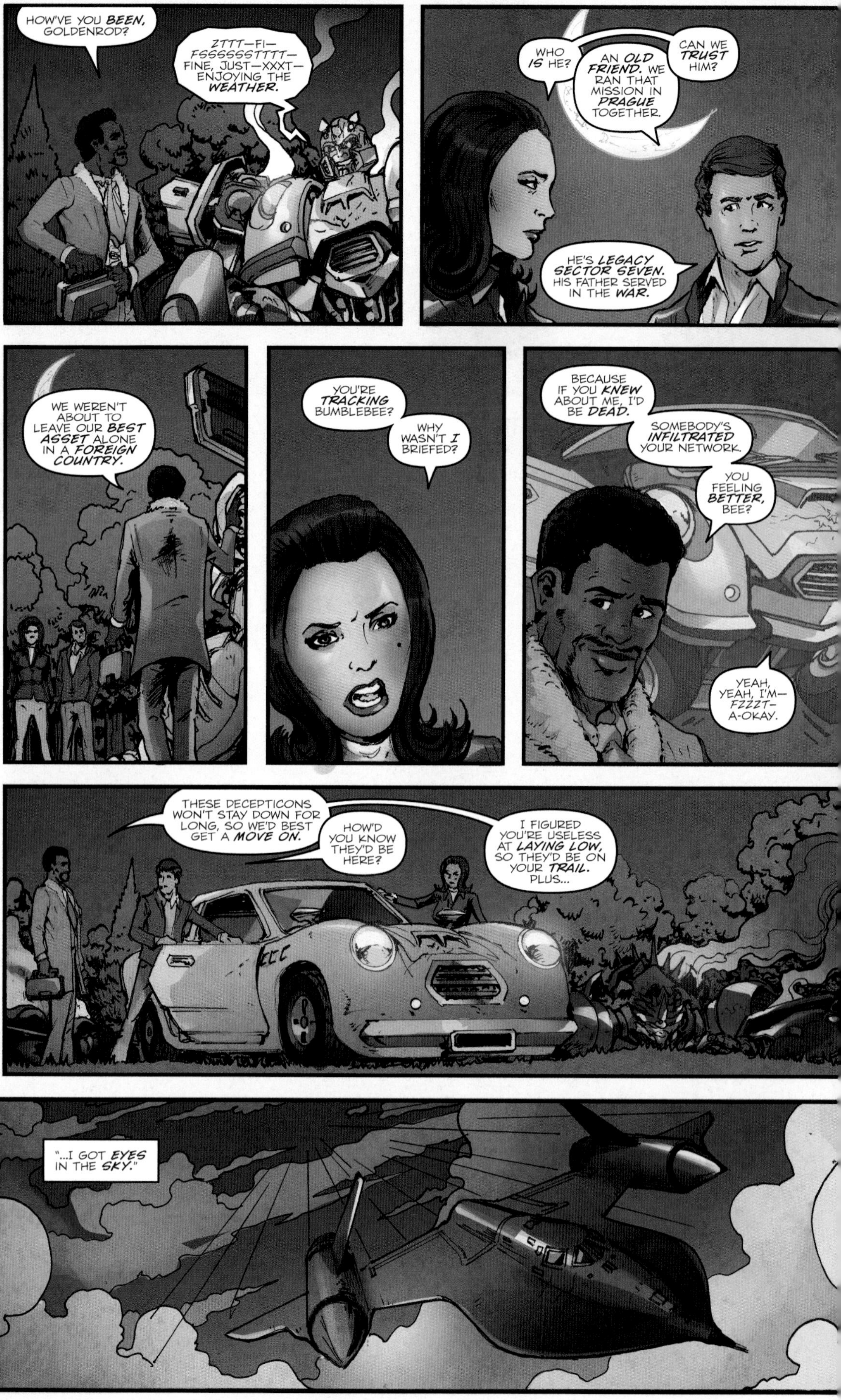
HOW'VE YOU BEEN, GOLDENROD?
ZTTT—FI—FSSSSSSTTTT—FINE, JUST—XXXT—ENJOYING THE WEATHER.
WHO IS HE?
AN OLD FRIEND. WE RAN THAT MISSION IN PRAGUE TOGETHER.
CAN WE TRUST HIM?
HE'S LEGACY SECTOR SEVEN. HIS FATHER SERVED IN THE WAR.
WE WEREN'T ABOUT TO LEAVE OUR BEST ASSET ALONE IN A FOREIGN COUNTRY.
YOU'RE TRACKING BUMBLEBEE?
WHY WASN'T I BRIEFED?
BECAUSE IF YOU KNEW ABOUT ME, I'D BE DEAD.
SOMEBODY'S INFILTRATED YOUR NETWORK.
YOU FEELING BETTER, BEE?
YEAH, YEAH, I'M—FZZZT—A-OKAY.
THESE DECEPTICONS WON'T STAY DOWN FOR LONG, SO WE'D BEST GET A MOVE ON.
HOW'D YOU KNOW THEY'D BE HERE?
I FIGURED YOU'RE USELESS AT LAYING LOW, SO THEY'D BE ON YOUR TRAIL. PLUS...
"...I GOT EYES IN THE SKY."

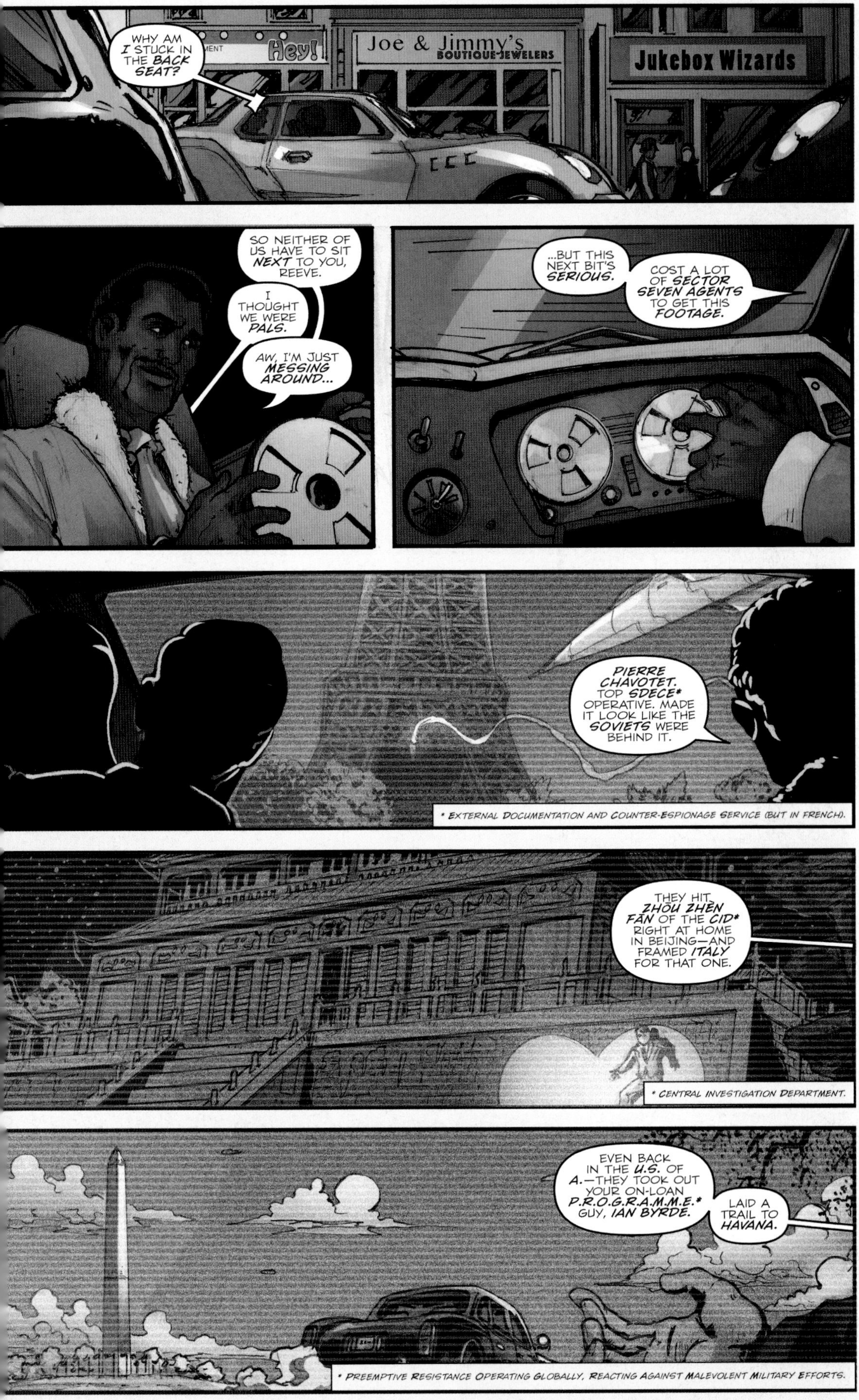
WHY AM I STUCK IN THE BACK SEAT?
Hey!
Joe & Jimmy's BOUTIQUE JEWELERS
Jukebox Wizards
SO NEITHER OF US HAVE TO SIT NEXT TO YOU, REEVE.
I THOUGHT WE WERE PALS.
AW, I'M JUST MESSING AROUND...
...BUT THIS NEXT BIT'S SERIOUS.
COST A LOT OF SECTOR SEVEN AGENTS TO GET THIS FOOTAGE.
PIERRE CHAVOTET. TOP SDECE* OPERATIVE. MADE IT LOOK LIKE THE SOVIETS WERE BEHIND IT.
* EXTERNAL DOCUMENTATION AND COUNTER-ESPIONAGE SERVICE (BUT IN FRENCH).
THEY HIT ZHŌU ZHÈN FĀN OF THE CID* RIGHT AT HOME IN BEIJING—AND FRAMED ITALY FOR THAT ONE.
* CENTRAL INVESTIGATION DEPARTMENT.
EVEN BACK IN THE U.S. OF A.—THEY TOOK OUT YOUR ON-LOAN P.R.O.G.R.A.M.M.E.* GUY, IAN BYRDE.
LAID A TRAIL TO HAVANA.
* PREEMPTIVE RESISTANCE OPERATING GLOBALLY, REACTING AGAINST MALEVOLENT MILITARY EFFORTS.

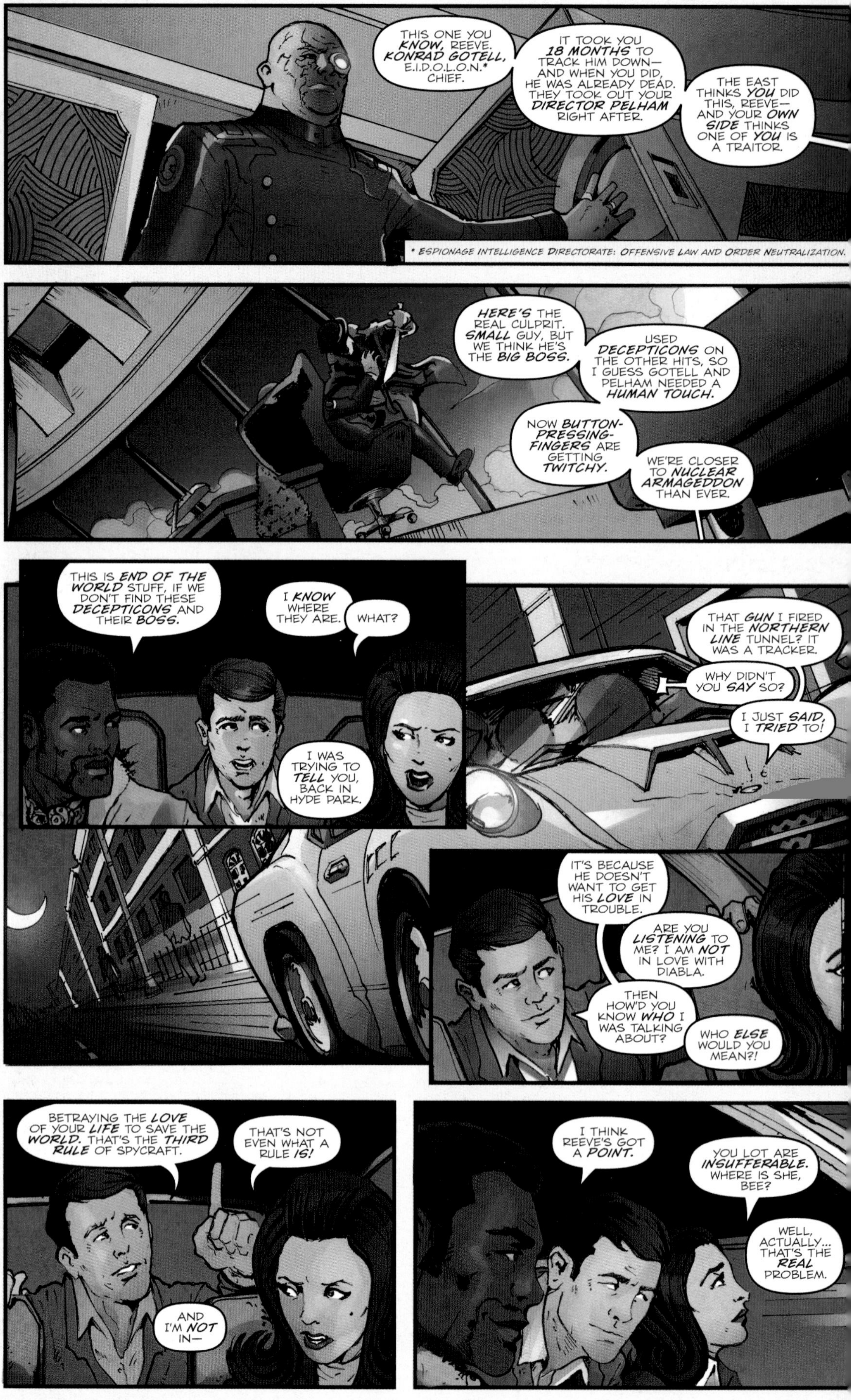
THIS ONE YOU KNOW, REEVE. KONRAD GOTELL, E.I.D.O.L.O.N.* CHIEF.
IT TOOK YOU 18 MONTHS TO TRACK HIM DOWN— AND WHEN YOU DID, HE WAS ALREADY DEAD. THEY TOOK OUT YOUR DIRECTOR PELHAM RIGHT AFTER.
THE EAST THINKS YOU DID THIS, REEVE— AND YOUR OWN SIDE THINKS ONE OF YOU IS A TRAITOR.
* ESPIONAGE INTELLIGENCE DIRECTORATE: OFFENSIVE LAW AND ORDER NEUTRALIZATION.
HERE'S THE REAL CULPRIT. SMALL GUY, BUT WE THINK HE'S THE BIG BOSS.
USED DECEPTICONS ON THE OTHER HITS, SO I GUESS GOTELL AND PELHAM NEEDED A HUMAN TOUCH.
NOW BUTTON-PRESSING-FINGERS ARE GETTING TWITCHY.
WE'RE CLOSER TO NUCLEAR ARMAGEDDON THAN EVER.
THIS IS END OF THE WORLD STUFF, IF WE DON'T FIND THESE DECEPTICONS AND THEIR BOSS.
I KNOW WHERE THEY ARE.
WHAT?
I WAS TRYING TO TELL YOU, BACK IN HYDE PARK.
THAT GUN I FIRED IN THE NORTHERN LINE TUNNEL? IT WAS A TRACKER.
WHY DIDN'T YOU SAY SO?
I JUST SAID, I TRIED TO!
IT'S BECAUSE HE DOESN'T WANT TO GET HIS LOVE IN TROUBLE.
ARE YOU LISTENING TO ME? I AM NOT IN LOVE WITH DIABLA.
THEN HOW'D YOU KNOW WHO I WAS TALKING ABOUT?
WHO ELSE WOULD YOU MEAN?!
BETRAYING THE LOVE OF YOUR LIFE TO SAVE THE WORLD. THAT'S THE THIRD RULE OF SPYCRAFT.
THAT'S NOT EVEN WHAT A RULE IS!
AND I'M NOT IN—
I THINK REEVE'S GOT A POINT.
YOU LOT ARE INSUFFERABLE. WHERE IS SHE, BEE?
WELL, ACTUALLY... THAT'S THE REAL PROBLEM.

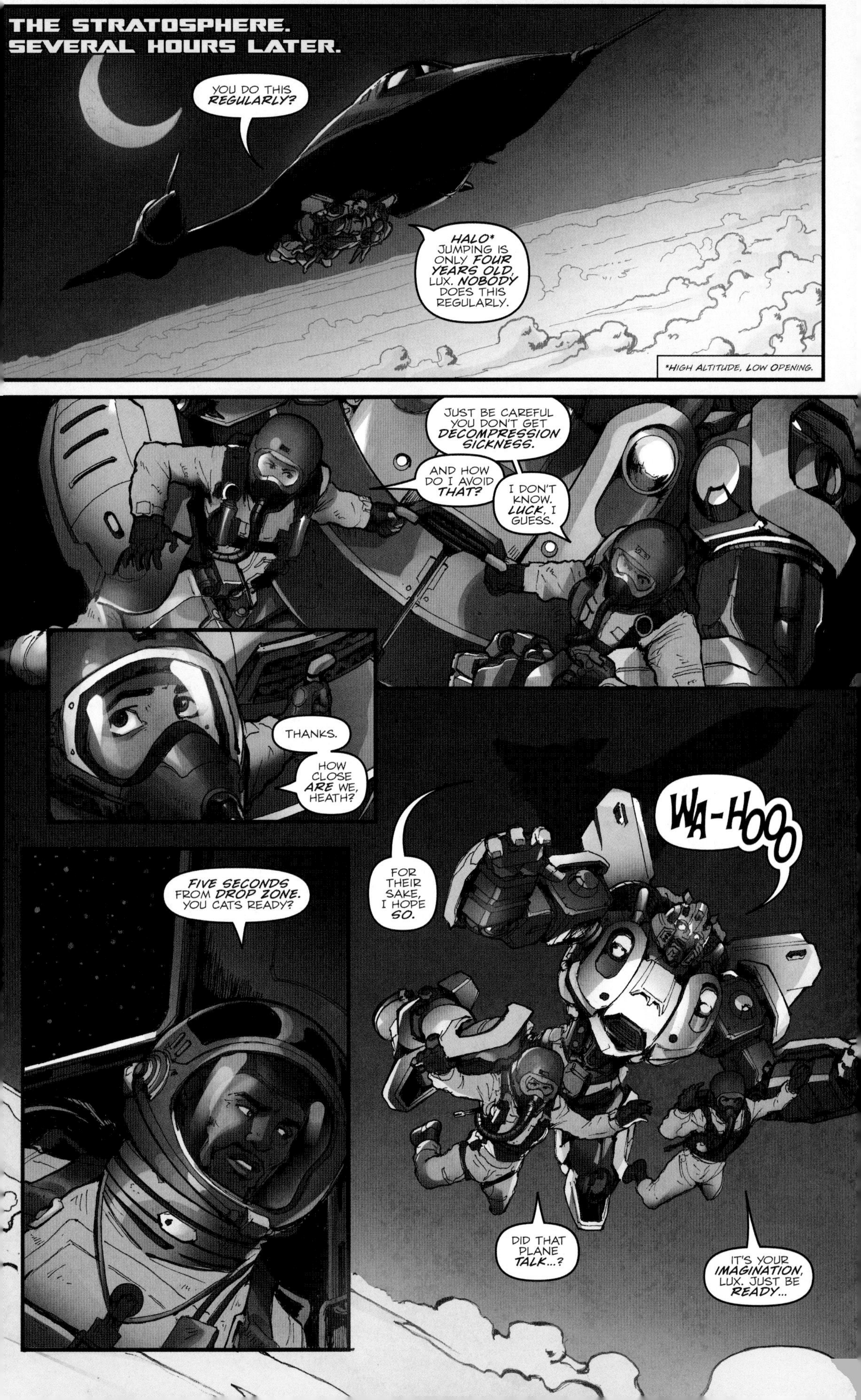
THE STRATOSPHERE. SEVERAL HOURS LATER.
YOU DO THIS REGULARLY?
HALO* JUMPING IS ONLY FOUR YEARS OLD, LUX. NOBODY DOES THIS REGULARLY.
*HIGH ALTITUDE, LOW OPENING.
JUST BE CAREFUL YOU DON'T GET DECOMPRESSION SICKNESS.
AND HOW DO I AVOID THAT?
I DON'T KNOW. LUCK, I GUESS.
THANKS.
HOW CLOSE ARE WE, HEATH?
FIVE SECONDS FROM DROP ZONE. YOU CATS READY?
FOR THEIR SAKE, I HOPE SO.
WA-HOOO
DID THAT PLANE TALK...?
IT'S YOUR IMAGINATION, LUX. JUST BE READY...

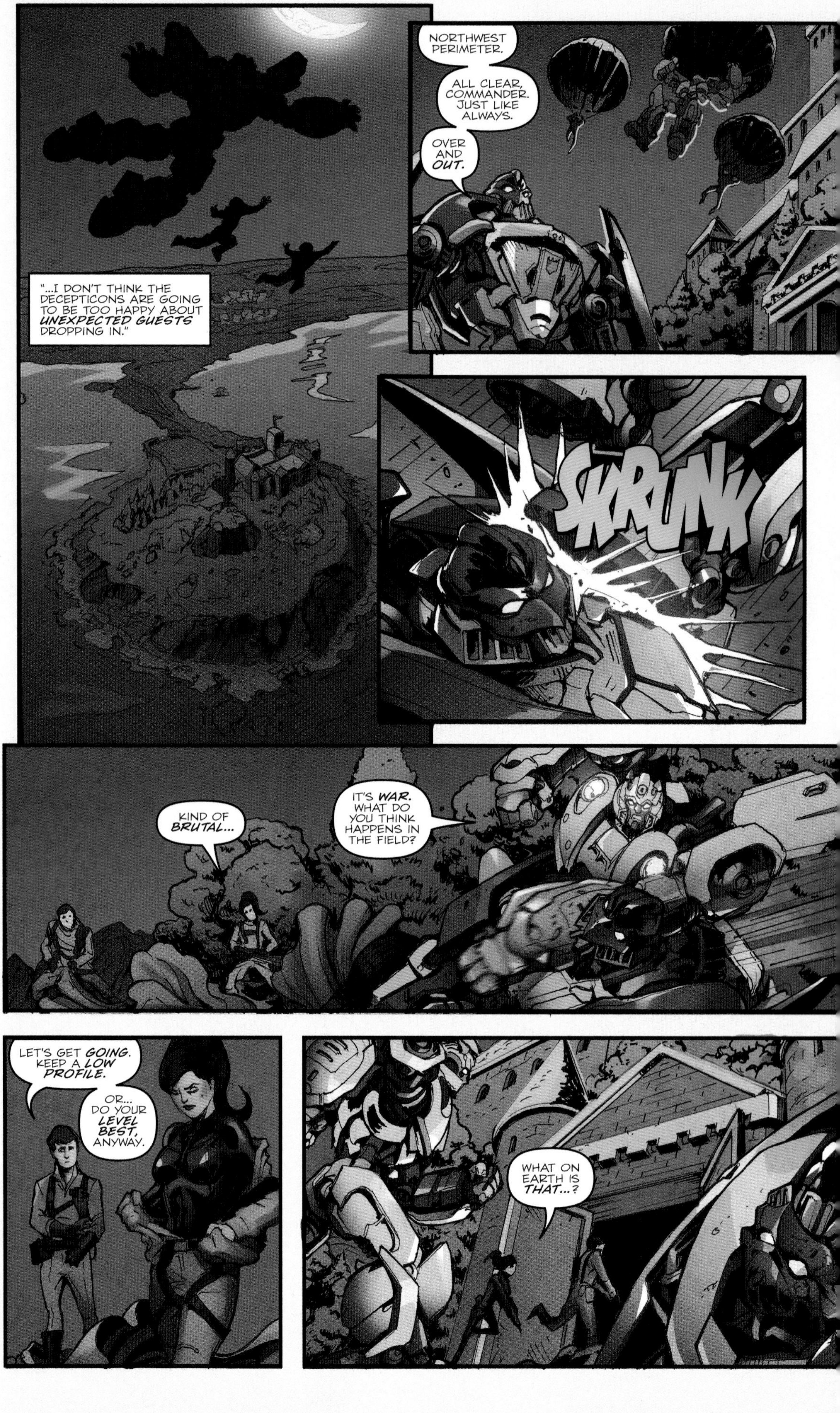

"...I DON'T THINK THE DECEPTICONS ARE GOING TO BE TOO HAPPY ABOUT ***UNEXPECTED GUESTS*** DROPPING IN."
NORTHWEST PERIMETER.
ALL CLEAR, COMMANDER. JUST LIKE ALWAYS.
OVER AND ***OUT.***
SKRUNK
KIND OF ***BRUTAL...***
IT'S ***WAR.*** WHAT DO YOU THINK HAPPENS IN THE FIELD?
LET'S GET ***GOING.*** KEEP A ***LOW PROFILE.***
OR... DO YOUR ***LEVEL BEST,*** ANYWAY.
WHAT ON EARTH IS ***THAT...?***

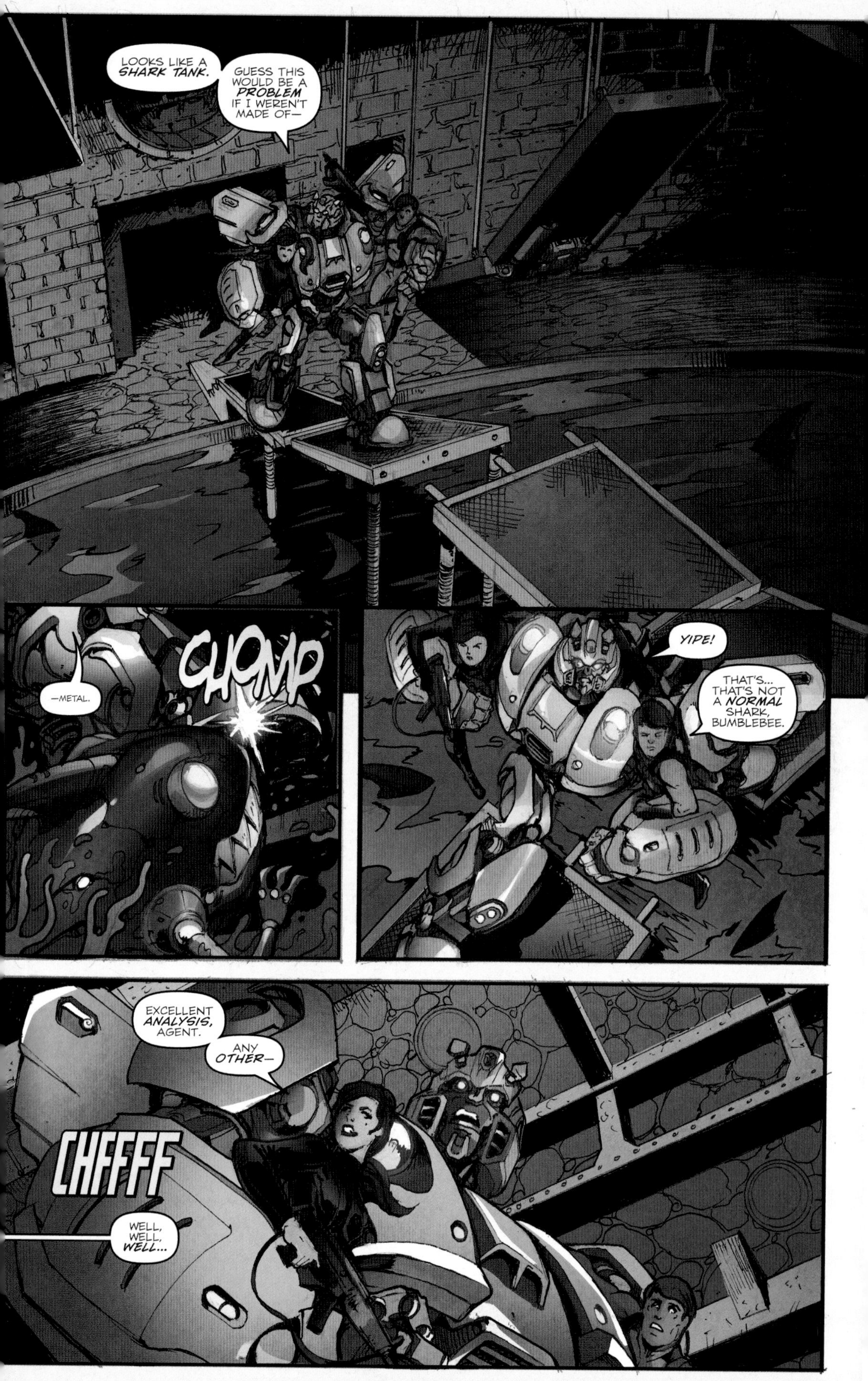
LOOKS LIKE A SHARK TANK.
GUESS THIS WOULD BE A PROBLEM IF I WEREN'T MADE OF—
—METAL.
CHOMP
YIPE!
THAT'S... THAT'S NOT A NORMAL SHARK, BUMBLEBEE.
EXCELLENT ANALYSIS, AGENT.
ANY OTHER—
CHFFFF
WELL, WELL, WELL...

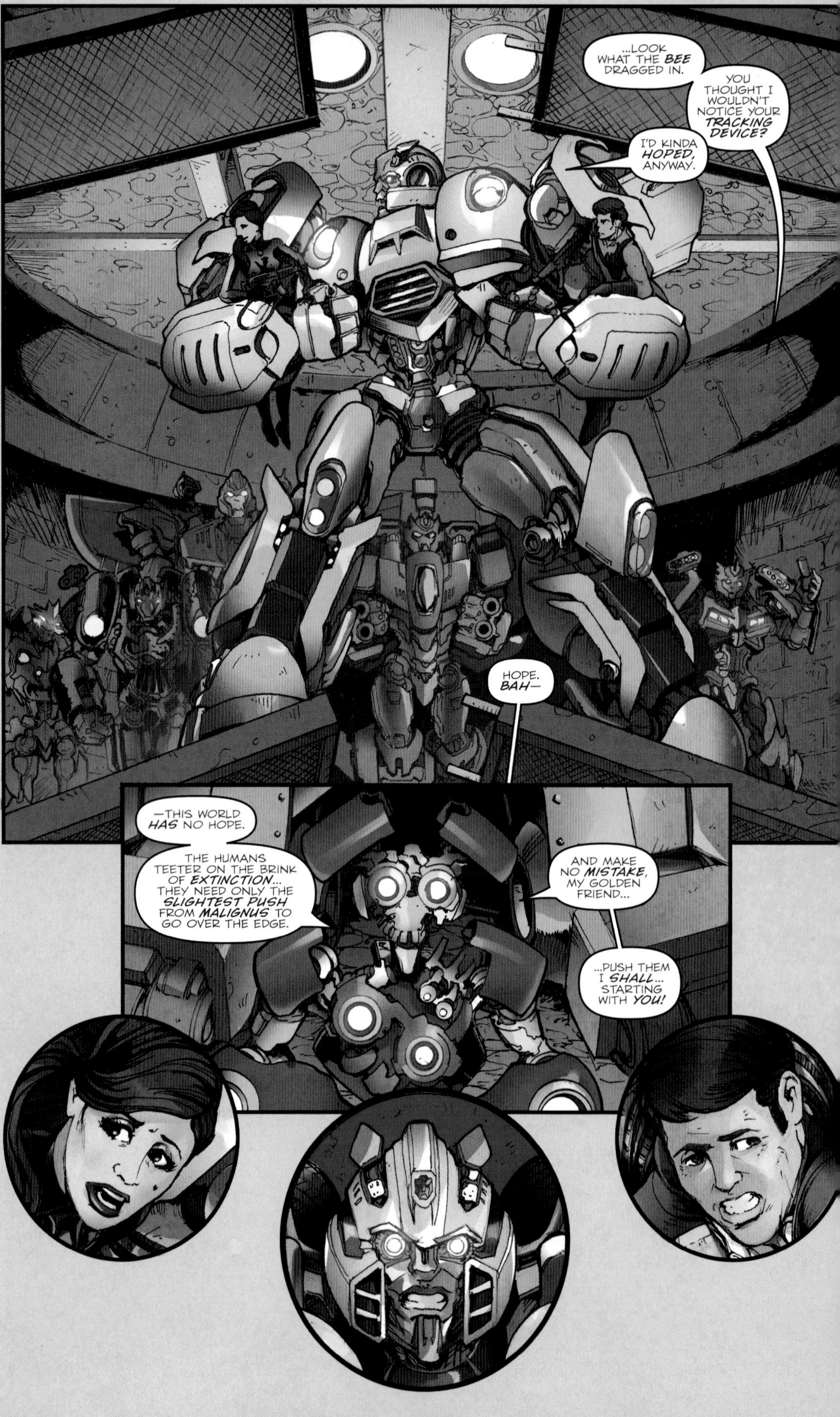
...LOOK WHAT THE BEE DRAGGED IN.
YOU THOUGHT I WOULDN'T NOTICE YOUR TRACKING DEVICE?
I'D KINDA HOPED, ANYWAY.
HOPE. BAH—
—THIS WORLD HAS NO HOPE.
THE HUMANS TEETER ON THE BRINK OF EXTINCTION... THEY NEED ONLY THE SLIGHTEST PUSH FROM MALIGNUS TO GO OVER THE EDGE.
AND MAKE NO MISTAKE, MY GOLDEN FRIEND...
...PUSH THEM I SHALL... STARTING WITH YOU!

TRANSFORMERS

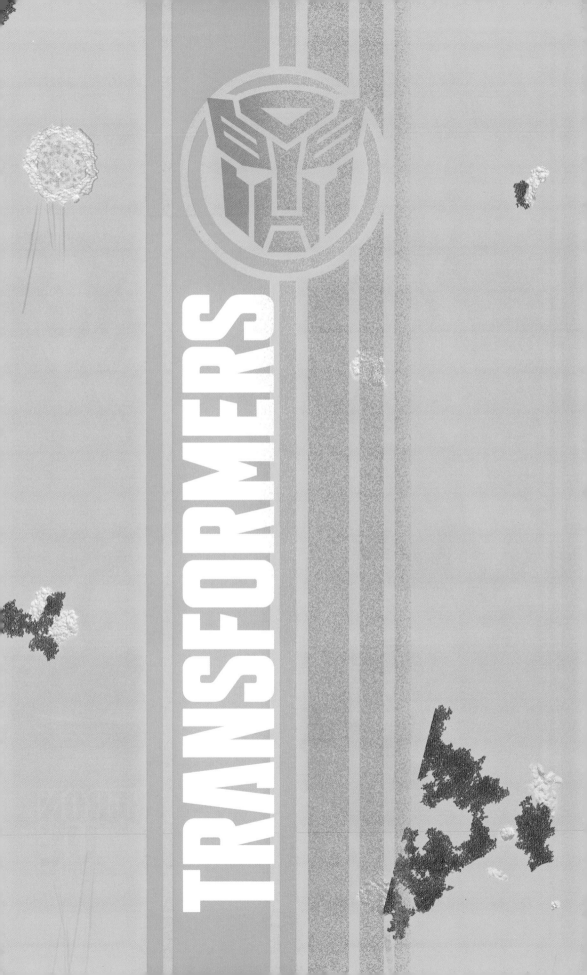

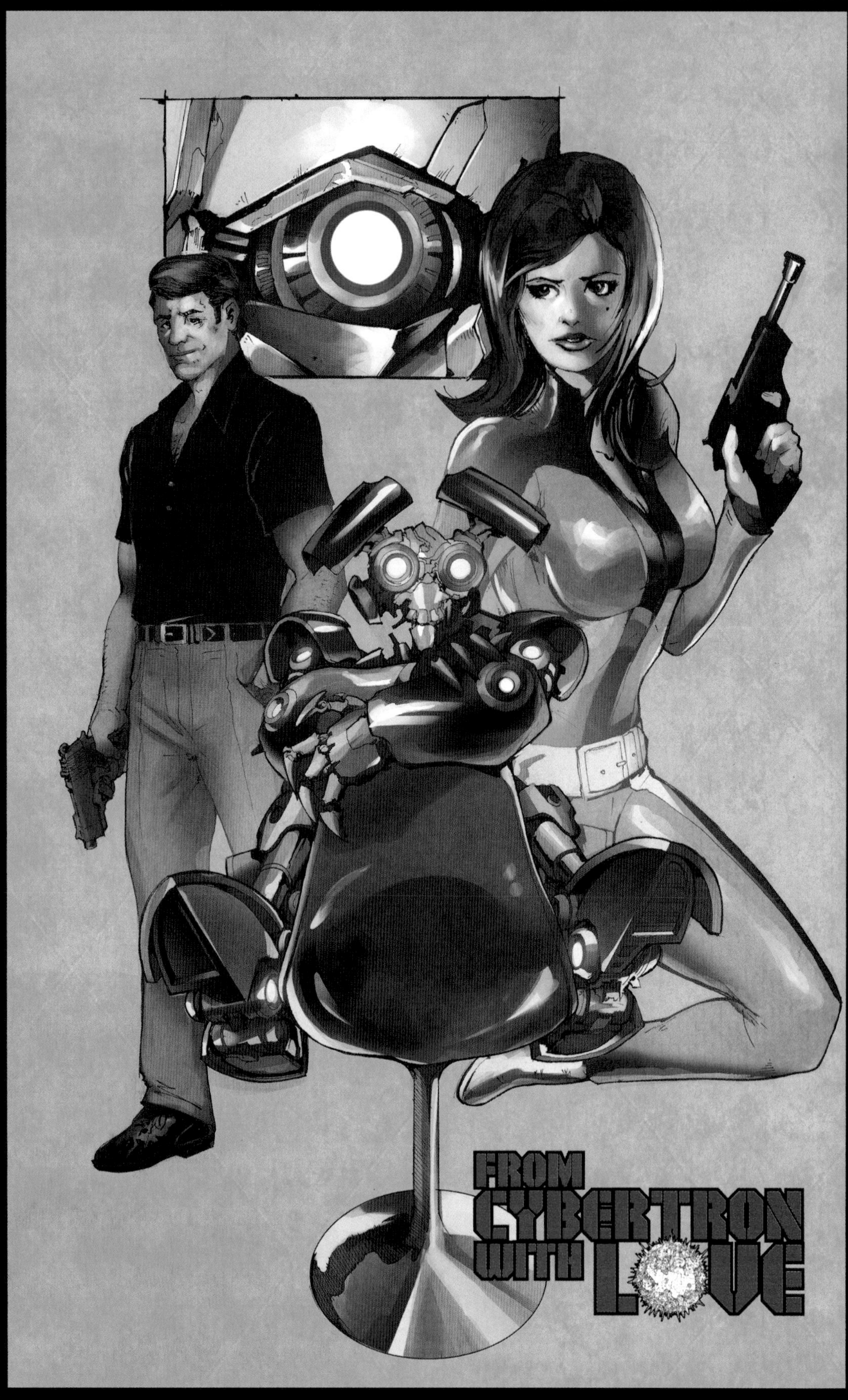
FROM CYBERTRON WITH LOVE

ART BY ANDREW GRIFFITH | COLORS BY PRISCILLA TRAMONTANO

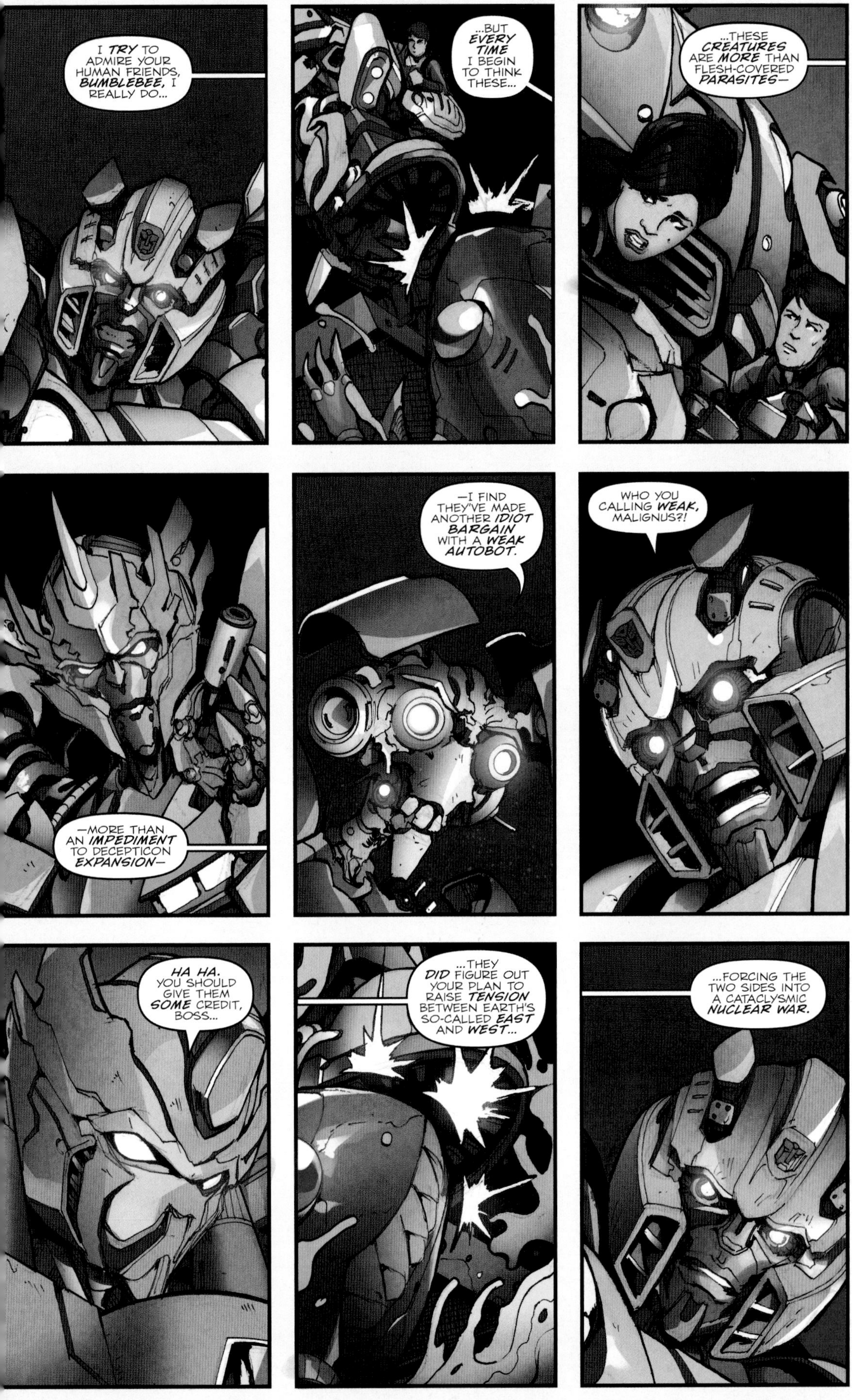
I TRY TO ADMIRE YOUR HUMAN FRIENDS, BUMBLEBEE, I REALLY DO...
...BUT EVERY TIME I BEGIN TO THINK THESE...
...THESE CREATURES ARE MORE THAN FLESH-COVERED PARASITES—
—MORE THAN AN IMPEDIMENT TO DECEPTICON EXPANSION—
—I FIND THEY'VE MADE ANOTHER IDIOT BARGAIN WITH A WEAK AUTOBOT.
WHO YOU CALLING WEAK, MALIGNUS?!
HA HA. YOU SHOULD GIVE THEM SOME CREDIT, BOSS...
...THEY DID FIGURE OUT YOUR PLAN TO RAISE TENSION BETWEEN EARTH'S SO-CALLED EAST AND WEST...
...FORCING THE TWO SIDES INTO A CATACLYSMIC NUCLEAR WAR.

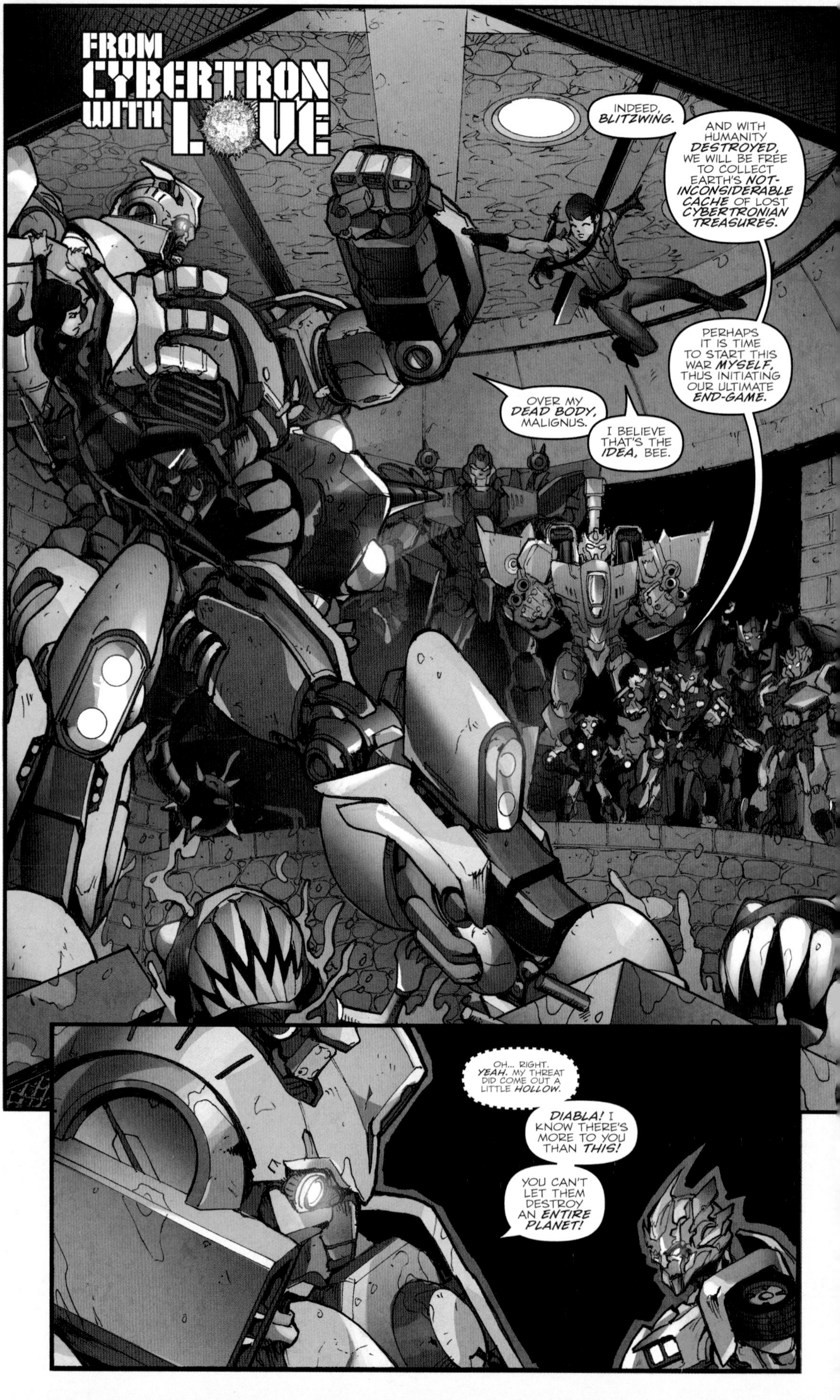
FROM CYBERTRON WITH LOVE
INDEED, BLITZWING.
AND WITH HUMANITY DESTROYED, WE WILL BE FREE TO COLLECT EARTH'S NOT-INCONSIDERABLE CACHE OF LOST CYBERTRONIAN TREASURES.
PERHAPS IT IS TIME TO START THIS WAR MYSELF, THUS INITIATING OUR ULTIMATE END-GAME.
OVER MY DEAD BODY, MALIGNUS.
I BELIEVE THAT'S THE IDEA, BEE.
OH... RIGHT. YEAH. MY THREAT DID COME OUT A LITTLE HOLLOW.
DIABLA! I KNOW THERE'S MORE TO YOU THAN THIS!
YOU CAN'T LET THEM DESTROY AN ENTIRE PLANET!

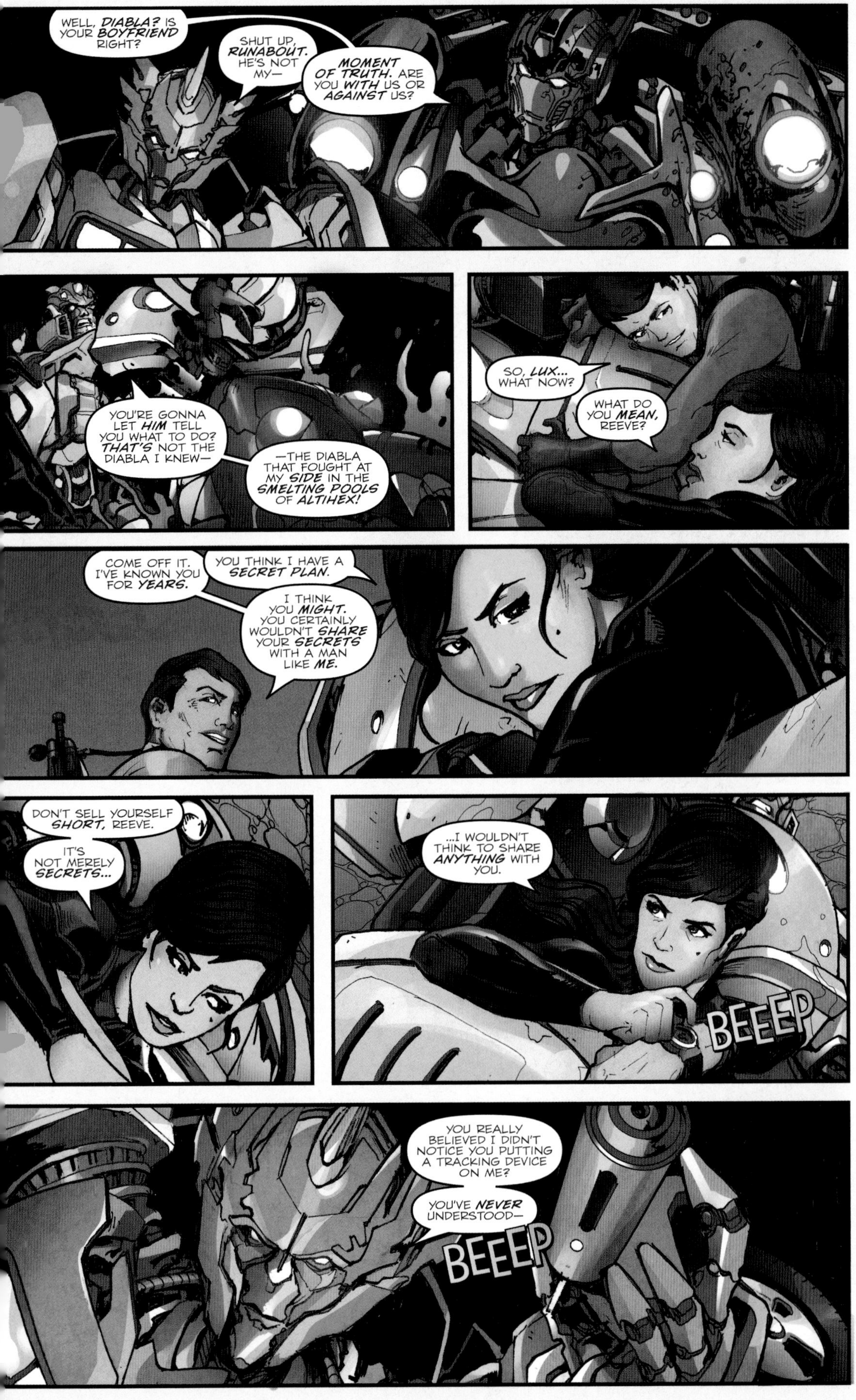

WELL, DIABLA? IS YOUR BOYFRIEND RIGHT?
SHUT UP, RUNABOUT. HE'S NOT MY—
MOMENT OF TRUTH. ARE YOU WITH US OR AGAINST US?
YOU'RE GONNA LET HIM TELL YOU WHAT TO DO? THAT'S NOT THE DIABLA I KNEW—
—THE DIABLA THAT FOUGHT AT MY SIDE IN THE SMELTING POOLS OF ALTIHEX!
SO, LUX... WHAT NOW?
WHAT DO YOU MEAN, REEVE?
COME OFF IT. I'VE KNOWN YOU FOR YEARS.
YOU THINK I HAVE A SECRET PLAN.
I THINK YOU MIGHT. YOU CERTAINLY WOULDN'T SHARE YOUR SECRETS WITH A MAN LIKE ME.
DON'T SELL YOURSELF SHORT, REEVE.
IT'S NOT MERELY SECRETS...
...I WOULDN'T THINK TO SHARE ANYTHING WITH YOU.
BEEEP
YOU REALLY BELIEVED I DIDN'T NOTICE YOU PUTTING A TRACKING DEVICE ON ME?
YOU'VE NEVER UNDERSTOOD—
BEEEP

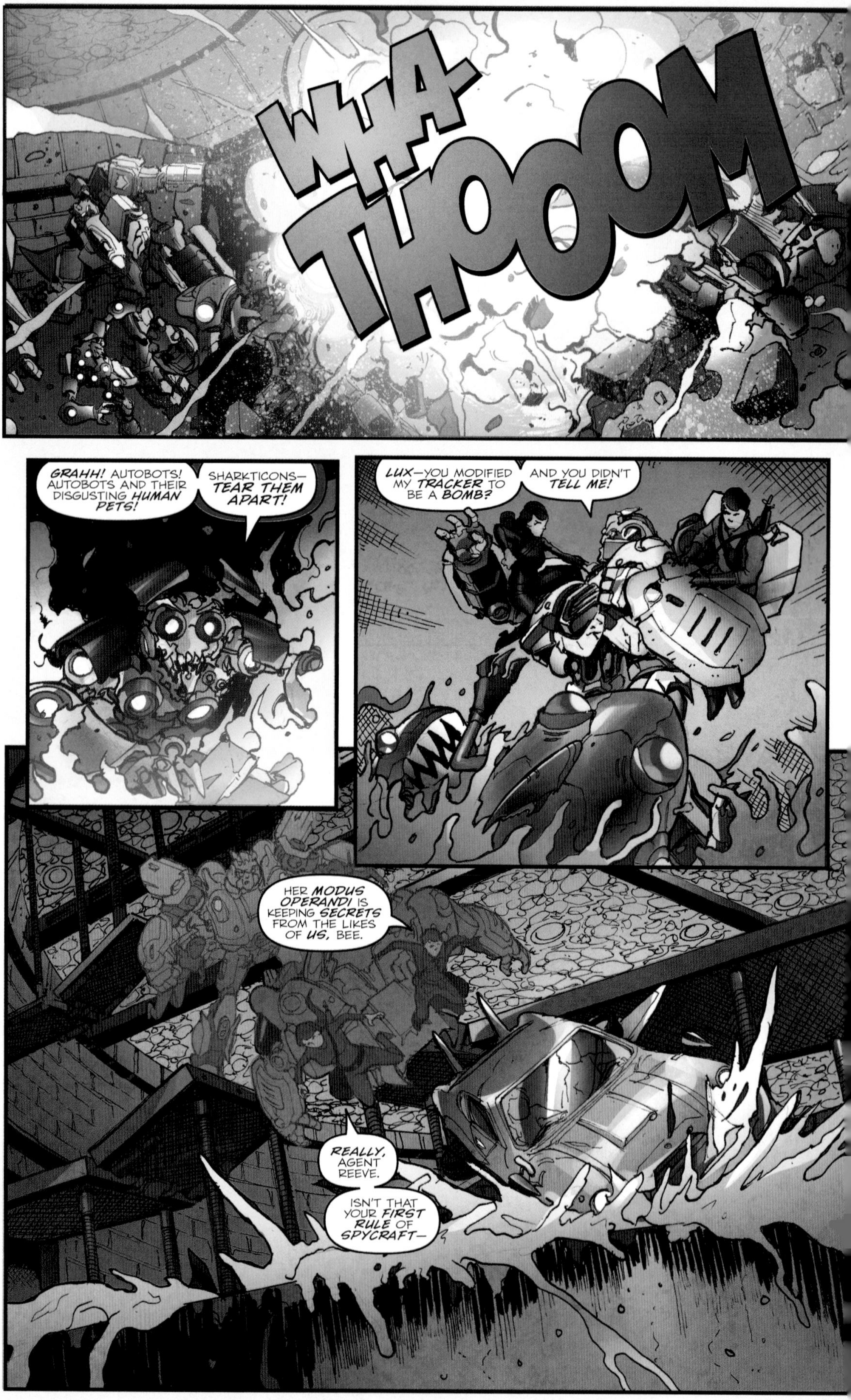
WHA-THOOOM
GRAHH! AUTOBOTS! AUTOBOTS AND THEIR DISGUSTING HUMAN PETS!
SHARKTICONS— TEAR THEM APART!
LUX—YOU MODIFIED MY TRACKER TO BE A BOMB?
AND YOU DIDN'T TELL ME!
HER MODUS OPERANDI IS KEEPING SECRETS FROM THE LIKES OF US, BEE.
REALLY, AGENT REEVE.
ISN'T THAT YOUR FIRST RULE OF SPYCRAFT—

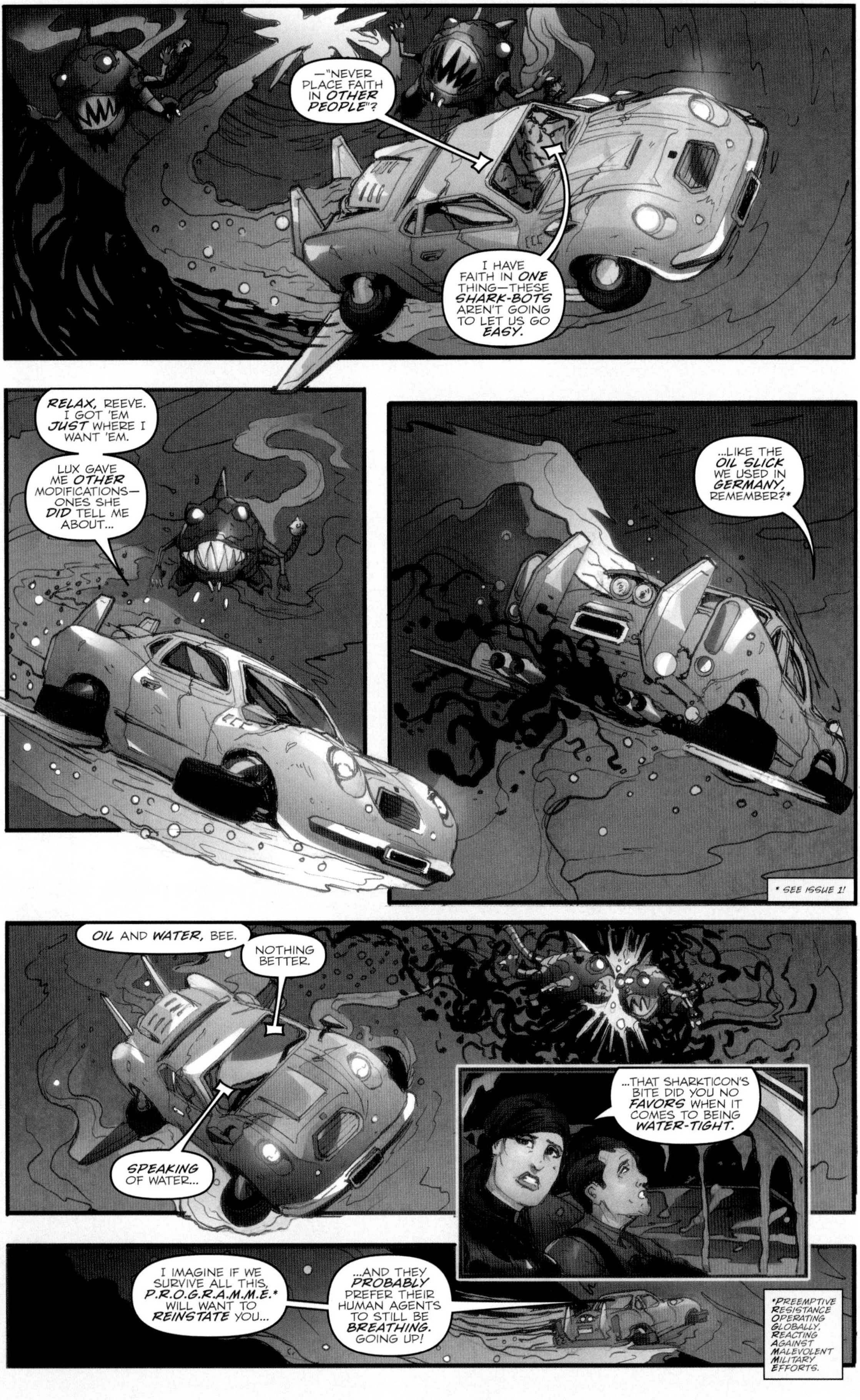
—"NEVER PLACE FAITH IN OTHER PEOPLE"?
I HAVE FAITH IN ONE THING—THESE SHARK-BOTS AREN'T GOING TO LET US GO EASY.
RELAX, REEVE. I GOT 'EM JUST WHERE I WANT 'EM.
LUX GAVE ME OTHER MODIFICATIONS—ONES SHE DID TELL ME ABOUT...
...LIKE THE OIL SLICK WE USED IN GERMANY, REMEMBER?*
* SEE ISSUE 1!
OIL AND WATER, BEE.
NOTHING BETTER.
SPEAKING OF WATER...
...THAT SHARKTICON'S BITE DID YOU NO FAVORS WHEN IT COMES TO BEING WATER-TIGHT.
I IMAGINE IF WE SURVIVE ALL THIS, P.R.O.G.R.A.M.M.E.* WILL WANT TO REINSTATE YOU...
...AND THEY PROBABLY PREFER THEIR HUMAN AGENTS TO STILL BE BREATHING. GOING UP!
*PREEMPTIVE RESISTANCE OPERATING GLOBALLY, REACTING AGAINST MALEVOLENT MILITARY EFFORTS.

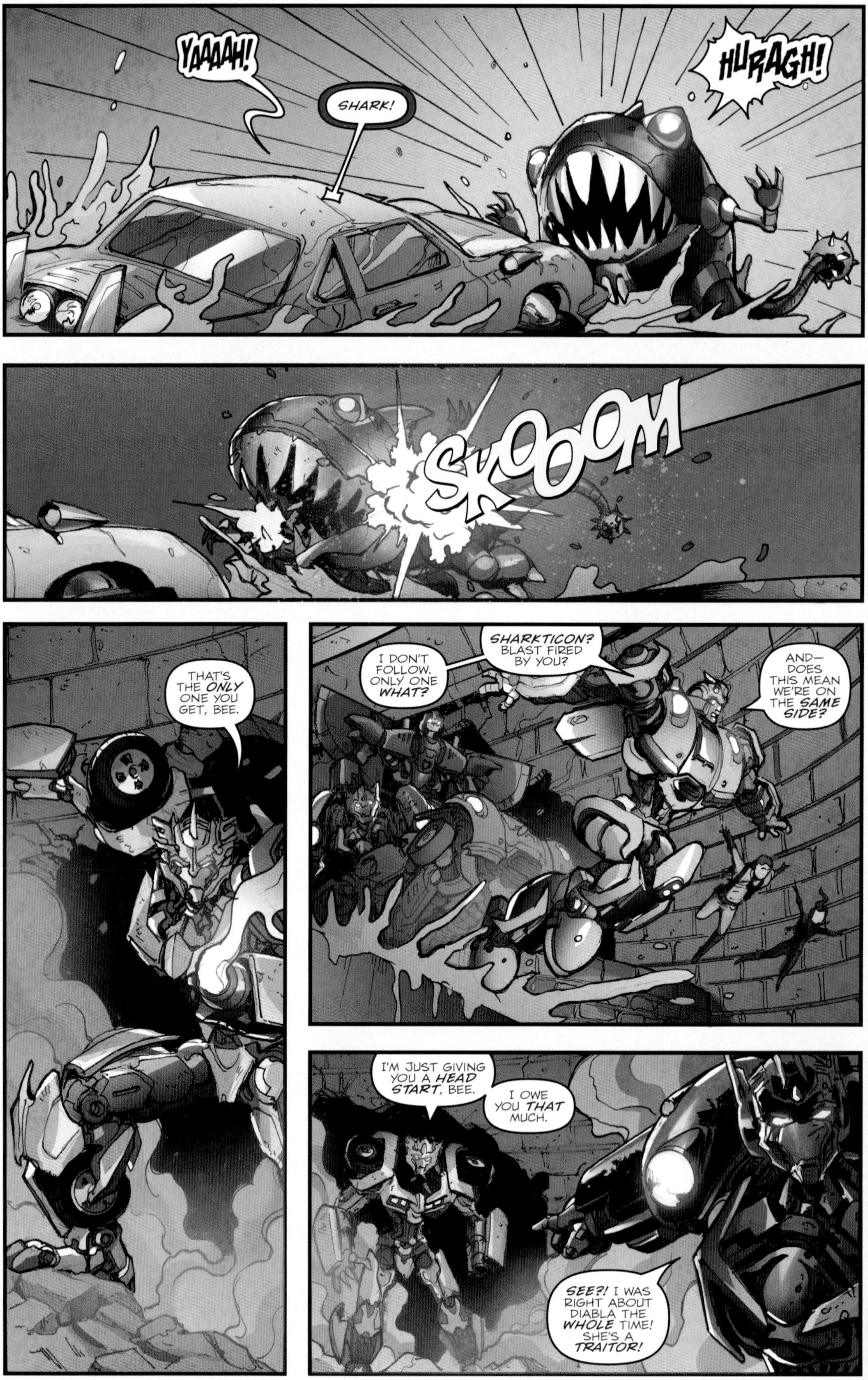
YAAAAH!
SHARK!
HURAGH!
SKOOOM
THAT'S THE ONLY ONE YOU GET, BEE.
I DON'T FOLLOW. ONLY ONE WHAT?
SHARKTICON? BLAST FIRED BY YOU?
AND— DOES THIS MEAN WE'RE ON THE SAME SIDE?
I'M JUST GIVING YOU A HEAD START, BEE.
I OWE YOU THAT MUCH.
SEE?! I WAS RIGHT ABOUT DIABLA THE WHOLE TIME! SHE'S A TRAITOR!

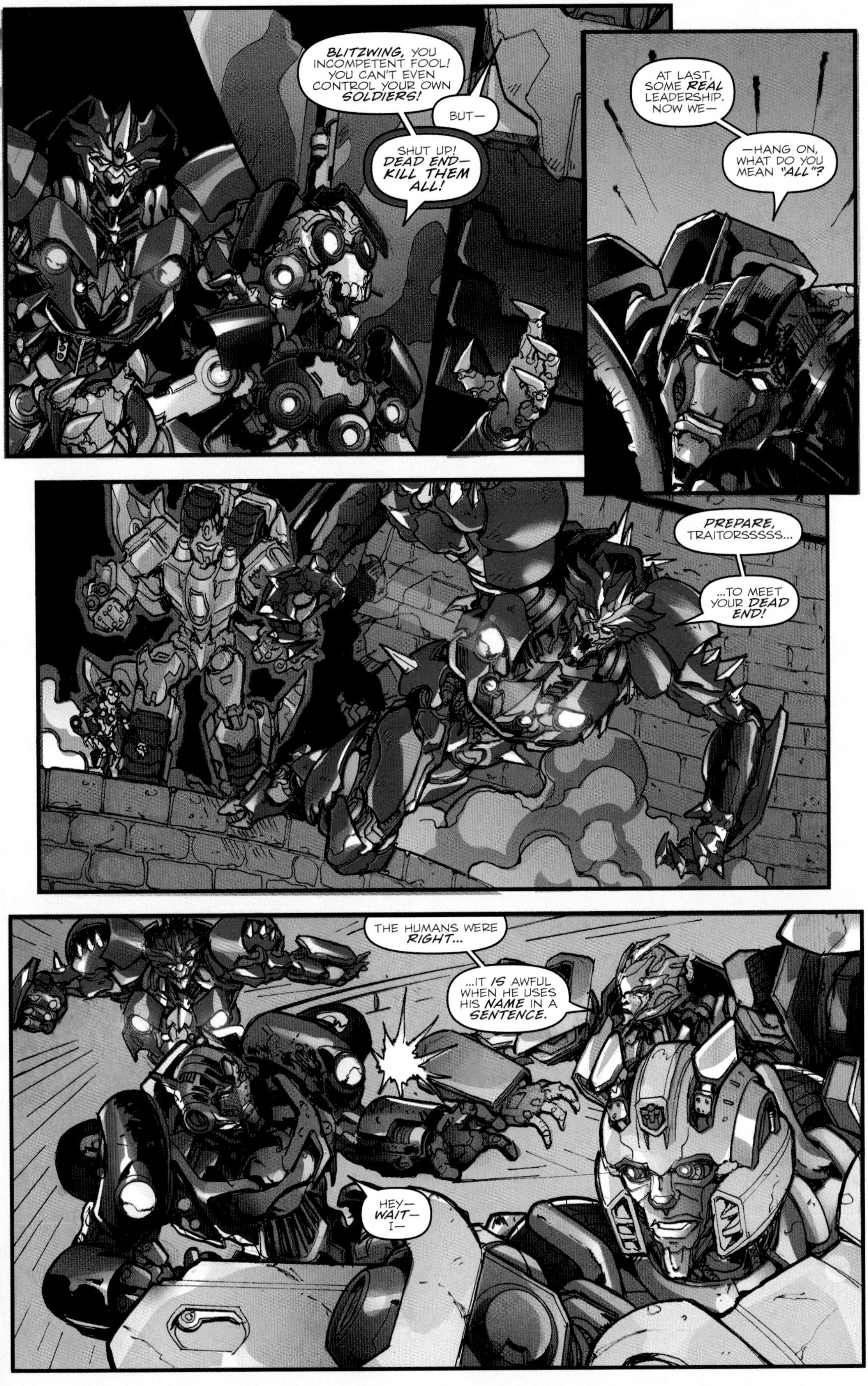
BLITZWING, YOU INCOMPETENT FOOL! YOU CAN'T EVEN CONTROL YOUR OWN SOLDIERS!
BUT—
SHUT UP! DEAD END—KILL THEM ALL!
AT LAST, SOME REAL LEADERSHIP. NOW WE—
—HANG ON, WHAT DO YOU MEAN "ALL"?
PREPARE, TRAITORSSSSS...
...TO MEET YOUR DEAD END!
THE HUMANS WERE RIGHT...
...IT IS AWFUL WHEN HE USES HIS NAME IN A SENTENCE.
HEY—WAIT—I—

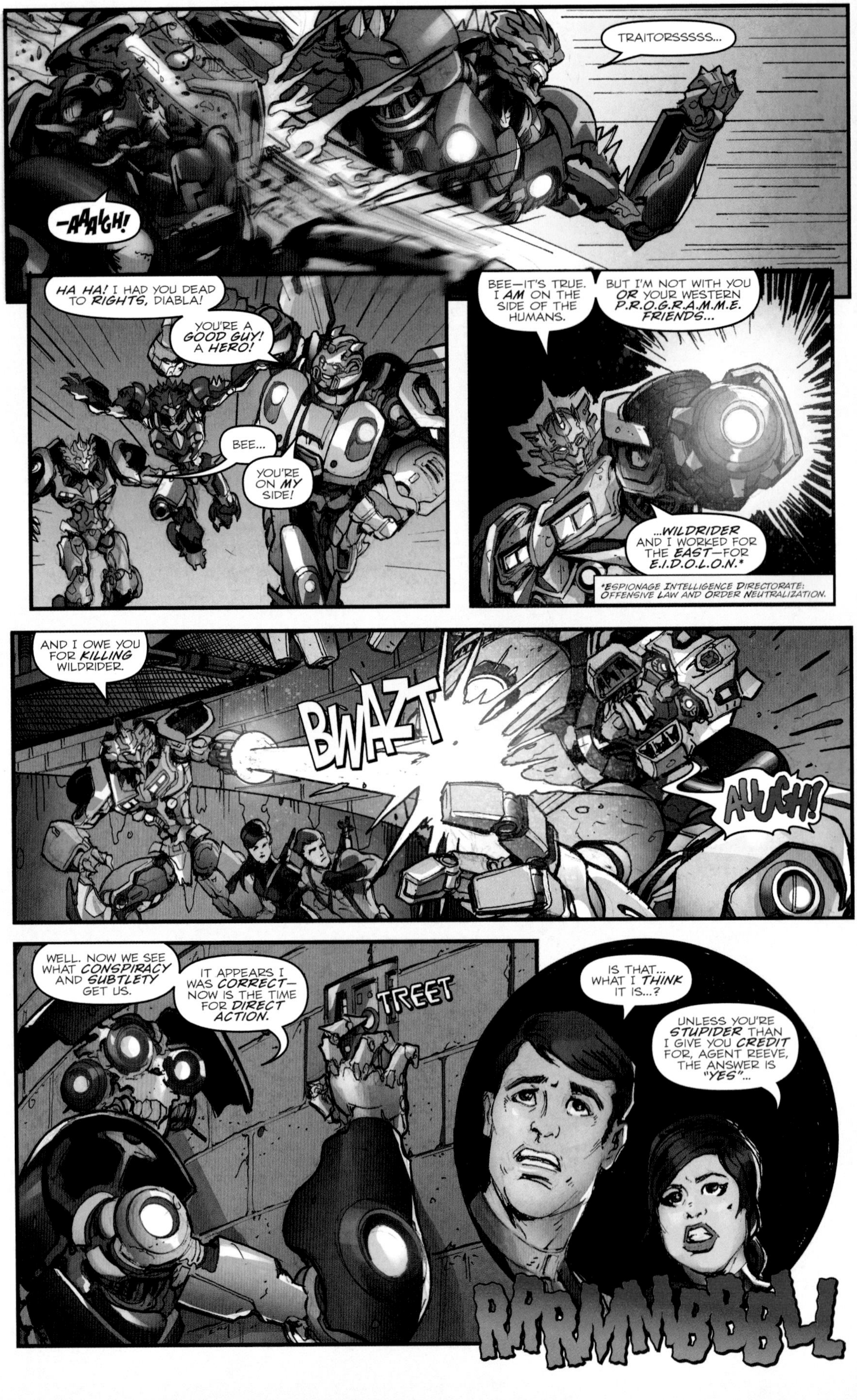
TRAITORSSSSS...
-AAAIGH!
HA HA! I HAD YOU DEAD TO RIGHTS, DIABLA!
YOU'RE A GOOD GUY! A HERO!
BEE...
YOU'RE ON MY SIDE!
BEE—IT'S TRUE. I AM ON THE SIDE OF THE HUMANS.
BUT I'M NOT WITH YOU OR YOUR WESTERN P.R.O.G.R.A.M.M.E. FRIENDS...
...WILDRIDER AND I WORKED FOR THE EAST—FOR E.I.D.O.L.O.N.*
*ESPIONAGE INTELLIGENCE DIRECTORATE: OFFENSIVE LAW AND ORDER NEUTRALIZATION.
AND I OWE YOU FOR KILLING WILDRIDER.
BWAZT
AUUGH!
WELL. NOW WE SEE WHAT CONSPIRACY AND SUBTLETY GET US.
IT APPEARS I WAS CORRECT—NOW IS THE TIME FOR DIRECT ACTION.
TREET
IS THAT... WHAT I THINK IT IS...?
UNLESS YOU'RE STUPIDER THAN I GIVE YOU CREDIT FOR, AGENT REEVE, THE ANSWER IS "YES"...
RRRMMBBBLL

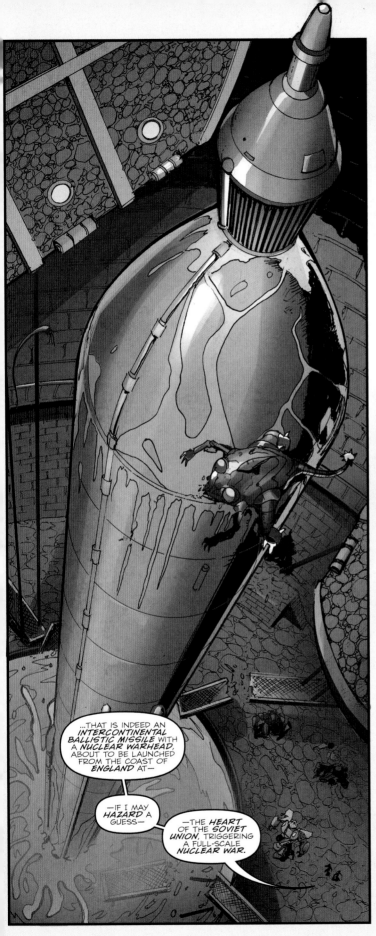

...THAT IS INDEED AN *INTERCONTINENTAL BALLISTIC MISSILE* WITH A *NUCLEAR WARHEAD*, ABOUT TO BE LAUNCHED FROM THE COAST OF *ENGLAND* AT—

—IF I MAY *HAZARD* A GUESS—

—THE *HEART* OF THE *SOVIET UNION*, TRIGGERING A *FULL-SCALE NUCLEAR WAR.*

DIABLA—YOU *GET* ALL THAT? *WHATEVER* HUMANS YOU'VE ALLIED YOURSELF WITH, WE GOTTA PUT THAT *ASIDE.*

IF WE'RE GOING TO SAVE THE EARTH, WE *HAVE* TO WORK TOGETHER.

MY *SOVIET* FRIENDS HAVE A *PHRASE*, BEE...

...*"FROM EACH ACCORDING TO HIS ABILITY, TO EACH ACCORDING TO HIS NEEDS"!*

TRAITORSSS!

HEY!

SO THEY WERE *ALL* RIGHT ABOUT YOU, DIABLA. I SHOULD HAVE *LISTENED.*

YOU *SOLD* US *OUT* TO THE *HUMANS.* WHAT DID THEY *OFFER* YOU? POWER? *ENERGON?*

NEVERMIND. IT DOESN'T MATTER. *ASTROTRAIN—* KILL HER.

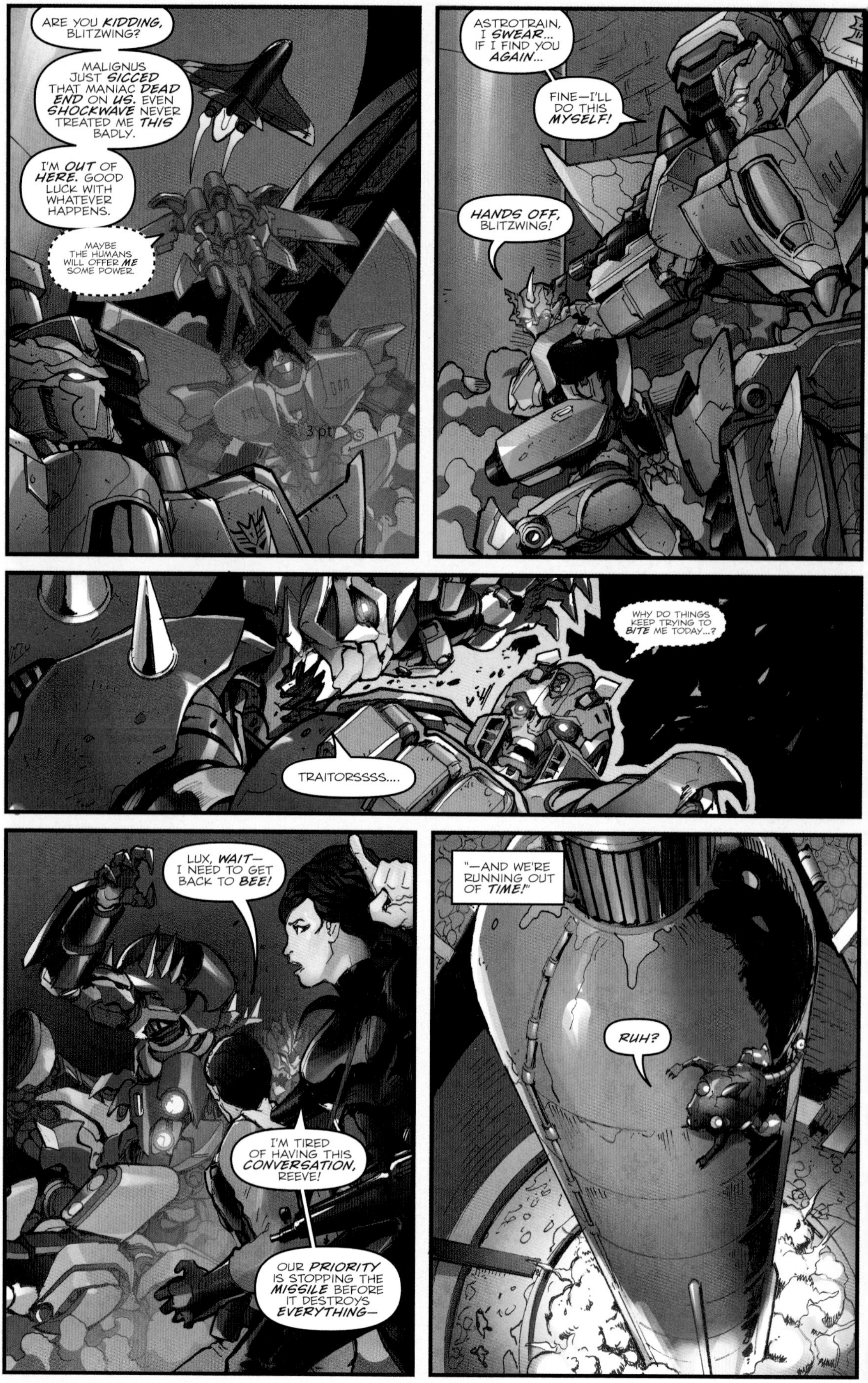
ARE YOU KIDDING, BLITZWING?
MALIGNUS JUST SICCED THAT MANIAC DEAD END ON US. EVEN SHOCKWAVE NEVER TREATED ME THIS BADLY.
I'M OUT OF HERE. GOOD LUCK WITH WHATEVER HAPPENS.
MAYBE THE HUMANS WILL OFFER ME SOME POWER.
ASTROTRAIN, I SWEAR... IF I FIND YOU AGAIN...
FINE—I'LL DO THIS MYSELF!
HANDS OFF, BLITZWING!
WHY DO THINGS KEEP TRYING TO BITE ME TODAY...?
TRAITORSSSS....
LUX, WAIT— I NEED TO GET BACK TO BEE!
I'M TIRED OF HAVING THIS CONVERSATION, REEVE!
OUR PRIORITY IS STOPPING THE MISSILE BEFORE IT DESTROYS EVERYTHING—
"—AND WE'RE RUNNING OUT OF TIME!"
RUH?

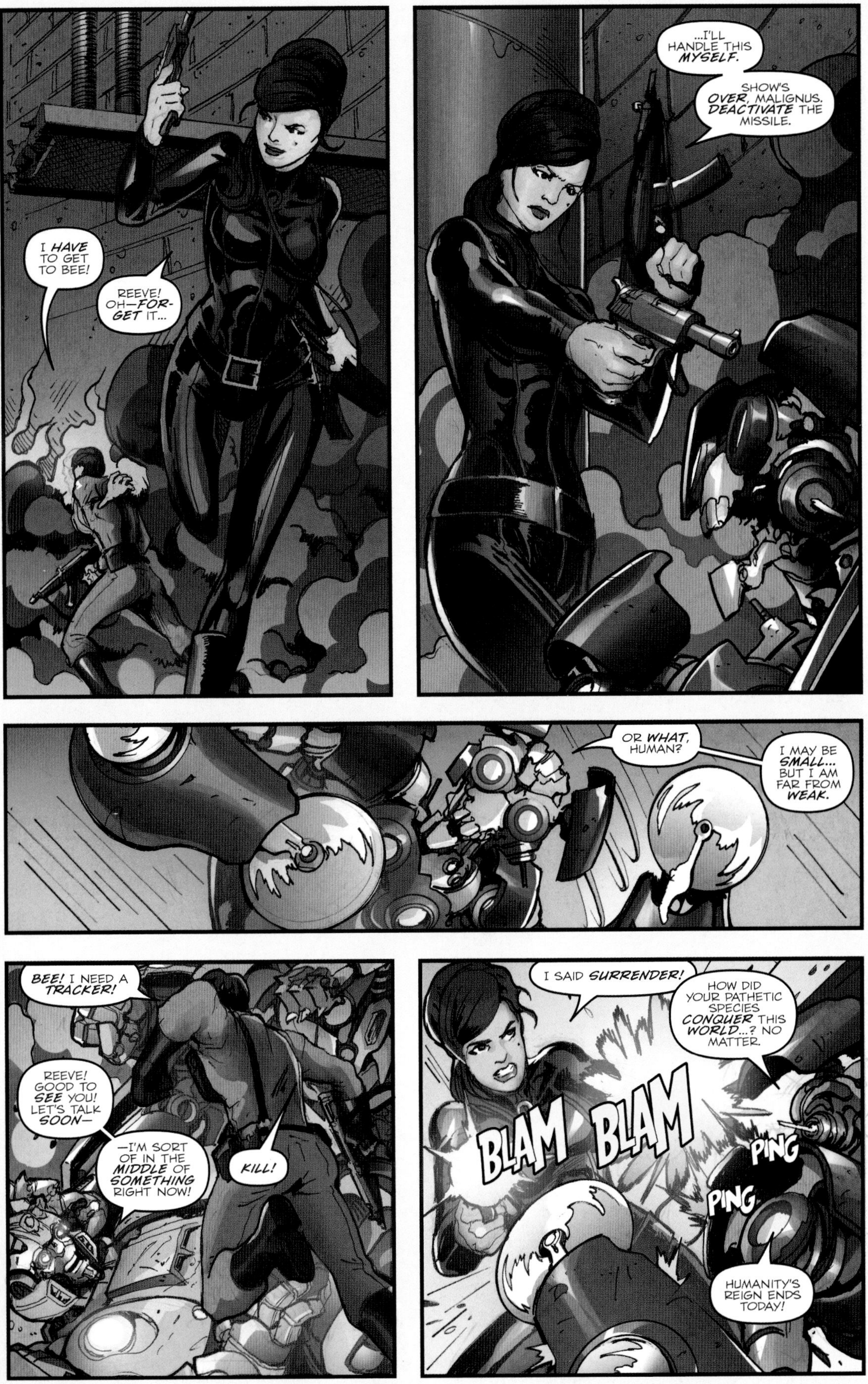
I HAVE TO GET TO BEE!
REEVE! OH—FORGET IT...
...I'LL HANDLE THIS MYSELF.
SHOW'S OVER, MALIGNUS. DEACTIVATE THE MISSILE.
OR WHAT, HUMAN?
I MAY BE SMALL... BUT I AM FAR FROM WEAK.
BEE! I NEED A TRACKER!
REEVE! GOOD TO SEE YOU! LET'S TALK SOON—
—I'M SORT OF IN THE MIDDLE OF SOMETHING RIGHT NOW!
KILL!
I SAID SURRENDER!
HOW DID YOUR PATHETIC SPECIES CONQUER THIS WORLD...? NO MATTER.
BLAM BLAM
PING
PING
HUMANITY'S REIGN ENDS TODAY!

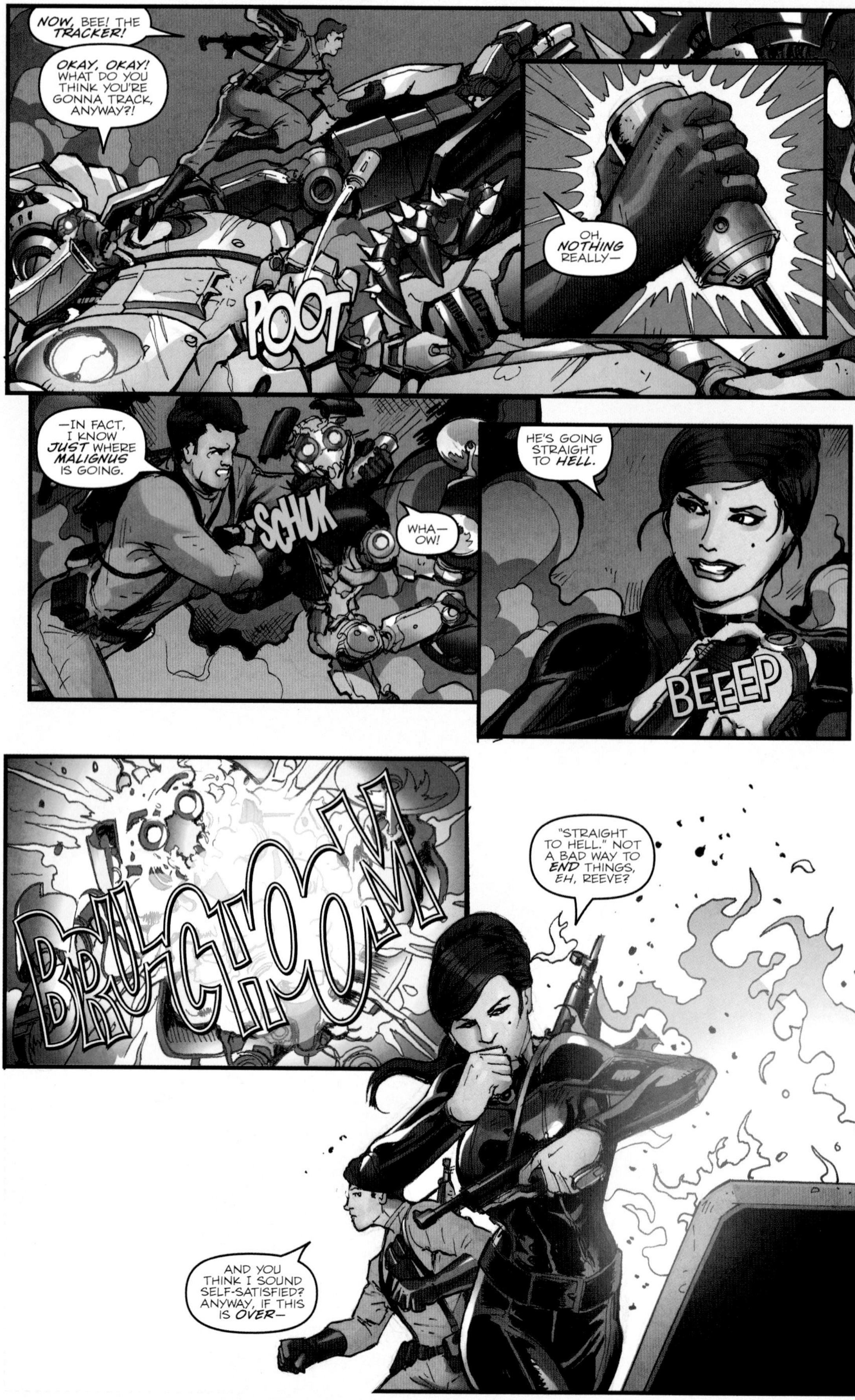

NOW, BEE! THE TRACKER!
OKAY, OKAY! WHAT DO YOU THINK YOU'RE GONNA TRACK, ANYWAY?!
POOT
OH, NOTHING REALLY—
—IN FACT, I KNOW JUST WHERE MALIGNUS IS GOING.
SCHUK
WHA—OW!
HE'S GOING STRAIGHT TO HELL.
BEEEP
BRUCHOOM
"STRAIGHT TO HELL." NOT A BAD WAY TO END THINGS, EH, REEVE?
AND YOU THINK I SOUND SELF-SATISFIED? ANYWAY, IF THIS IS OVER—

"—NOBODY TOLD THE *MISSILE*. IT'S STILL *LAUNCHING!*"

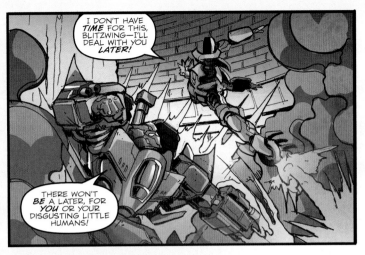

I DON'T HAVE *TIME* FOR THIS, BLITZWING—I'LL DEAL WITH YOU *LATER!*

THERE WON'T *BE* A LATER, FOR *YOU* OR YOUR DISGUSTING LITTLE HUMANS!

WE'LL *SEE.*

BEE! IT SEEMS THIS *SHARKTICON'S* LEARNED THE *SKY'S* THE *LIMIT.*

GOOD LESSON.

HISSSS!

HERE'S ONE FOR *BOTH OF US*, DEAD END:

THUNK

THERE'S *PLENTY* OF *FISH* IN THE SEA.

CHOMP

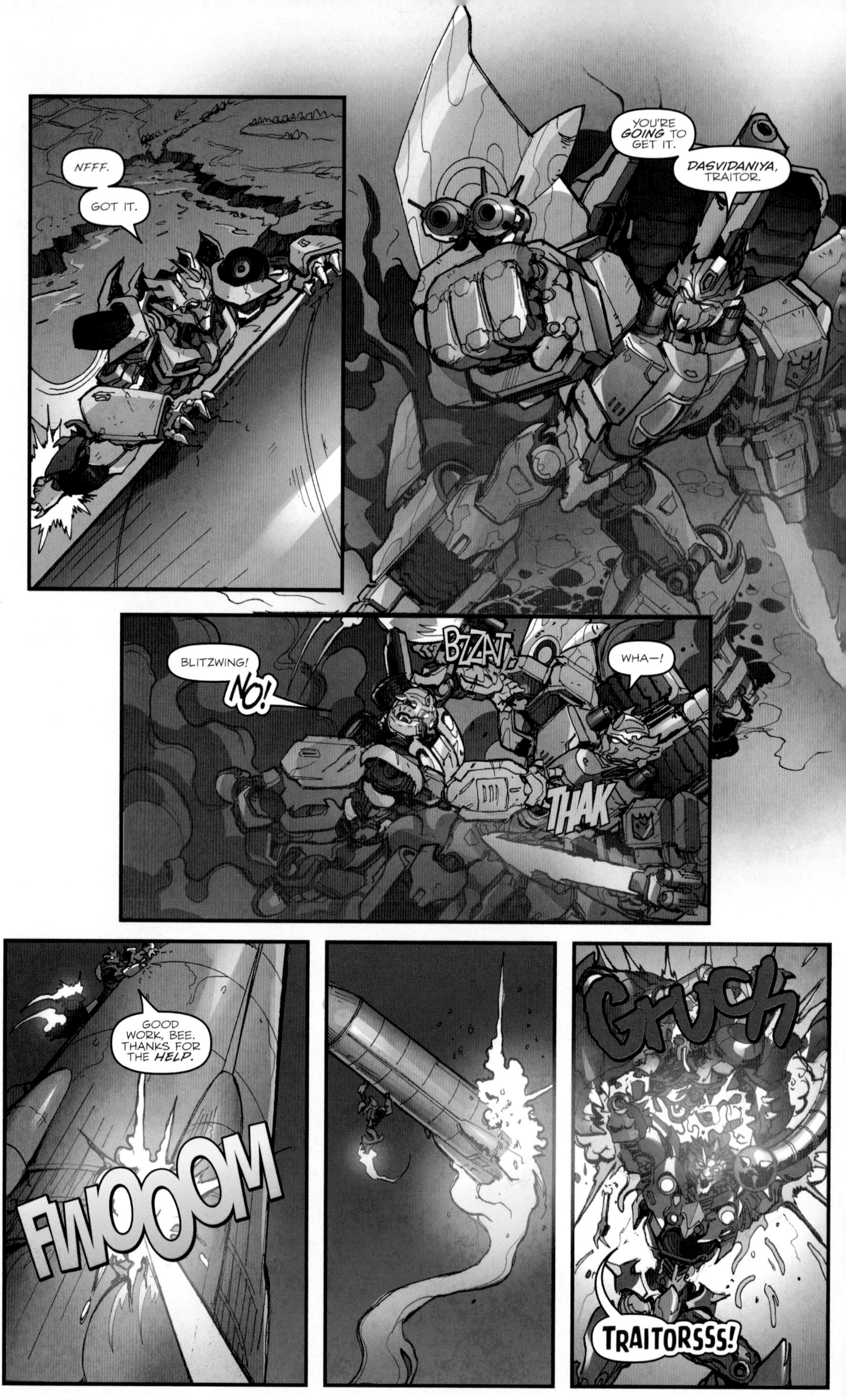
NFFF.
GOT IT.
YOU'RE *GOING* TO GET IT.
DASVIDANIYA, TRAITOR.
BLITZWING! NO!
BZZAT
WHA—!
THAK
GOOD WORK, BEE. THANKS FOR THE *HELP*.
FWOOOM
GRUCK
TRAITORSSS!

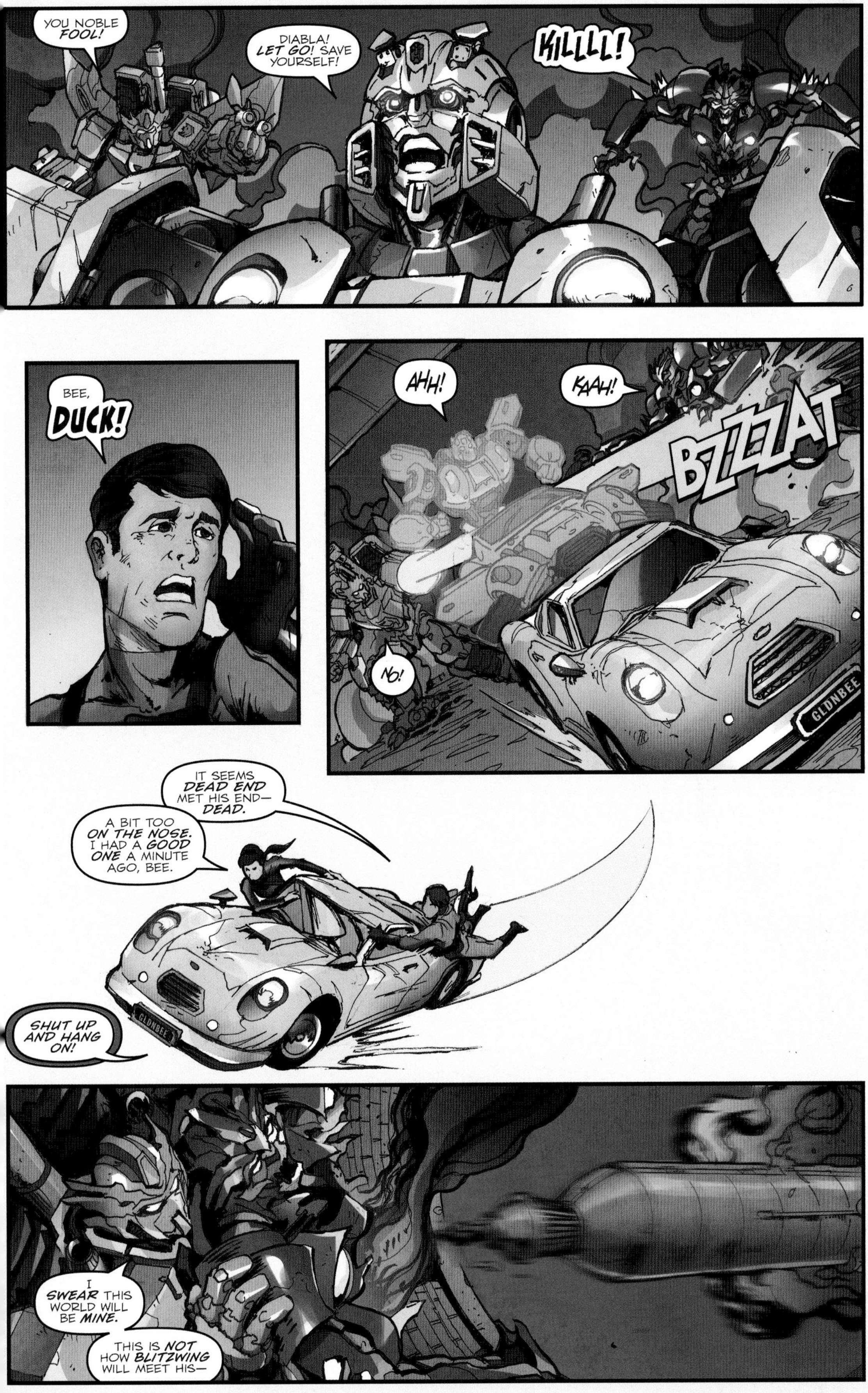

YOU NOBLE FOOL!
DIABLA! LET GO! SAVE YOURSELF!
KILLLL!
BEE, DUCK!
AHH!
KAAH!
BZZZZAT
NO!
GLDNBEE
IT SEEMS DEAD END MET HIS END— DEAD.
A BIT TOO ON THE NOSE. I HAD A GOOD ONE A MINUTE AGO, BEE.
GLDNBEE
SHUT UP AND HANG ON!
I SWEAR THIS WORLD WILL BE MINE.
THIS IS NOT HOW BLITZWING WILL MEET HIS—

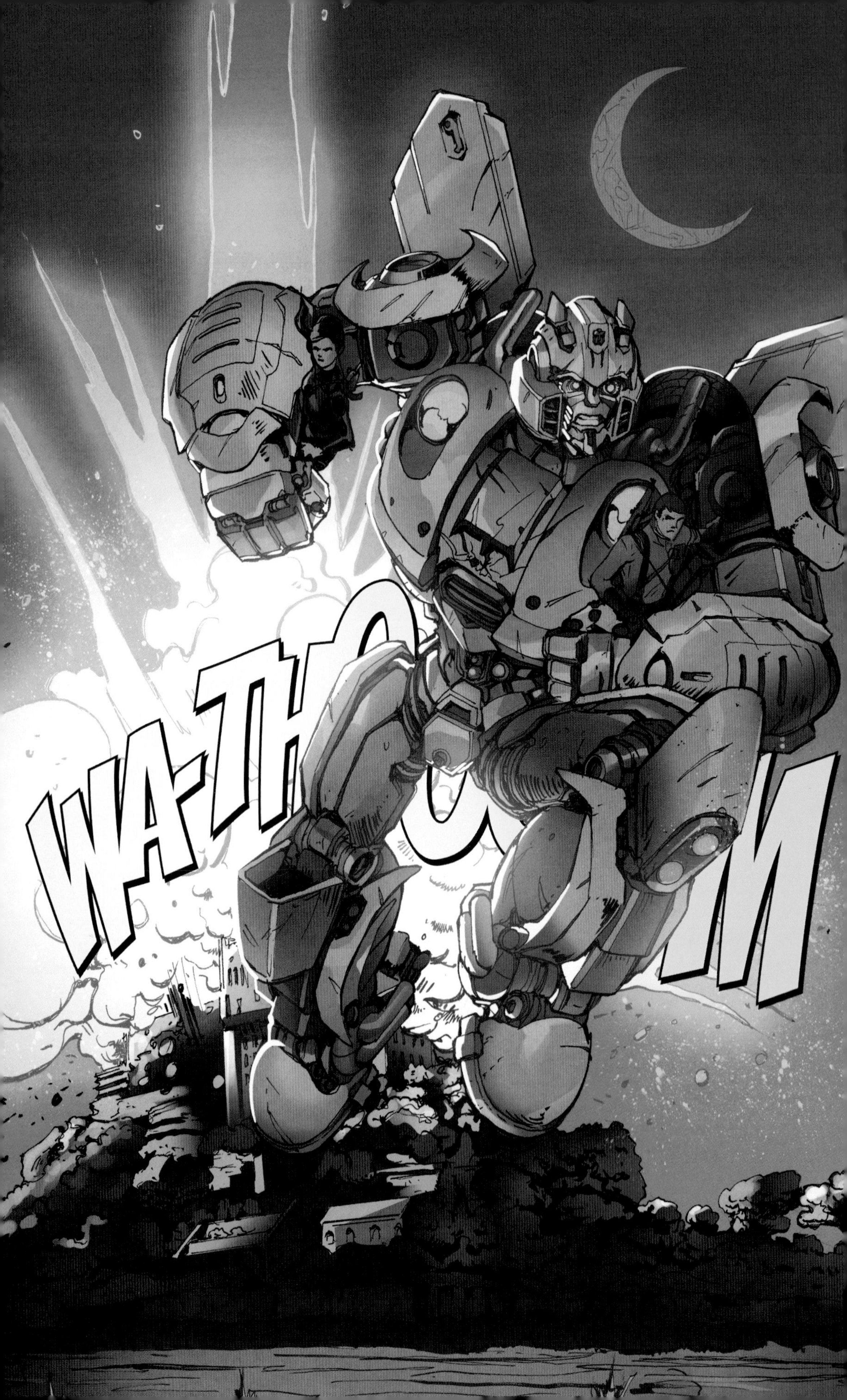
WA-TH
M

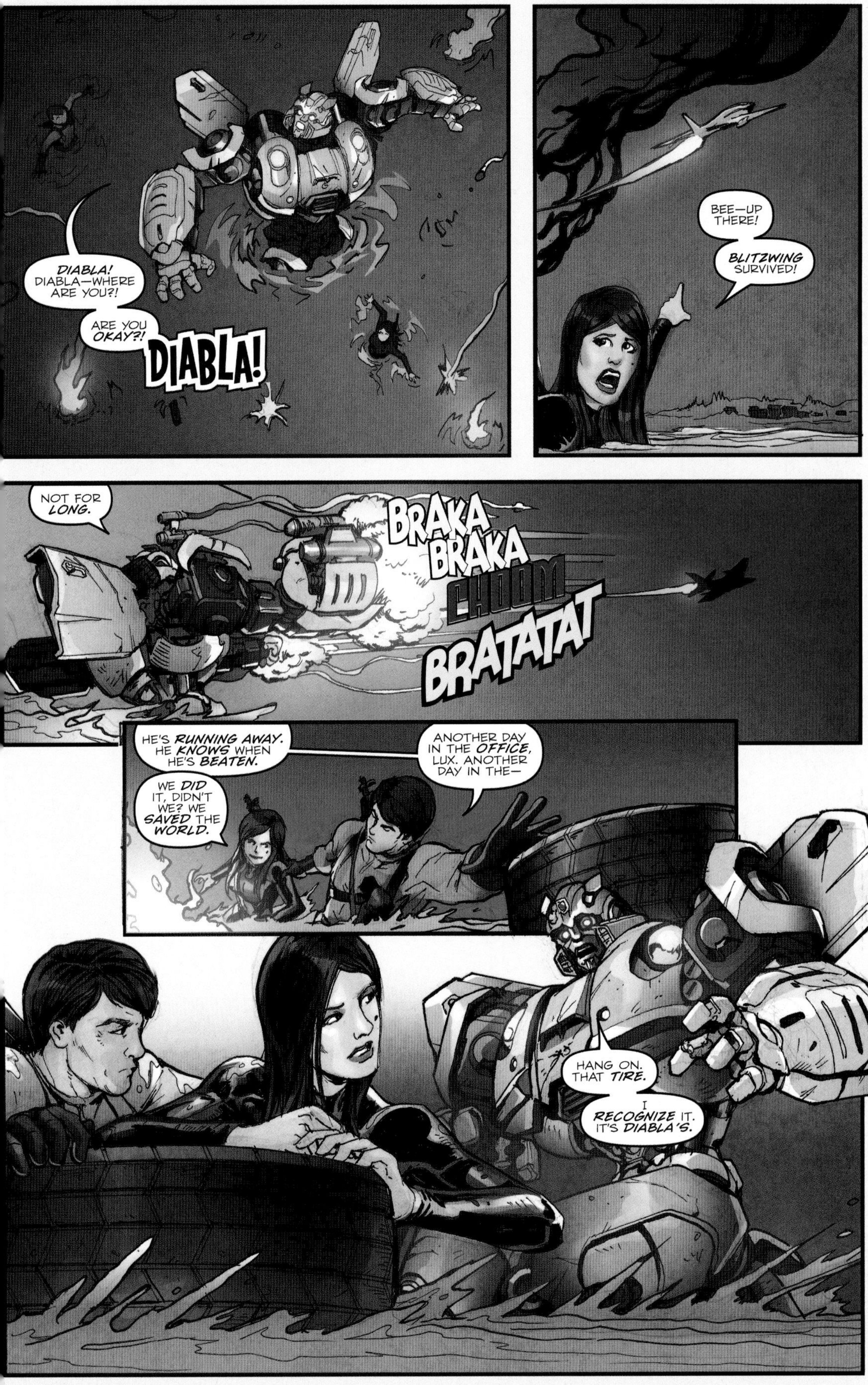
DIABLA! DIABLA—WHERE ARE YOU?!
ARE YOU OKAY?!
DIABLA!
BEE—UP THERE!
BLITZWING SURVIVED!
NOT FOR LONG.
BRAKA
BRAKA
CHOOM
BRATATAT
HE'S RUNNING AWAY. HE KNOWS WHEN HE'S BEATEN.
ANOTHER DAY IN THE OFFICE, LUX. ANOTHER DAY IN THE—
WE DID IT, DIDN'T WE? WE SAVED THE WORLD.
HANG ON. THAT TIRE.
I RECOGNIZE IT. IT'S DIABLA'S.

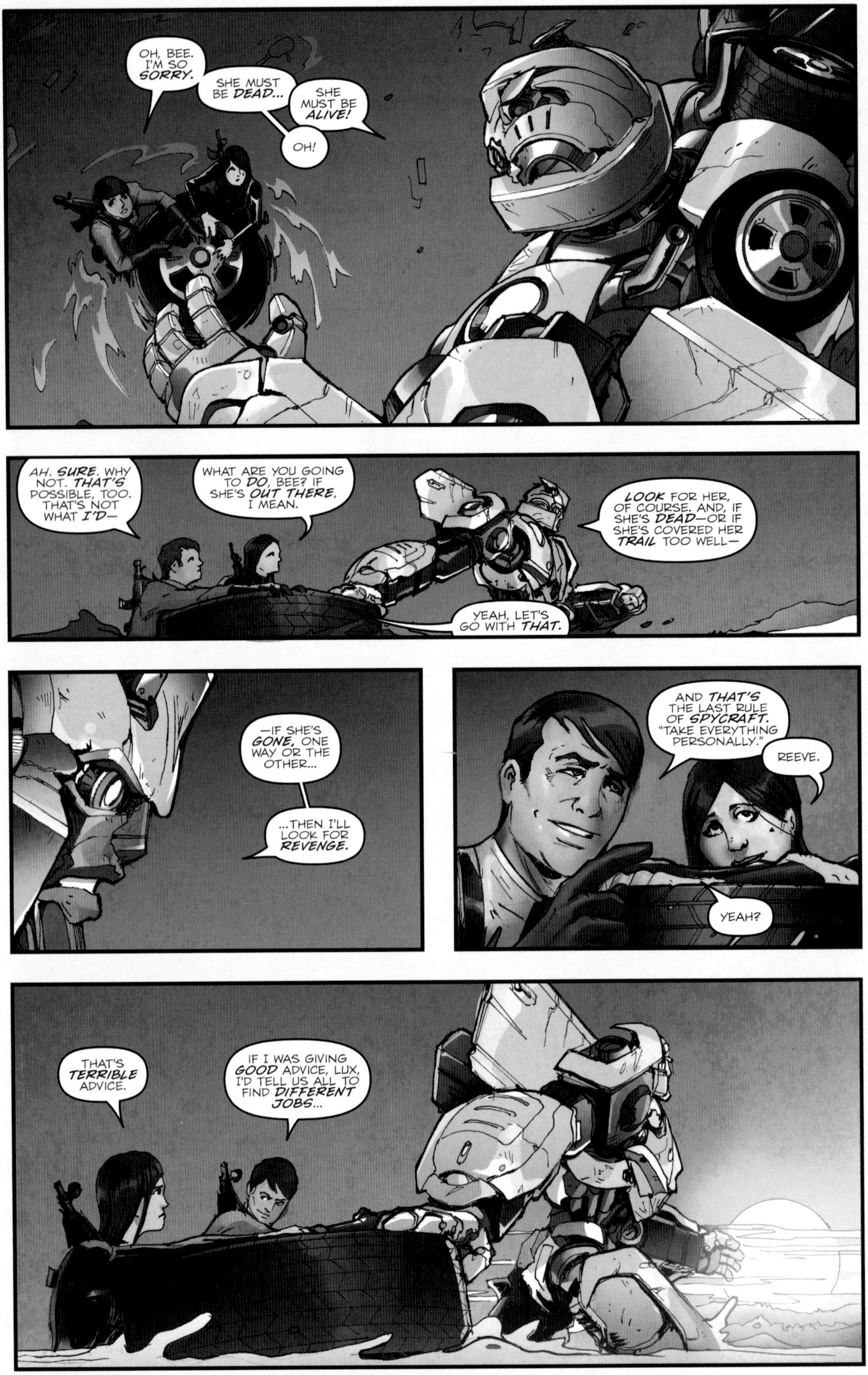
OH, BEE. I'M SO SORRY.
SHE MUST BE DEAD...
SHE MUST BE ALIVE!
OH!
AH. SURE. WHY NOT. THAT'S POSSIBLE, TOO. THAT'S NOT WHAT I'D—
WHAT ARE YOU GOING TO DO, BEE? IF SHE'S OUT THERE, I MEAN.
LOOK FOR HER, OF COURSE. AND, IF SHE'S DEAD—OR IF SHE'S COVERED HER TRAIL TOO WELL—
YEAH, LET'S GO WITH THAT.
—IF SHE'S GONE, ONE WAY OR THE OTHER...
...THEN I'LL LOOK FOR REVENGE.
AND THAT'S THE LAST RULE OF SPYCRAFT. "TAKE EVERYTHING PERSONALLY."
REEVE.
YEAH?
THAT'S TERRIBLE ADVICE.
IF I WAS GIVING GOOD ADVICE, LUX, I'D TELL US ALL TO FIND DIFFERENT JOBS...

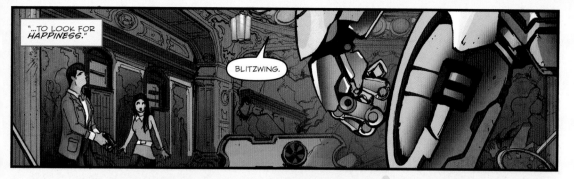

"...TO LOOK FOR *HAPPINESS*."

BLITZWING.

"TO LEARN TO HAVE *FAITH* IN YOUR FELLOW *HUMAN*— OR *CYBERTRONIAN*."

BLITZWING...

"TO COME TO RECOGNIZE HOW FAR IS *TOO FAR*."

BLITZWING!

"TO LIVE A LIFE WHERE EVERY *KISS* ISN'T A PRELUDE TO *BETRAYAL*."

BLITZWING!

"BUT PEOPLE LIKE *US*...

"...WE'RE JUST NOT *BUILT* THAT WAY."

LONG TIME NO SEE, *BLITZWING—*

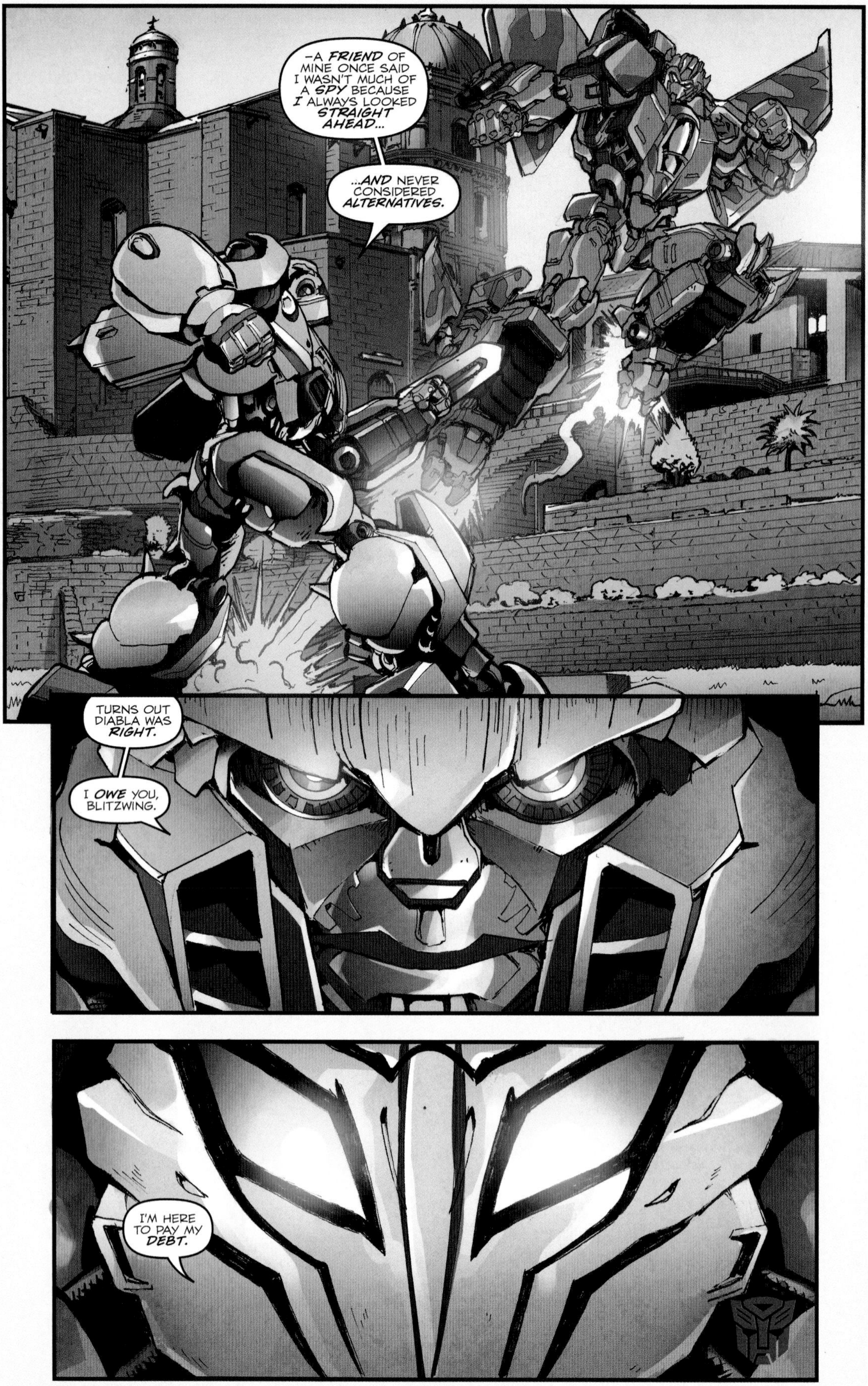

–A FRIEND OF MINE ONCE SAID I WASN'T MUCH OF A SPY BECAUSE I ALWAYS LOOKED STRAIGHT AHEAD...
...AND NEVER CONSIDERED ALTERNATIVES.
TURNS OUT DIABLA WAS RIGHT.
I OWE YOU, BLITZWING.
I'M HERE TO PAY MY DEBT.

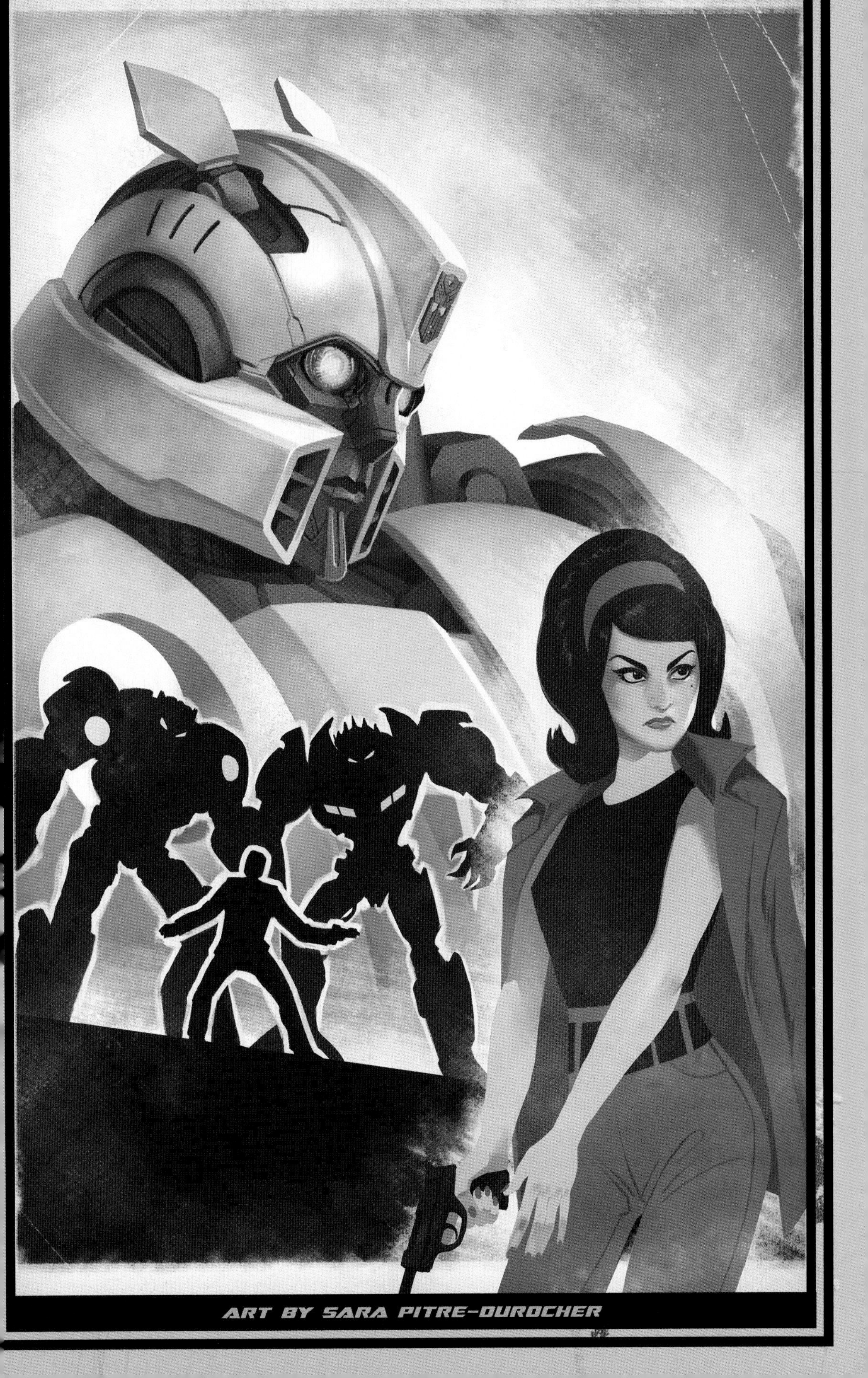

ART BY SARA PITRE-DUROCHER

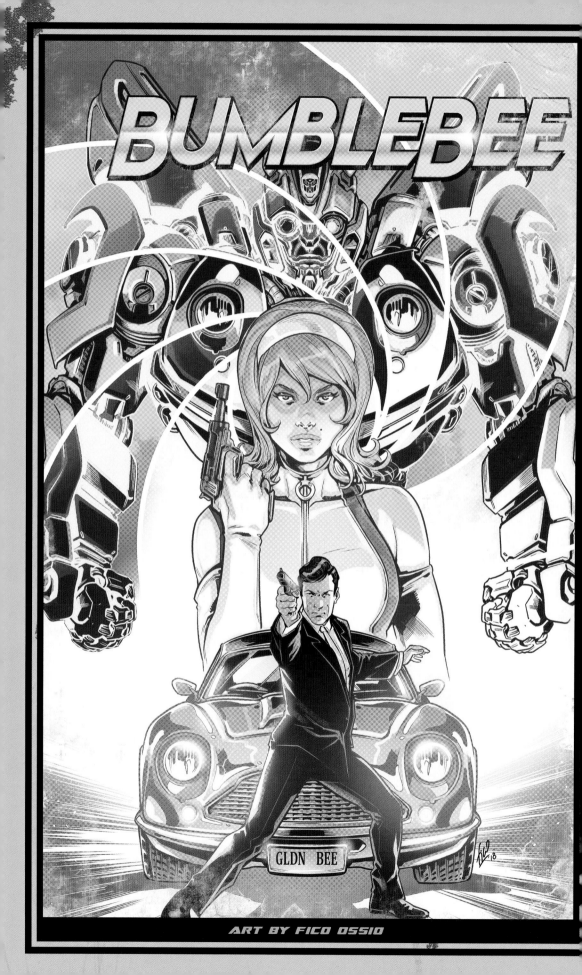

BUMBLEBEE

GLDN BEE

ART BY FICO OSSIO

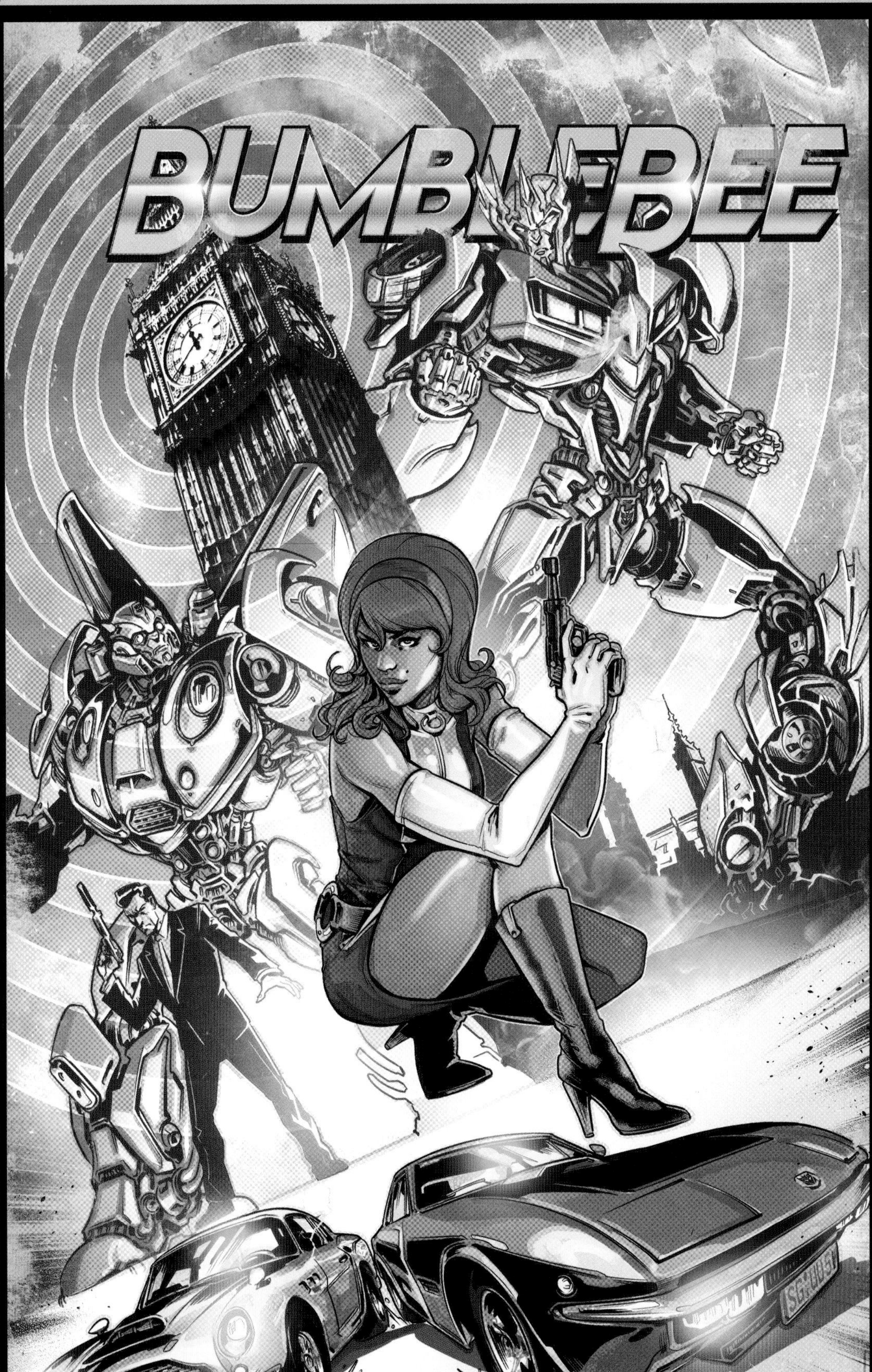
BUMBLEBEE
GLDN BEE

ART BY FICO OSSIO

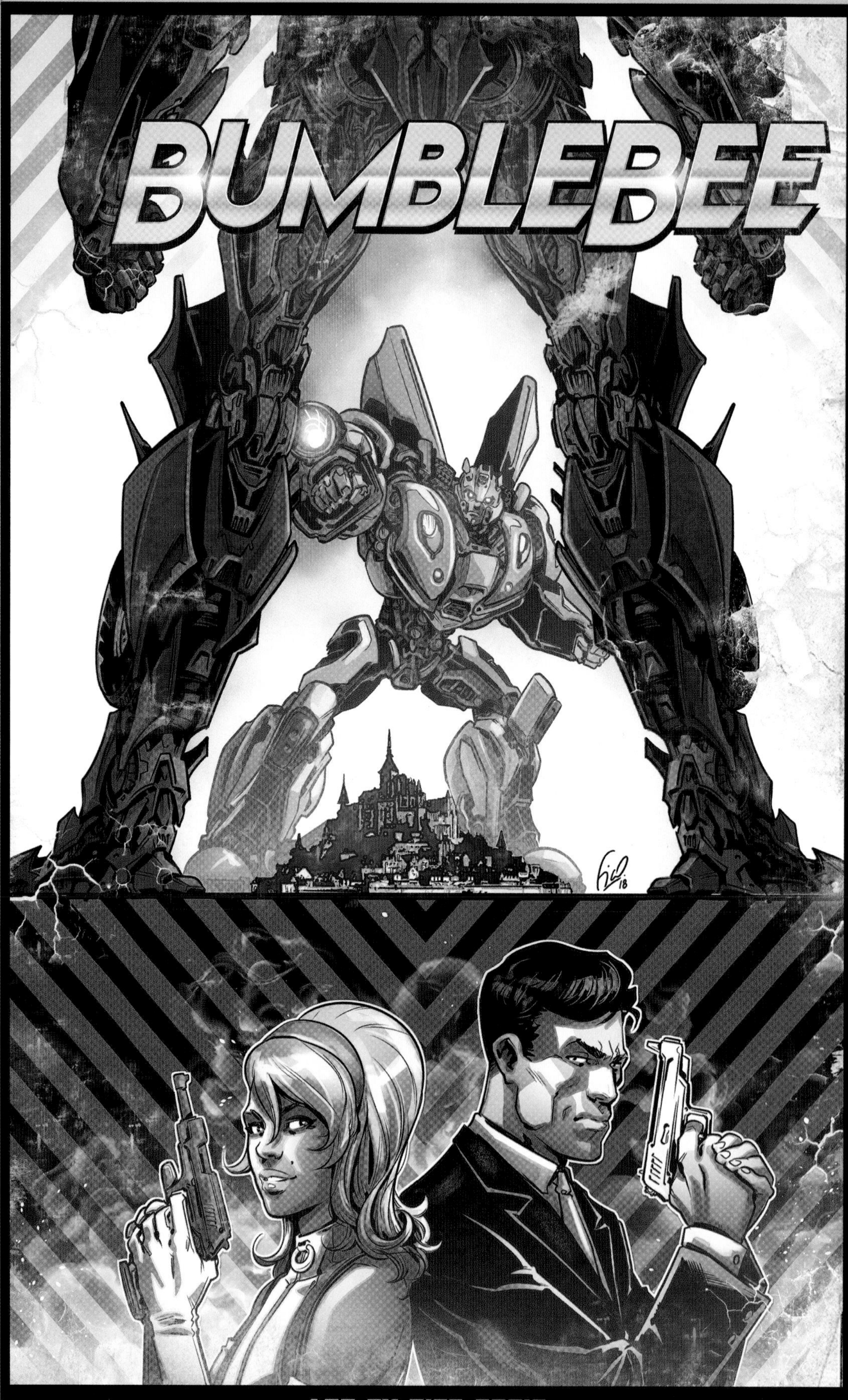
BUMBLEBEE

ART BY FICO OSSIO

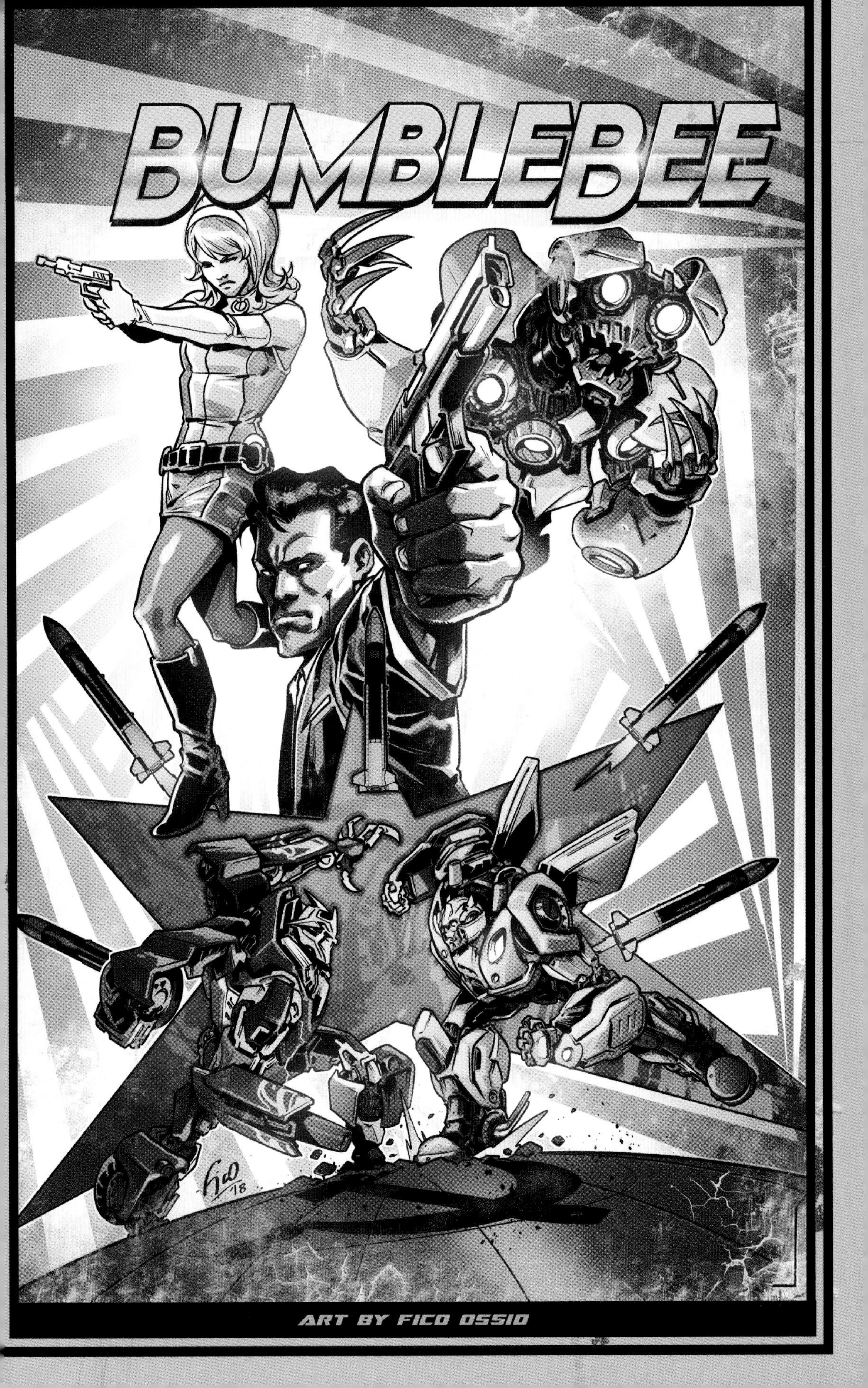
BUMBLEBEE

ART BY FICO OSSIO

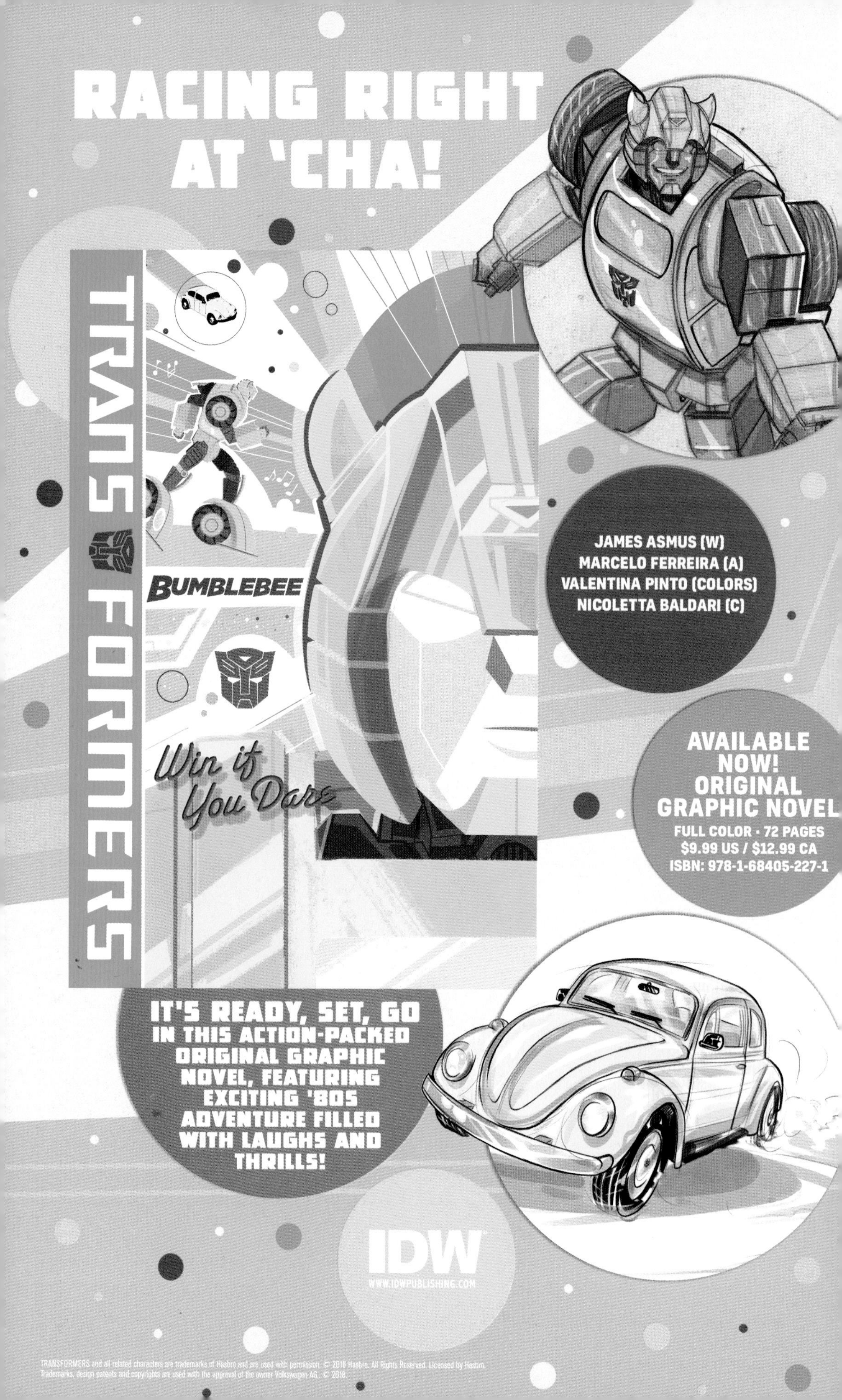
RACING RIGHT AT 'CHA!
TRANSFORMERS
BUMBLEBEE
Win if You Dare
JAMES ASMUS (W)
MARCELO FERREIRA (A)
VALENTINA PINTO (COLORS)
NICOLETTA BALDARI (C)
AVAILABLE NOW! ORIGINAL GRAPHIC NOVEL
FULL COLOR • 72 PAGES
$9.99 US / $12.99 CA
ISBN: 978-1-68405-227-1
IT'S READY, SET, GO IN THIS ACTION-PACKED ORIGINAL GRAPHIC NOVEL, FEATURING EXCITING '80S ADVENTURE FILLED WITH LAUGHS AND THRILLS!
IDW
WWW.IDWPUBLISHING.COM
TRANSFORMERS and all related characters are trademarks of Hasbro and are used with permission. © 2018 Hasbro. All Rights Reserved. Licensed by Hasbro.
Trademarks, design patents and copyrights are used with the approval of the owner Volkswagen AG.. © 2018.